PRAISE FOR

BLOO~ ~~
THE S

"This is steampunk clanking to life on the page."
—Jay Lake (*Mainspring*)

"G. D. Falksen's witty, anachronistic, and downright fun writing style makes him a storyteller to watch."
—Terrance Zdunich (*REPO! The Genetic Opera*)

"A piston blast of pure pulp adventure"
—John Leavitt (*Dr. Sketchy's Official Rainy Day Colouring Book*)

"A rousing adventure filled with a wealth of imagery, action and technological wonders."
—Chet Phillips

"G.D. Falksen is not only one of the most important authors in Steampunk literature, he is arguably the most enjoyable."
—Art Donovan (*The Art of Steampunk*)

"A delightfully crunchy alternate reality that lets you feel the gears grinding."
—Phil Foglio (*Girl Genius*)

THE HELLFIRE CHRONICLES

BLOOD IN THE SKIES

G. D. FALKSEN

WILDSIDE PRESS

THE HELLFIRE CHRONICLES: BLOOD IN THE SKIES

Copyright © 2011 by G. D. Falksen

Use of the AIR setting is licensed by Hatboy Studios, Inc.
www.hatboystudios.com

Cover art by Bethalynne Bajema
Interior art by Jeni Hellum, Evelyn Kriete, and Nicolas Palmer

Published by Wildside Press LLC.
www.wildsidebooks.com

Ebooks available at
www.wildsidepress.com

To my family.

PROLOGUE

June 30, 1908 AD
Tunguska, Siberia

It was morning over the boreal forests of central Siberia, and the wilderness had awakened, just as it had since time immemorial, to the rustling of branches, the songs of birds and the buzzing of insects. Deep beneath the ground inside a bunker of concrete and steel, Maxim Rykov sat in his small, Spartan office and poured over a pile of notes and charts with the vigor of a fanatic. He had not slept the night before, such was the significance of his work, and now his bleary eyes were kept open only by the knowledge that today would be the day that he would deliver Russia from her enemies.

There was a noise at the door, and Rykov looked up to see his fresh-faced aide, Lieutenant Pavlov, watching him.

"What is it, Alexi?" he asked.

"It's time, sir," Pavlov said. "The machine is ready."

Rykov's face lit up. He leapt to his feet, knocking aside his chair.

"Then we've no time to lose!" he cried, rushing to the door. "Come, Alexi, it is time to change the world!"

* * * *

They hurried into the belly of the bunker, through concrete tunnels lined with pipes and wires. At every turn, soldiers and engineers going about their business passed them and gave the two officers salutes that they had no time to return. At length, Rykov arrived at the heart of his creation, a vast engine room filled with boilers and generators, thunderous machinery and working men. The air was heavy with steam and smoke and an all-pervasive heat that made him sweat beneath his uniform the instant he crossed the threshold. Pavlov followed, his breath quickening.

"I want pressure at full!" Rykov shouted to the engineers. "Keep those furnaces going!"

He walked to the center of the chamber, where there stood a massive column of metal covered in belts, wires, and gears. All of the pipes and wires in the engine room converged on this single machine, and the engine's many dials shook violently as the pressure behind them threatened to break them into pieces.

"Is the program loaded?" Rykov demanded.

"Yes, sir," Pavlov said.

Rykov drew a small punch card from the tunic of his uniform and studied it, his face distorted by a strange half-smile. The card had been made from a piece of tempered steel, its holes cut with the most advanced precision machinery to ensure clean and perfect circles.

"Smile, Alexi," he said, placing his hand on Pavlov's shoulder. "Today is the start of a new age." He swept a hand through his sweat-matted hair. "Fetch me the megaphone. I would like to address the men."

"Of course, sir."

When Pavlov had done as instructed, Rykov stepped to the front of the balcony and raised the megaphone. His voice echoed throughout the engine room, drawing his troops to him like a priest calling his congregation. As he spoke, the noise of the room seemed to fade away into the background.

"Soldiers! Brothers! Sons of Mother Russia! Today is a great day! Today is the day when all the world shall be remade by our hands!"

There was a cheer from the crowd, but Rykov waved them into silence.

"We have all toiled so very long and so very hard for this great goal," he continued. "Some of you have worked for these many months constructing this great engine of Russia's destiny. Others of you have served alongside me in pursuit of this goal since its first inception years ago. But all of you can hold yourselves proud that what you are doing is for the greatness, the glory, and the preservation of our Empire!"

Rykov's tone became more serious.

"I cannot stress too greatly the urgency of our situation and the necessity of our cause. Russia's enemies are many, and they will stop at nothing to destroy our beloved empire. In Crimea, the British and the French allied with the godless Turks for no cause greater than to oppose the rightful will of the Tsar. It was ordained that Russia should control all of Asia, the great frontier to our east, and yet the British have stalked us at every turn in their so-called 'Great Game.' Now, in desperation, the French turn to us to free them from their isolation, to use us as a weapon against Germany! Now, the hated British seek to lure us into complacency, so that they and their Japanese dogs can tear the Empire into pieces!"

Rykov leaned forward over the balcony, the light of the furnace fires casting his face in orange and crimson.

"Enough, I say!" he cried. A cheer echoed from the crowd. "No longer shall mongrels like the British bite at our heels! No longer shall the craven Austrians and Turks lord over proud Slavs and noble Christians! No longer shall Japan seek to bar our rightful possession of East Asia! With this machine, brothers, we shall harness the very power of the Earth itself, and with the fiery might of *gods*, we shall shatter our enemies and lay waste to their cities! I swear to you that before this day is out, London and Paris, Berlin and Vienna, Tokyo and Peking will all burn! We shall defend Church and Tsar whatever the cost our foes must pay!"

Another great cheer rose from the soldiers and engineers, but it was to be short-lived. As Rykov stood, arm outstretched as if to take the very future within his grasp, the air became heavy as if a storm was about to break, and the stench of ozone rose to assail the noses of the men. A torrent of sparks erupted from the generators, followed by bursts of electrical discharge. The pressure gauges went mad under the strain, and pipes began to burst as steam struggled to vent between the joins.

Though almost overcome with panic, the engineers rushed to their stations and began struggling with the machinery. Under the increased pressure, the belts and flywheels thundered louder than ever, drowning out the screams that arose when clouds of boiling vapor erupted around the men. The bunker shook as if rocked by the blows of heavy artillery.

Rykov bounded down from the balcony and grabbed one of the engineers by the arm.

"What happened?" he demanded.

"Some sort of electrical surge!" the engineer cried. "It is running along the metal supports in the walls, and the boiler pressure has doubled without any increased heat. I do not understand it!"

Pavlov grabbed his commander's arm. "Major, we must give the order to evacuate! The engines could explode at any moment! If we don't leave now, we could be boiled alive!"

The chamber shook again.

"Good God!" Pavlov cried. "I think we're sinking into the ground!"

"I will not give up when we are so close!" Rykov rushed for the central machine. "We must activate the machine now, before it is too late!"

"Activate it?" Pavlov gasped. He rushed forward and tried to bar Rykov's way. "If the machine is turned on now, there's no way of knowing what it might do! There's too much pressure and electricity for it to handle!"

"Out of my way, Alexi!" Rykov shouted.

Pavlov pressed his back against the machine's control panel, blocking Rykov's access to it.

"You'll kill us all!" he cried.

There was a dreadful fire in Rykov's eyes as he drew his revolver and leveled it at Pavlov.

"I will kill any man who stands between me and Russia's destiny. Even you, Alexi."

"No . . ." Pavlov said.

"Move!"

"No!"

Rykov fired without hesitation.

The gunshot was scarcely heard above the noise of the engines, and none of the soldiers showed any sign of noticing. By then they were all too intent upon their own survival, some struggling to relieve the pressure of the boilers, others fleeing for their lives, certain that doom had come.

Rykov kicked Pavlov's body aside and raised the command card. He shoved it into its slot.

A cascade of sparks showered down around him and lightning arced across the room. Rykov placed his hand on the machine's control switch. A hymn to glory pounded with the blood in his ears.

"Today is the day we change the world!" he cried and threw the switch.

ONE

2120 AD (211 Post Upheaval)
The Badlands, western fringe of the Known World

Two hundred years later and several thousand miles away from the shattered remains of Tunguska, another day dawned just as pleasantly. In the rocky and rubble-strewn Badlands, birds sang in the early light, and then took to wing as the sounds of gunfire broke the stillness of the morning sky.

On the bridge of the merchant airship *Fortuna*, Captain Adams struggled to keep from panicking as his ship fled at full steam with a flotilla of pirates trailing close behind it. Adams looked out of a nearby window as the *Fortuna* made an evasive turn. He saw three light airships packed down with black market artillery spread out in a line that formed the core of the pursuing gang. The immediate danger, however, came from a wing of biplanes of mixed models and designs that crisscrossed the *Fortuna*, raking it with machine gun fire.

"Captain, they're gaining on us!" the navigator, Wilcox, cried from the other side of the narrow bridge. "We can't outrun them much longer!"

Adams rubbed his mouth. "We have to try. If we can make it to Commonwealth airspace, they'll have to break off."

More gunfire sounded from outside, and a few moments later Adams watched as a man in a warm leather jumpsuit—one of the machine gunners positioned on the top of the *Fortuna*'s envelope—tumbled down past the window and vanished into the clouds below them.

"Our machine guns are gone!" cried the communications officer.

Wilcox paled. "We're defenseless!"

"Pull yourselves together, boys!" Adams said. "Batista, keep on that aethercaster. Call for help until you can't call anymore."

"Yes, sir!" the communications officer replied. He turned back to the aethercast transmitter and began broadcasting on all available frequencies. "Mayday, mayday. Merchant ship *Fortuna* under attack from pirates. Taking heavy fire. Requesting any assistance. Coordinates as follows—"

Adams drew his revolver and held it aloft. "You're all acting like a lot of sissies from out east, and I won't have it on my ship! We live with the threat of piracy hanging over our heads every day, and do we hide at home in fear?"

"Hell no!" someone shouted from the other side of the bridge.

"Damn right!" Adams said. "We're Badlanders, born and bred to take risks that 'civilized' folks can't stomach! You all knew this day might come. What the Hell are you carrying guns for if not for this?"

He fixed every man on the bridge with a stern glare. He was met with silence.

"That's what I thought," he said. "Now get back to your stations, do your jobs, and we might make it out of this alive!"

The first officer, James Peck, burst into the bridge from the top deck. He held one arm and blood dripped from the end of his sleeve. He stumbled over to Adams and grabbed his captain by the shoulder.

"They've punctured the gas cells!" he said.

"Which ones?" Adams demanded.

"*All of them*! And most of the punctures are in the upper quarter! We're venting hydrogen!"

"Can you patch the blasted things?" Adams asked.

Peck wiped sweat from his forehead, leaving a trail of blood in his hair. "The men are trying, but it's next to suicide with those fighters shooting at us. We're going down, Cap'n, and there's nothing we can about it."

"Good, God," Adams said.

The airship pitched in the wind, and Adams stumbled against a nearby support.

"We're finished," Peck growled. "We'll never make Kilkala in time."

"God damn it," Adams said, "but I think you're right."

Peck snapped his head toward Adams. "We never should have given the old man passage. He's the one they're after, you know! I warned you when we left port at Turtle Island!"

Adams said, "His price was too good to turn down. It's too late now, at any rate."

He watched as the *Fortuna* began to sink through the clouds. Fragments of floating rock flew past them, some narrowly missing the airship, others striking and rebounding off the metal hull or fabric envelope. One of the region's many smaller eyots appeared from beneath a cloud directly in the falling *Fortuna*'s path, and Adams knew they were going to crash onto it.

He grabbed a nearby voicepipe. "All hands, brace for impact!"

Turning back to the window, he saw the ground rushing toward them. A tree struck the bottom of the *Fortuna*, rocking the ship and making it pitch sideways. The bridge crew grabbed onto any handholds they could find, and Adams held onto a handle next to the window with one hand. With the other, he supported his wounded first officer.

The impact was softer than he had expected. Only two men were knocked from their feet; the rest were merely jostled. Releasing Peck, Adams rushed out onto the deck. What was the damage?

The airship had landed at a slight angle, and its envelope was offset just enough for him to make out the sky. Above, pirate fighters swept around for another pass. They fired a few more bursts into the airship, but there was little that gunfire could do now that it had not already done. Then one of the pirate airships eclipsed the sun, descending toward the eyot. They meant to land.

"Hell's bells!" Adams said.

Peck joined him.

Adams said, "Open the arms locker. Distribute weapons to the crew."

"We're finished anyway," Peck said, but he did as instructed.

As the pirate ship landed, its crew dropped grappling anchors. The moment their ship stabilized, dozens of pirates burst from cover, rushing down a metal walkway and sliding down ropes to the ground.

Adams dashed back to the bridge. "We'll make a stand here," he said. "Wilcox, Burns, get the rest of the men and secure the engine room and the catwalks inside the envelope. The rest of you, get this bridge locked down!"

"What about the crew quarters?" asked Wilcox. "If the pirates get in there—"

Peck grabbed Wilcox and shook him. "Get some sense into your head! If they steal the contents of our lockers, it'll be a small price to pay so long as we get out of here alive!"

"Yes, sir!" He nodded to Burns, and the two dashed out. The communications officer dogged the door shut behind them.

When Wilcox and Burns had gone, Adams rejoined Peck. "Inspiring words, James. I thought you'd written us off as done for."

"We *are* done for," Peck said, "but the last thing we need is a panic. I may be a pessimist, but I'm not stupid."

Adams looked out the window. The pirates were a motley lot: dirty and unshaven, dressed in patched and worn garments stolen or taken from the dead. They carried an assortment of rifles, pistols, axes, and swords. Many had their oily hair cut short or tied into long braids to protect it from the wind; others wore knit caps pulled tightly over their heads. All were haggard and had a barbarous look in their eyes.

Adams selected a shotgun from the arms locker, then crouched by one of the bridge windows and pushed it open. The remaining bridge crew followed his lead. As the pirates neared, he shouldered his weapon.

"Take aim!" He drew a bead on a burly man with an axe in one hand and a pistol in the other. "Fire at will!"

Bullets and shot poured into the pirate mob, which let out a startled cry and surged forward with even greater vigor. A few pirates fell; others returned fire, while the rest swarmed onto the deck to loot less well-defended portions of the airship. Two men with sledgehammers darted just at the edge of the window's field of view, and a few moments later the thunderous pounding of steel on steel echoed from the bridge door. The bridge crew shuddered as one, knowing that they would soon be overrun, but they kept up their fire at the windows.

All the while, the sounds of aeroplanes circling overhead could be heard over the noise of gunfire. Peck looked upward quickly and scowled.

"Those blasted aeroplanes," Adams said, sharing the first officer's expression. "They'll be the death of us."

"You're right about that," Peck told him. "Even if we somehow fight off these pirates, we'll be gunned down by the rest of the flotilla before you can say 'Bob's your uncle.'"

"At least they'll kill us fast and clean," Adams said.

"You find the silver lining in everything."

Bullets ricocheted off the metal of the bridge's hull. One or two even punched through the metal, killing a member of the crew. Adams and his men continued to fire out of the windows, but the pirates were no fools. They kept away from the windows' sight angles and focused their attentions on breaking down the door. Adams heard machine gun fire echoing from somewhere outside, but he was too occupied by the threat of death to pay it much attention.

His first indication that something had changed was when the burning hulk of a pirate biplane crashed against the ground some dozen feet from the window. Adams jumped in surprise and stared in confusion at the wreckage. As he watched, another biplane fell to the ground further away, and Adams strained his eyes to make out what was happening. He jumped in fright as a third biplane tumbled against the eyot, shattered its wheels and wings, and barreled aflame toward the *Fortuna*. It stopped barely five feet from the bridge window and sat there, a funeral pyre for its pilot.

The bridge door came down with a terrible clang, and Adams jerked his gaze toward it. In the doorway stood the two pirates holding sledgehammers. Behind them stood more of the mob, weapons brandished and ready to turn the narrow confines of the bridge into an abattoir.

The closest pirate hefted his sledgehammer and took a single step toward the doorway, eyes fixed on Adams. A moment later, a spray of gunfire ripped into him and flung him onto the deck in a bloody heap. More bullets rained down upon the pirate mob from the side, and they were suddenly struck by panic. Those who survived dropped to the ground or crawled for cover, some even using their dead and dying comrades to shield themselves. Rifles and pistols went off, peppering the unseen enemy, who returned fire in another lengthy burst.

Gripping his shotgun, Adams burst out of the door and fired off both barrels into the cluster of men closest to the bridge door. Two were knocked to the ground. The third turned his eyes toward Adams and raised his cutlass with a howl. Adams felt the adrenaline take him, and he struck the pirate with the butt of the shotgun over and over again until the attacker stopped moving. He leaned heavily against the bridge room's outer wall, nausea and shudders gripping his body.

In the sky above, he saw aeroplanes twisting about in tight spirals and dives, dogfighting with all the viciousness of wild beasts. The pirates were still there, now fighting desperately against a squadron of sleek monoplane fighters that darted in and out of their enemy's ranks, trading fire with the biplanes and even engaging the pirate airships with almost suicidal daring. The monoplanes looked like a vision of the future, with metal bodies rather than the canvas and wood of the pirates. Their cockpits were enclosed in glass canopies to protect their pilots from the tremendous winds their high-speed flight produced. It was little wonder that they seemed to outmaneuver the pirate fighters at every turn.

"Commonwealth Kestrels . . ." Adams mumbled to himself. "Thank God!"

Two of the Kestrels had broken away from the rest of the squadron to see to the *Fortuna*'s relief. Having whittled down the pirates on deck, they now were attending to the pirate airship on the eyot. A barrage of incendiary rounds soon had the pirates' envelope aflame. After a couple more passes for good measure, the two monoplanes dove toward the ground and came in to land a short distance from the *Fortuna*.

Adams watched as the pilot of the lead fighter shoved open the plane's canopy and stood, one foot up on the cockpit's side as she took in the situation on the ground. She wore a leather flight suit and gloves, with a revolver in a holster strapped at the top of her boot. She pulled off her flying helmet, releasing a bundle of golden hair that fluttered magnificently in the breeze.

Fixing her eyes on the *Fortuna*, the pilot drew her revolver and jumped down from the plane. She was quickly joined by her wingman, a swarthy woman with short dark hair. The two of them hurried to the *Fortuna*'s side and climbed up onto the deck, keeping their pistols at the ready. They were met by a token force of surviving pirates who, now on the verge of panic, were quickly dispatched in a blaze of gunfire.

Adams rushed to meet the pilots, holding his shotgun by the barrel to show that he meant no harm. "Thank God you've come!" he exclaimed. "You're just in time."

The blond woman gave Adams a pat on the shoulder. Her companion kept her aim on the open deck and the bodies that covered it.

"I'm Wing Commander Steele of the Commonwealth Air Force," the blond said. "This is Flight Lieutenant Nadir. We caught your distress call and thought you might need a hand. Good for you we were in the area."

"Good for us indeed! We'd be dead if it weren't for you."

Steele gave a sardonic smile. "Better death than slavery, right?"

She snapped open her revolver and began reloading it with bullets held in a pocket on the chest of her flight suit. Adams opened the breech of his shotgun and reloaded as well.

"What's the status of the ship?" Nadir asked over her shoulder.

"My men have the bridge and engine room locked down. Thanks to you, most of the pirates who came aboard are dead, but some of them headed down into the crew quarters below decks."

"Any of your people still down there?" Steele asked.

Adams wiped his brow. "None of the crew. Just the old man. He refused to leave his berth when I gave the order."

"Old man?"

"We took on a passenger at our last port of call. He was on the run from somebody."

"Clearly they found him," Nadir said.

"Clearly," Steele agreed. "Taking on a stranger on the run in the Badlands? You should know better."

"I know," Adams said, "but we needed the money."

Steele looked at Nadir. "There might still be a chance to save him."

"*Might*," Nadir said.

Steele turned to Adams. "Stay here. We'll get him."

TWO

Steele made for the airship's lower levels, Nadir in tow. Below deck, the *Fortuna* was divided into a narrow row of crew compartments, the barricaded engine room, the galley and, at the very bottom, the cargo hold. The space was terribly claustrophobic, and it reminded her of a sleeping car on a train. The corridor ran along one side of the ship and accessed a row of rooms as it led toward the galley at the far end. All of the doors had been flung open, and she saw several pirates bustling about. No doubt they were searching for the old man, but some were not above rifling through the crew's footlockers in search of booty.

Steele spotted one man on guard near the foot of the stairs, but he was too busy smoking a cigarette to notice their approach. Best to take him out before he saw them and raised the alarm. She crept down the steps as softly as she could, reversed her revolver, and delivered a sharp blow to the back of his head with the weapon's butt. Nadir caught the body and eased it to the deck.

From a room near the end of the hallway, Steele heard shouting. Was it one of the pirates?

"Where is it, old man?" demanded a young, powerful voice.

A muffled response came.

"Not good enough!"

She heard a blow, followed by a cry of pain.

She exchanged a glance with Nadir, who nodded, and she readied herself to charge. But before she took a step, a pirate emerged from one of the crew rooms carrying a clock covered in gold leaf.

Steele drew up short. The man froze for a heartbeat, dropped the clock with a crash, and grabbed for his gun.

Nadir leveled her revolver and shot him cleanly through the head before he could draw. Quick thinking, but would it give them away?

Sure enough, the sound brought more pirates into the hall, this time with weapons ready. Steele pulled Nadir into the nearest crew compartment. A cry went up behind them, and bullets struck the doorframe in a burst of splinters.

Steele peeked into the hall for a look at the pirates. There were five of them, armed with a mixture of rifles, pistols, and wicked-looking blades.

Damn! she swore to herself. *Bad odds.*

She had barely enough time for a glance before she was answered with another volley.

"Five," she said to Nadir, ducking away from the door. "Three in front."

"How do you want to do this?" Nadir asked. "Low-high?"

"Yeah. You take low left; I'll go high right.

Nadir shook her head. "You're the ranking officer. You go low."

Steele opened her mouth, but Nadir interrupted.

"We don't have time to argue," she said. "I'm your wingman, let me do my job."

"Fine," Steele said. "And remember, your aim at range is better than mine, so once you have a shot on those rifles in the back, take them out."

"Roger."

Steele chanced a glance out into the hallway again.

Fifteen feet and closing.

"Now!" she said.

Steele leapt out into the hallway and began firing. Nadir followed close behind her. Steele dove onto the floor and began shooting upward at the front rank of pirates, while Nadir crouched at her side and gave her supporting fire. The pirates were taken by surprise at the unconventional firing arcs. As the men returned fire, bullets whizzed just over Nadir's head and missed Steele completely.

Steele and Nadir shot like madwomen, emptying their revolvers into the pack of pirates with precision and ferocity. The front rank went down almost immediately, and Nadir dropped onto her belly beside Steele just in time to evade a second volley by the riflemen, who then bolted behind the cover of another crew compartment.

Steele was on her feet in a flash. She and Nadir dashed forward just in time to see one of the riflemen jump out in front of them. Steele caught the pirate's rifle barrel with her free hand and shoved it away as it fired. Nadir dove in and smashed her revolver against the pirate's head, dropping him to the ground. Wasting no time, they stepped over the man's body and burst into the compartment. The remaining pirate appeared from the side and jabbed Nadir in the belly with his rifle barrel—had it been fixed with a bayonet, the blow would surely have been fatal. Nadir let out a pained gasp and fell backward against the wall, but Steele shoved past her and shot the pirate point-blank.

She quickly knelt and helped Nadir up.

"Are you ok?"

Nadir gasped for air and waved Steele away. "Don't worry 'bout me. I get hit harder doing corkscrews." Nadir looked down at the dead pirate. "Why didn't he fire?"

Steele picked up the rifle and checked the bolt. "His gun jammed." She gave Nadir a cheerful pat on the back. "Looks like it's your lucky day."

Nadir made a noise. Steele knew she was still shaken at the thought of how close she had just come to death.

"You know what they say: when you fly with 'Lucky Lizzy' Steele, sometimes a bit of her luck rubs off on you."

Steele flashed a grin at Nadir's words and then became serious again. "C'mon, let's find the old man."

She and Nadir found the mysterious passenger lying on the floor of the last compartment before the galley. In their search, the pirates had thrown about the room's few furnishings. Some of the mattresses had been pulled out of their berths and now lay on the floor. In one corner lay the crumpled form of an elderly man with gray hair, severely tanned skin, and a worn expression. His clothes were mismatched, dirty, and threadbare, as was common among natives of the Badlands. But, Steele noticed, behind the lines of wear and exhaustion he had the narrow features and high brow of a Commonwealth man. That was not unusual—Commonwealth criminals sought refuge in the Badlands all the time—but it was odd.

The man had been beaten by his assailants and now was covered in his own blood. At the sight of Steele, he grabbed a small penknife out of his boot and began crawling toward the other side of the room. He had been so brutalized by the pirates, he was afraid of anyone he saw.

"Calm down, you're safe," Steele said, kneeling by the man's side. "We're with the Commonwealth Air Force. We're not going to hurt you."

The old man pulled away. The force of the movement made him bleed all the more. In spite of his pain and weakness, he cut open the side of a nearby mattress with several jerky stabs of the penknife and thrust his hand inside the stuffing. He pulled something out, clutched it against his chest and then rolled over onto his back. He was on the verge of passing out.

He reached out with one bloody hand and grasped Steele's forearm. Sitting up as best he could, he managed to rasp out, "Too late for me. . . ." He shoved something cold and hard against Steele's belly and looked into her eyes in desperation.

"Don't let *him* find it!"

Steele looked down at the object in her lap. It was a small, unassuming metal strongbox. "What is it?" she asked.

"The power to change the world!" the old man gasped.

He breathed his last and slumped to one side, dead.

* * * *

Steele returned to the top deck with Nadir and found the crew busy shoving the bodies of the dead pirates off the airship. The crew was out in force and armed to the teeth. Captain Adams rushed to meet the two pilots as they emerged from the hatch.

"Well?" he asked.

"The old man's dead," Steele replied. She kept the strongbox tucked under one arm, partly but not suspiciously concealed behind her back. "But the pirates are as well. I'd suggest you get some of your crew together to do a follow-up sweep to be sure, but if any pirates are still alive, chances are they'll have made their escape by now."

"Thank you," Adams said. He motioned to Peck. "James, get some of the men and make sure all the pirates are off the ship. If you find any, by God shoot them."

"If you'll give me a moment, Captain, I'd like to check in with my squadron," Steele said.

"Yes, of course."

Steele led Nadir off the *Fortuna* and they hurried back to their waiting planes.

"Not a word of the box to anyone, Azra," Steele said, tossing the strongbox into her cockpit.

"Of course," Nadir replied.

Steele snatched up her aethercast headset and switched the communication device to the frequency being used by her squadron. After a moment of static, she caught the familiar chatter of her pilots, all having a grand old time as they finished off the remnants of the pirate flotilla.

They're having themselves a bloody party while I'm away, Steele thought. *Typical.*

"Bazaine, come in, over," she said, calling for the Squadron Leader she had left in charge.

There was a break in the chatter and Bazaine's deep voice sounded over the line. "Welcome back, Wing Commander. We were getting worried."

"You know me. Just stretching my legs. Any word on reinforcements?"

"Yes, there's an air frigate operating out of Singhkhand on its way. ETA fifteen minutes."

"Roger that," Steele said. "Keep the boys and girls on patrol while we wait. I'll get the civvies packed up. Out."

"Roger, out."

Steele climbed back out of the cockpit and waved to Nadir.

"Azra," she said, "I'm going to make sure the merchants don't keep the frigate waiting when it arrives. You know how Badlanders are with punctuality."

Nadir laughed.

"Get the planes warmed up while I'm away," Steele continued.

"Roger, roger." Nadir snapped a quick salute.

Steele returned to the *Fortuna* and found Captain Adams waiting on deck, supervising a growing stockpile of arms that had been collected from the dead.

"We've got reinforcements arriving in fifteen minutes," she told him. "Make sure your people are ready to go as soon as they get here. We don't dally in the Badlands."

"What about my ship?"

"Can she fly?"

"All of our cells are punctured," Adams replied. "We don't have enough gas to float, let alone fly."

"Then it's staying behind," Steele said.

Adams gritted his teeth. "Please, this is our livelihood. If we lose the ship and cargo, I don't know how we'll recover."

Steele thought for a moment as she studied the envelope resting above them.

"Ok, if you can patch up your cells enough to hold gas before aid arrives, we'll give you enough to fly. But if this ship isn't airworthy by the time we have to leave, it's staying behind. Understood?"

"Yes!" Adams exclaimed. "Thank you!"

"Don't waste time thanking me," Steele said. "Get this thing patched up so we can get out of this wasteland."

* * * *

Steele was too intent on returning to her aeroplane and getting back into the sky to notice any peculiarities in the local flora or fauna; likewise, the crew of the *Fortuna* were too busy rushing to repair their ship to worry about such trivialities. But had anyone been in the mood for bird watching, they would have noticed a peculiar sight. In the branches of a nearby tree sat a bird that had no proper place in nature. It was not living, being composed entirely of metal and machinery, but its maker had perfected its appearance down to the finest detail such that it could have been mistaken for one of the many eagles that populated the Badlands. Tiny gears in its body whirred softly as it twitched in a deceptive parody of life, and its eyes—the lenses of a camera—studied the entire proceeding as a reel of expensive celluloid film ran inside its head.

The bird that was a machine waited until the noise of Steele and Nadir's engines starting drowned out the chance of any more audio recording—courtesy of a gramophone and wax cylinder hidden just under its neck. Then, with all the movements of a startled animal taking flight, it shot into the air and took to wing, flying off into the depths of the Badlands to report these new developments to its master.

THREE

Circling the eyot in her Kestrel, Steele led her squadron in an aerial skirmish order while she waited for reinforcements. Any opportunistic vultures who might have ideas about preying upon the fallen merchant ship would be met with a hot-headed bunch of fighter pilots eager for a fight. Steele almost wished more pirates *would* happen by.

There's nothing worse than the chatter of bored Air Force officers, Steele thought to herself.

She watched as the air frigate arrived, on time of course, traveling at full steam to reinforce them before more pirates arrived. Steele smiled as she heard a collective groan of disappointment over the aethercast channel now that a warship had joined the fighters. Even if pirates attacked now, it wouldn't be half as challenging or half as fun.

The aethercast crackled as a message came in on a different Commonwealth channel. Steele switched over.

"Fighter wing, come in. This is the Commonwealth airship *Zafer*. What is your status? Over."

"Right as rain, *Zafer*. This is Wing Commander Steele, Frontier Reconnaissance Group. Call sign *Mongoose*. Glad you could join us."

The communications officer on the *Zafer* laughed. "Did we miss all the fun?"

"I'm afraid so," Steele said. "It's been quiet skies since we downed the first batch of pirates. We've been playing governess to the civvies for the past fifteen minutes."

The aethercast crackled with some more static.

"Good," the *Zafer* officer replied. "We'll give the salvage teams another fifteen to go over the wreckage of that pirate airship down there and then we'll get out of this wasteland."

Steele sighed softly. *Of course you have to send down the salvage teams. Pirate hunting's too expensive without commandeering supplies and contraband from the enemy. And meanwhile, we get to fly around doing nothing while the quartermaster mucks about with itemized lists.*

Aloud, she said, "While you're down there, see if you can spare some gas for the merchantman. It took a beating before we arrived. Might not have enough to stay aloft on the return journey."

"Roger that. We'll take care of it. Over and out."

Steele switched back to the squadron channel and relayed the news to her pilots. She was met with a chorus of groans.

* * * *

THE FLYING FOXES

Steele had to admit that, tiresome as they were, the salvage teams at least knew how to do their jobs quickly. Within half an hour the small convoy was on its way eastward, limping along slowly so that the *Fortuna* could keep up.

The Air Force units were operating out of the Rahul Air Force Base on the eyot of Singhkhand, but for the return trip they selected the nearby port of Kilkala, the westernmost point of Commonwealth territory. Kilkala was located within Singhkhand's administrative region, and its population was dominated by the

Mahari, the native people of the Singhkhand state. Its governance, however, was given over almost entirely to the powerful United Colonial Trading Company, a corporation that ran Kilkala and several other holdings like private estates. The UCTC even maintained its own security force to police the area, which rankled the men and women of the Air Force to no end.

Leaving the *Fortuna* in the care of the *Zafer*, Steele landed her squadron at the extensive network of airfields located just outside the city. While some of the eyot boasted heavy forestation, the land around Kilkala was extremely flat, making it an ideal shipping hub.

After collecting the cartographic data assembled by her pilots, Steele left Bazaine in charge of the squadron and made her way into Kilkala proper. Like most of the Singhkhand region, Kilkala's climate was extremely hot, and there was ample activity out of doors. Merchant stalls and boxwallahs lined the main roadway, and the air was filled with exotic sights and smells from across the world.

The scent of fresh produce and spiced meat grilling made Steele's stomach rumble, and she turned her steps toward the nearby food markets. They were the best in the world, in her opinion, and no visit to Kilkala was complete without them.

She passed carts of apples and oranges, pots of spices, and even foreign delicacies like peppers, yams and olives. She paused at one stall and inhaled the invigorating smell of fresh basil.

Now where are they? Steele wondered to herself, as she moved from one merchant to the next, searching through the produce.

"Ah ha!" she exclaimed aloud as she finally found the object of her search: fresh sun-ripened tomatoes. They never seemed to grow outside of the Badlands, which made them a rare delicacy. In the Commonwealth, the only tomatoes to be had were produced in environmentally-regulated greenhouses, and they never tasted the same.

As she ate her afternoon snack, Steele meandered into downtown Kilkala, finally stopping outside a simple two-story shop painted an austere white and constructed in the traditional Mahari style. It had a sign over the door that read "Special Survey Bureau, Kilkala Office" with an accompanying notice proclaiming the purchase and sale of "Maps, Statistics, and Other Cartographic

Information"; a smaller sign placed in a window surreptitiously advertised the sale of mining licenses.

Finishing her last tomato, Steele walked inside. The storefront looked like any other in Kilkala, with a counter broken up by workstations running lengthwise against one wall. On the opposite wall, posters advertised the wide range of maps and charts available for sale. A door at the back of the room led into the offices of the cartographers, who turned survey data into the maps that would be sold to the general public.

The room was warm but not hot, the temperature managed by a series of machine-regulated fans that moved lazily up near the ceiling. Steele closed her eyes for a moment and imagined that she was being cooled by a pleasant spring breeze. There were two clerks in linen suits working behind the counter. One was busy serving the office's only customer—a prospector after ore deposits by the looks of him—while the other carried out the SSB's unofficial first rule: "when in doubt, tidy up."

Steele left her name with the clerks at the desk, asking to speak to their superior, and then went to look at the advertisements on the wall. Hidden in among them sat a recruitment poster depicting a young man and a young woman in khaki sporting broad, patriotic smiles, who looked off into an unknown world that was just waiting to be discovered, mapped, indexed and filed. The headline read "DO YOU HAVE WHAT IT TAKES TO BE A *CARTOGRAPHER?*" accompanied by the invitation to "Join the Special Survey Bureau Today!"

"Thinking of joining up, Ms. Steele?" asked a soft voice at Steele's elbow.

Steele nearly jumped in surprise. She turned to see a dark-skinned Mahari man standing next to her with a grin just barely suppressed under his bureaucratic formalness. Like most people of the Commonwealth, he was tall and slender, with a high forehead and a narrow face. Dressed impeccably in a suit and cravat, he was handsome enough to charm, but he would never stand out in a crowd.

The perfect spy, Steele thought as she looked at him. *The last person you'd expect to be one.* She took a deep breath and caught the faint scent of clove oil and cinnamon. *And such a lovely taste in aftershave too.*

Steele smiled warmly at the man, placed her hands together, and bowed her head slightly, a gesture that the man repeated.

"Namaste, Mr. Ray," she said, in the traditional Commonwealth greeting.

"Namaste, Wing Commander." Ray returned Steele's smile. "I'm glad to see you back in one piece."

"Was there any doubt?" Steele asked.

Ray's smile became narrow and sly. "I'm not one to make assumptions where the Badlands are concerned." He reached into his vest pocket and checked his watch. "And I see you're early at that."

"We had to break off reconnaissance to rescue a merchantman and escort it back here. I came to Kilkala directly without stopping at Rahul."

"A good thing you did. I was about to step out for a late lunch." Ray nodded at the satchel held under Steele's arm. "Ah, you have presents for me I see."

Steele gave Ray a cheeky wink. "Well, you know how I dote on you, Ray."

She tossed the satchel to Ray, who caught it easily with one hand. He began rummaging through the bag's contents.

"It's all the usual," Steele said. "Maps, charts, barometric pressure readings, a few photographs. I even managed a little film footage with one of those new aerial cameras from New London."

Ray had the gleeful look of a child opening birthday presents, an inscrutable reaction common among SSB agents, who never seemed happy unless they had a mass of incomprehensible numbers in front of them.

"This is simply wonderful," he said. Turning toward the counter, he motioned to one of the clerks. "Smith, take all this into the back and start analyzing it."

Young Smith—a fair-haired Londinian like Steele—hopped to the task with vigor. "Yes, sir, Mr. Ray," he said, taking the satchel as if it were a beloved child and hurrying into the back rooms.

Steele watched the boy go and shook her head in wonderment.

"I don't understand how you can get so excited about *numbers*," she said.

"I don't understand how you can get so excited about machine guns and whizbangs," Ray replied, "but we get on all the same, don't we?"

"We do indeed."

"Care to join me for a late lunch?"

"Sure," Steele replied. "But first I've got a favor to ask of you. Can we speak privately in your office?"

"But of course," Ray replied. *"Chez moi est chez toi."*

* * * *

Steele had been privy to the interior of Ray's office many times before. It was a dark and cozy place, a cross between a gentleman's study and a cartographer's workroom. The windows were closed and shuttered, and light came from the blue-white flicker of arc lamps mounted on the walls. The walls were covered in maps and charts, which had undecipherable things written on them in Ray's customary scrawl. Handwriting did not appear to be one of Ray's strengths. The room smelled pleasantly of old books and sandalwood, with an elusive hint of shoe polish lurking in the background.

"Well now, we're in private," Ray said, sitting behind his desk. "What can I do for you, Steele?"

Steele held up the box she had been given on the *Fortuna* and set it down on the desk.

"While I was on patrol, this ended up in my possession. The man who had it before me was killed trying to hide it, so I want to know what's inside and why it's so important. Unfortunately, the damn thing's locked, and I don't want to force it."

"Ah," Ray said, with a gentle nod of his head. "Let me have a crack at it."

Steele stepped around behind the desk as Ray pulled a set of lock picking tools out of a drawer.

"May I ask what happened to the previous owner?" Ray asked, putting on a jeweler's eyepiece and setting to work on the lock. "You said he was on the run?"

"Pirates caught up with him," Steele replied, "which makes me wonder all the more what's inside."

"Agreed," Ray said. "What sort of person was he? A Badlander?"

"Could have been," Steele replied. "His clothes were right for it, but I swear his face looked Commonwealth. Possibly Londinian, possibly Melmothian."

And behind the lines of age and wear, the old man had had the face of a scholar. That was odd.

"He might have been an academic," Steele added.

"A Commonwealth academic in the Badlands?" Ray asked. "That's almost too much to be believed."

"You're telling me."

"Very interesting indeed," Ray said, flicking his wrist to adjust the pressure of one of the tools. "Hmm. . . . This lock is trickier than it—"

Ray abruptly dropped his tools and jerked his hands away from the strongbox. The speed of the movement took Steele quite by surprise. There was a lengthy silence in which she stared at Ray curiously, and Ray in turn stared at the box.

"What just—"

"Did you see that?" Ray asked. "It was bloody fast!" He looked over his hands. "No. . . . No. . . ." He sighed in relief. "No cuts. Good."

Cuts? What cuts?

"Ray, what are you going on about?" Steele asked.

"Watch," Ray said.

Steele watched Ray pick up his tools and begin working the lock again. Every muscle in Ray's forearms seemed ready for action: not tense *per se*, but relaxed and prepared to flex at a moment's notice. He seemed more intent on feeling the tension on his tools than actually seeing anything with his eyes. For all his bureaucratic demeanor, he was a remarkable man to watch on the job.

Still, as the minutes wore on, Steele grew impatient.

Come on, Ray, hurry it up. I want some answers.

"Ah ha!" Ray suddenly exclaimed, and he shoved one of his tools sideways against the lock. He switched hands on the tool to make it easier to hold and then passed his eyepiece to Steele. "Here, look."

Steele leaned over his shoulder and peered at the lock. Through the magnifier she could make out the narrow point of a needle extending out of the keyhole where Ray's lock pick had pinned it.

"That's nasty," she said.

"Isn't it just?"

Ray removed a pair of pliers from his tool kit and used them to yank the needle out of the lock opening. After a lengthy application of pressure, it came free, and Ray held it up for Steele to see.

"Now that's a tricky little number," Ray said. "Poisoned no doubt. And it only released when I started to make progress on the lock. This is a surprisingly complicated box you've brought me."

Steele patted Ray on the shoulder. She hated putting him out like this, and this time it seemed she had nearly gotten him killed.

"Sorry for the inconvenience, Ray. I promise I wasn't trying to kill you."

"Not at all," Ray said with a grin. "This is the most fun I've had all week."

Steele rolled her eyes at him and folded her arms. There was no point in being contrite if Ray insisted on enjoying his death-defying experiences.

"Carry on then."

Ray resumed his lock picking with great care, all the more cautious having only narrowly escaped poisoning. Still, for all the stress of the activity, he truly seemed to be enjoying himself. Finally he finished working his way through the tumblers and the lock turned. Ray took a long probe and carefully raised the lid of the box. Steele could hardly blame him for not wanting to put his hands near it.

"Another nasty number," Ray said, motioning toward a small metal bottle that was placed in one corner.

"Pressurized container?" Steele asked.

"Yes, of the sort that we in the trade normally use for holding chemical vapors. See how the bottle's catch is connected to the lock and the hinges? A good thing you brought it to me. If you'd tried to force it open, you'd have found yourself with a face full of poisonous gas."

Steele threw an arm around Ray's shoulders and gave him a friendly shake. "A good thing indeed. If it had gone off, you'd have been the one to end up dead, and I'd have an exciting new story to tell."

"I'm glad you're looking on the bright side."

Ray pulled on a glove and reached into the box. He drew out a flat metal object perforated by a series of perfectly circular holes. Where the holes were not present, it was covered with strange symbols of great obscurity.

"Well, that was anticlimactic," Ray said.

Steele took the object and turned it over in her hands.

"A *punch card?*" she asked aloud. Why would anyone go to such lengths to protect a single punch card?

"Judging by the security precautions, it must be a very important punch card," Ray said. "I wonder what it's for."

"The man I got it from said the box contained 'the power to change the world.' I can only assume he meant this card."

Ray frowned. "I realize the Badlands are a bit behind the times in terms of modern technology, but I'd have thought that they'd at least have *heard* of punch cards. A programmable loom may be a marvel of engineering, but it won't change the world."

Steele agreed that it made very little sense.

"It must be what's on the card," she said. "Maybe it's . . . hmmm . . . account information? Or military secrets?"

"All on a single card? Impossible."

Ray was right, of course. A single card simply could not hold enough information to make it useful. Dozens would be needed to store something useful.

"What are these symbols?" Ray asked. "Have you ever seen anything like them before?"

"Never," Steele said.

"Nor have I." Ray furrowed his brow in concentration. "Maybe . . ." he mused.

Steele pursed her lips, similarly deep in thought. "Perhaps . . ."

After a moment, they turned toward one another, each intent upon an idea that had suddenly come to them. They paused, fingers raised and mouths open to speak. Then, as one, they both realized that their ideas were quite implausible and fell silent.

"No . . ." they said simultaneously.

Steele sighed. "All right, let's be honest. We've got nothing."

"There's only one thing to do now," Ray said.

"Ask a professional?"

Ray slammed his fist down on the desk with great finality.

"Have some *lemonade.*"

FOUR

During the heat of the day, Kilkala's open-air cafes were always filled with people enjoying iced drinks, fruit and yoghurt, anything to help keep cool in the bright mid-day sun. Steele always found herself drawn to Kilkala's public spaces when she was in town, especially around mid-day. The heat reminded her of her birthplace, the dry tropical eyot of Saba.

Broad umbrellas and canopies covered the area, keeping the patrons free from both direct sunlight and the periodic showers that were known to appear without warning and vanish just as abruptly. Steele especially appreciated the art that went into the positioning of the cafe tables. They created the illusion of meandering, serpentine space, but, in fact, the layout was carefully engineered to make it easy for waiters to reach their sections without creating the appearance of a grid. That was the Commonwealth in a nutshell: a unity of art and engineering.

Steele sat in the shelter of one of the canopies, absently stirring her bowl of *cacik* with a spoon, while she stared intently at the punch card in her hand. Her mind whirled with intense agitation. What was the card's purpose? What did the symbols mean? And why would anyone want to kill for it?

Across the table, Ray sipped his drink with the languor of a man who knew how to relax in between periods of intensive work.

How does he do it? Steele wondered. *He was nearly poisoned just half an hour ago, and now he's acting like he hasn't a care in the world.*

"Well then," Ray said, dabbing his lips with a napkin, "what can we deduce from this mysterious punch card of yours?"

"The card's metal, not paper," Steele replied. That much was obvious, but there had to be a reason for it. After a moment's thought, she added, "That says to me that it's supposed to withstand a lot of wear and tear."

"And that it's difficult to replace," Ray said. "Otherwise, why not just make a stack of paper ones and exchange old for new if it wears down?" He set his napkin down. "Steele, have some lemonade."

"I'm not thirsty."

"For my sake, then."

Ray tilted his head slightly and gave her a pleading look.

Oh, not the big brown eyes, Ray, Steele thought. *You know I can't say no to them!*

"Fine," she said, and took a long gulp of lemonade. The mixture of lemon, water, sugar and the faintest hint of spice was marvelously refreshing, and in spite of herself, she took a second drink after she had swallowed the first. She had not realized how hungry or thirsty she was.

Well, I suppose the last time I ate was breakfast before patrol this morning—

"Also, there's only the one card," Ray said, interrupting Steele's thought. "Either it represents an absurdly small program or it's part of a larger stack. I suppose there could be some machine out there that won't run without it."

Steele found the stack of metal punch cards theory far-fetched. A person would need dozens of them, and that would quickly become expensive.

"Maybe it's some kind of command card," she said, before eating a mouthful of mint-flavored yoghurt. "Perhaps the rest of the cards are paper, but the program won't run unless this one's there to translate the code."

"Now that's an interesting possibility," Ray said. Something nearby drew his eye, and he sighed a bit. "The waiter's hovering again."

Steele glanced over her shoulder and saw a man with an apron watching them expectantly, one hand holding his notepad of orders. Seeing that he had been noticed, the waiter paused for a moment as if expecting to be called over. When this did not occur, he quickly busied himself with serving the patrons at another table.

Steele sighed. "They'll do anything for a tip, won't they?"

She quickly returned to the matter of the punch card. "What really puzzles me are these markings. They have to be words of some sort. If we could translate them, we'd have a much better idea of what this thing is for."

Ray held out his hand for the card.

"If you like," he said, "I'll have my cartographers look it over to see if any of them recognize the characters. Failing that, I know a chap over at Vihara University who specializes in esoteric languages. He might be of some help."

"That would be perfect." Steele passed the card to Ray. "I don't have time to bother with the bloody thing, but I'll admit it's got my curiosity now."

Ray tucked the card into one of his coat pockets. "My pleasure, Steele. You know I'll do anything for a woman who keeps me supplied with numbers and barometric pressure readings."

Steele grinned. "Cheeky devil."

"Heads up, the tip hunter is back."

Steele looked over her shoulder to see the waiter return. He had a scrap of paper in one hand.

"Ma'am, you're Ms. Steele, correct?"

"That I am," Steele replied. "Why?"

"Urgent message for you at the telegraph exchange, and they need an immediate reply."

Steele sighed and took another sip of lemonade. Her morning had been long enough without interruptions getting in the way.

"Honestly, my day keeps getting better and better," she said.

"Trouble?" Ray asked.

"Probably UCTC bureaucrats giving Bazaine a hard time about resupplying," Steele replied, standing. "I swear, I've had it up to *here* with private companies acting like they own the place. I've half a mind to take my squadron and do a strafing run on their corporate headquarters."

In that moment, she meant it.

"You'd be doing us all a favor," Ray said with a grin. "Don't be long, or else I might finish off your yoghurt."

Steele made a noise and rolled her eyes at him. She could always count on Ray to provide an interjection of sarcasm.

Turning, she accompanied the waiter toward the telegraph building shared by the café and the adjoining businesses.

* * * *

As Ray watched them go, his trained eyes took in a detail about the waiter that neither he nor Steele had previously noticed. It was a small point, easily overlooked, and at first Ray merely saw it without observing. Then, as he raised a spoonful of *cacik*, his conscious mind noticed what was wrong. The waiter had had a revolver tucked into the back of his trousers, barely concealed beneath his jacket.

Ray's eyes went wide, and he dropped his spoon. Bolting to his feet, he raced for the telegraph office, already reaching into his coat for a weapon.

* * * *

Impatient and direct, Steele walked past the waiter and went directly up to the counter of the telegraph office. The room was small and stuffy. A lone fan turned up near the ceiling, providing more noise than cool air.

It must be Hell to work in here, Steele thought as she waited for the operator to appear. There was no one in the chair behind the desk. It was probably boring as well with no one else to talk to in the office. No wonder telegraph operators were known to chat with one another over the lines in between messages.

Irritated at the delay, Steele tapped the bell on the counter a few times and looked around for the operator. As she did, she caught a glimpse of something heaped on the floor near the batteries and equipment in the back.

"What the—"

Steele spun about on her toes just in time to see the waiter draw a revolver topped with a silencer from behind his back.

A trap!

Although taken by surprise, Steele had dealt with enough ambushes in the air to know when to act first and think second. Ducking under the gun, she lunged with her shoulder forward and caught the waiter just under the arm. The revolver went up and fired into the ceiling. Steele twisted around, fighting to keep the gun pointed away from her.

She spotted an opening and jabbed the waiter hard in the stomach with her elbow. The man grunted and doubled over. As his weight shifted, Steele crouched and heaved him over her shoulder. The waiter struck the floor with a thud. Steele quickly kicked the revolver away and knocked him senseless with a jab of her fist.

Steele dusted herself off and adjusted her collar. *There's that sorted.*

Behind her, Ray appeared in the doorway, breathless from running.

"Steele!" he cried. "It's a . . . Oh."

Steele cracked her knuckles and grinned at him. "Hey Ray. Glad you could join us."

Ray did his best to look nonchalant. "So you don't need any help then?"

"No."

"And here I was rushing to your rescue."

"Silly you," Steele said. "What made you follow us?"

"I saw he had a gun," Ray replied. "Took me a moment to put two and two together."

Steele watched as Ray knelt by the waiter's body and began searching him. After finding nothing of use in the man's pockets, Ray pulled back the man's sleeve to reveal a blue tattoo of a skull surrounded by a five-pointed star. Steele could tell that it was not the most professional of inking jobs, but it was clear enough to make out. She suddenly had a much better idea of who the man might be.

"What have we here?" Ray asked aloud.

"That looks like a pirate mark," Steele said.

"Do you recognize it?"

Steele thought hard, but nothing specific came to mind. This came as little surprise. The number of pirate emblems in use across the Known World was staggering. It seemed like every year a dozen new ones appeared on the scene, replacing others whose users had died off or been absorbed by rival gangs.

"No," Steele admitted, "but it's the sort of composition they all use. They're not always the most creative of people. Everyone wants a death's head or a few weapons."

"I suppose it gets the point across," Ray said.

He was right.

Ray might have said more, but a sound from outside interrupted him. He and Steele looked up as the sounds of voices approached the door. A pair of large, weather-worn men in dirty clothes entered the room in the midst of conversation.

"If Pugly's done his job, she should be dead by now," said the first man as they rounded the corner. "Now we just—"

The second man's eyes went wide at the sight of Steele. "She's alive!"

"Hello there," Steele said, giving her best winning smile. "You must be here for our drink orders."

The first man lunged at Steele, hands outstretched to strangle her. His companion drew a knife and raised it above Ray's head. Steele saw Ray reach beneath his coat and grab for some concealed weapon. The two of them exchanged a quick glance.

Now!

Steele bounded forward to meet her assailant. She brought her arms up to knock the man's grasp away and then stepped inside his reach and landed a pair of solid jabs to the chin.

One! Two! Down you go!

The assailant tumbled backward and hit the ground in a heap. Steele bounded back lightly, keeping on her toes and maintaining her boxer's stance. She was suddenly having a marvelous time of things.

At Steele's side, Ray bounded to his feet and drew his concealed weapon: a length of metal wrapped in wire with a pair of prongs at one end and a wooden handle at the other. The second attacker brought his knife down at Ray, screaming bloody murder. Ray nimbly sidestepped the blow and shoved the pronged end of the rod into the man's neck. There was a jolt and a crackle. The man shook, convulsed, and collapsed in a heap.

Steele dusted her hands off as Ray shoved the shock stick back into its holster to recharge.

"That was *fun*," she said, and she meant it.

"Immeasurably," Ray agreed.

"Are there more?"

Ray peered out the door. "No, thankfully."

"Pity," Steele said, disappointed. "I was just getting warmed up."

They knelt down and began searching the bodies of the unconscious men. There were more tattoos, including pirate marks identical to the one on the waiter. In one man's pocket, Ray found a folded piece of paper. As he looked it over, his eyes narrowed.

"This is troubling."

"What?" Steele asked, taking the paper from Ray. It was a note typewritten on coarse paper. As she read the contents, her expression darkened in anger. "Bloody Hell!"

FIVE

"'Kill the woman,'" Steele said, reading aloud from the note they had found, "'and take what she carries. When the task is done, send signal and wait for instructions.' This is about me and the bloody punch card!"

She threw the note down on Ray's desk and began pacing back and forth across the office. Bloody pirates! Who else would resort to murdering a pilot in the street when they could not match her in the air?

"The fact that they're after you is no great surprise," Ray said from behind his desk. He was busy proofing a collection of survey charts for sale and did not even look up as he spoke. "Their knowledge of the punch card, or at least of the box, is more interesting. That, and the fact that they were clearly following someone's orders rather than acting on their own initiative."

Cool as ice, Steele thought, *as usual. Does nothing upset that man?*

"How can you be so calm at a time like this?" Steele asked. "We were just attacked, *in broad daylight*, and I have assassins after me who clearly lack the common decency to fight a girl face to face."

"We already made our report to the police," Ray said without looking up. "Now please calm down, Steele. You're just making yourself more agitated while you wait."

Calm down? Wait?

Steele stopped for a moment and flashed Ray an irritated look. "I'm a fighter pilot, Ray. We don't 'wait'. We're not used to inactivity in the face of danger. When I've got people who want to kill me, my instinct is to go out and kill them first. This whole waiting around thing is a foreign concept to me."

Ray smiled demurely and cleared his throat. "In that case," he said, "why don't we give you something more productive to think about? What do we know about the people behind this?"

Steele took a deep breath. At least it was better than pacing.

"Fine," she said, and set to thinking. What were the facts? What did they know for certain? "Well, whoever's behind this is after the box, and wants me dead."

"True enough," Ray said. "*And* they're connected to pirates. I suspect the same group that attacked that airship you rescued. Do any possible suspects spring to mind?"

"Ha!" Steele laughed. "Pirates who want me dead?" There was probably a line out the door on that count.

Ray moved on to the next chart on his desk, not in the least bit concerned. "'Everyone loves a pirate-hunter,'" he said, quoting a popular Commonwealth recruitment slogan.

"Everyone except pirates," Steele replied. "There must be half a dozen bounties on my head by now."

"Perhaps you should fake your death and collect the reward. You could retire early."

Now that was a thought. But retirement was bound to be boring. Not nearly enough dogfights.

"Maybe I could," Steele said.

"What would you do with the money?" Ray asked.

What would I do? Steele wondered. *Perhaps settle down and get a bungalow on Singhkhand? Or a townhouse in New London? A chalet in Devraz up north? Or maybe I could start my own aircraft company— Wait a minute!*

"Now you're just trying to distract me," she said, looking cross.

"Of course not." After a pause, Ray added, "Is it working?"

"Not in the slightest." Steele hid a smile.

"Well, while we wait to hear back from the police, let us go over the facts. You find a civilian airship carrying a hunted man that has just come under attack by pirates. The hunted man gives you a box and then expires. You come to me, and together we find that the box contains a punch card of uncertain purpose. Then, only a couple of hours after the attack, you're assaulted by men who are after something you have, presumably the box, which is to say the punch card."

"Yes," Steele agreed. "It begs the question, how did someone on Kilkala know I had it?"

"Any thoughts?"

Steele shrugged. There were any number of possible answers, and none of them were conclusive.

"Someone might have seen me take it, I suppose," she said. She sounded extremely doubtful even to herself. "But really, anyone who could have would have died shortly after or been stranded on that eyot. And I'm positive no one followed us back to Kilkala."

"Could it have been the captain of the merchantman?" Ray asked.

"Captain Adams?" Steele considered this. But no, Adams hadn't seemed like the sort of man to commit murder, let alone conspire with pirates. "No, I wouldn't think so. He was a Badlander, but he was all right. Besides, if it was him, why didn't he just kill the old man and take the box from him when he had the chance? He'd have had a damn sight easier time of it in the wilderness than when he reached port."

Ray nodded. "Perhaps one of his crew then?"

Always a possibility.

"Could be," Steele said. But most Badlander crews were extremely close-knit, kept together on strong bonds of trust. A new member would have aroused suspicion. "Then again, I can't imagine they took on a new member right before being attacked by pirates and then *forgot to mention it*."

"Point taken," Ray said, rubbing his chin as he pondered Steele's words. "Hard to say if it's more or less plausible than the alternative."

"Which is?" Steele asked.

"Which is that someone on the eyot saw you leave the ship with the box and identified your destination as Kilkala, then contacted the person behind the attack, who just happens to have agents already in position to ambush you when you arrive. And all that in the space of a few hours."

"It's not impossible," Steele said, wishing with all her heart that it were.

"No," Ray admitted. "But it's not in the least bit comforting."

You're telling me. Steele shivered a little at the thought of such wide-reaching power.

"Well," she said, "I'll leave you to ponder the disconcerting implications of such possibilities. If you'll excuse me, I'm headed back to the airfield. Call me when something productive happens."

With that, she turned and walked toward the door. Behind her, Ray cleared his throat.

Don't try to stop me, Ray.

"You're doing no such thing," Ray said. "You're going to wait here until Inspector Marceaux sends us the results of his interrogation. He has three prisoners under lock and key, and then there's the matter of those tattoos. There must be *something* he can find out."

Steele turned around and glared at Ray with her hands on her hips and a scowl across her lips.

"Ray, I don't have time for this! I'm burning up my ground leave waiting for some police inspector to rifle through his rogues' gallery on the off-chance that he might have the right pirate thug on file!"

Ray kept his voice calm. "Steele, please relax. The prisoners are bound to start talking eventually."

"You overestimate the police," Steele replied. "And I'm not going to waste my evening on the off-chance that men willing to commit murder in broad daylight are going to be intimidated by the likes of the Kilkala constabulary! Hell, I've got to be on patrol again in *twelve hours*, Ray! I'm not staying here."

Ray removed his spectacles and rose, his expression clouded in anger and frustration.

"Steele, be reasonable! People are trying to *kill you!*"

Steele laughed at the thought.

"People are *always* trying to kill me! I'm a fighter pilot. It comes with the job."

Ray leaned over his desk, eyes locked firmly on Steele. Never one to back down from a challenge, Steele met his gaze. She walked to the desk and leaned across it as well, matching Ray in stance and stubbornness, daring him to fight with her.

"Wing Commander Steele," Ray said, "someone out there is after your head, and I will be damned if you walk into a trap on my watch! You are staying here!"

"How do you plan to make me?" Steele asked. She grinned. It was the sort of smile she reserved for times of conflict.

Ray's expression remained calm and firm as he looked at her.

"By physical force, if necessary," he said.

He probably meant it. That thought made Steele's aggressive smile widen further.

Try it, Ray. Try it. And don't think I won't hit you just because you're pretty.

At that moment, the office door opened slightly and young Smith poked his head in. At the sight of Ray and Steele squared off against one another, he gave an awkward cough and spoke.

"Mr. Ray, Inspector Marceaux is on the line. He says it's urgent."

Steele and Ray continued staring at one another for a few moments more. Then Ray looked over at Smith and smiled.

"Just in time, I think," he said.

Ray reached across the desk and picked up the telephone. "Hello, Inspector?" He said. "Yes, go ahead." He paused as the man on the other end of the line spoke. "Really?" A smile slowly crossed his lips. "That *is* good news. We'll be there in five minutes."

"*Well?*" Steele demanded, as Ray hung up.

"Wing Commander, get your gun. We're going to have some fun."

* * * *

In the first strains of twilight, Steele crouched in the undergrowth of the Kilkala jungle some distance outside of town. Ray was at her side. Through the foliage ahead, Steele could make out a wooden cabin sitting in the midst of a small clearing. She pushed a low branch out of the way and approached a little closer, sizing up the building.

Someone had gone to great trouble to protect the cabin from detection by the aerial patrols that periodically made fly-bys over the wilderness. Rocks, brush, and even a few fallen trees covered the top of the building, making it invisible to aerial surveillance. But from the ground, Steele could see the walls and windows with little difficulty. The building even had an aethercaster, identified by a set of aerials that Steele spotted protruding through the top of the camouflage. Apparently no one in the cabin thought they would be observed from ground level, although Steele could hardly blame them. The strange noises and rustling sounds that filled the jungle set her hair on end. No sensible city-dweller would venture this far into the wilderness without a damn good reason.

Two uniformed policemen waited just at the edge of the clearing. Their superior, Inspector Ahmed Marceaux—a dark-haired Melmothian with a neatly trimmed moustache—crouched next to Ray with a shotgun lying across one knee. Steele could hear the two of them whispering to one another behind her.

"What are we looking at, Inspector?" Ray asked.

"The men who attacked you belong to a local gang," Marceaux said. "They're strictly small-time, you understand. A little petty crime here or there, sometimes a protection racket, most often smuggling. We raid their hideouts from time to time, but it rarely amounts to much. We've suspected that they had a headquarters somewhere, but we've never been able to find it."

"Until now," Ray said.

Marceaux gave a little nod. "Yes, one of the fellows had the good sense to realize that attempted murder of an Air Force officer was a little more than he'd bargained for. After the right application of pressure, he gave up his comrades in exchange for clemency."

Ray chuckled. "No honor among thieves."

"Not where a hanging's concerned, no," Marceaux said. "Especially after I explained what would happen if the hangman miscalculated the proper length of rope. Photographs often help illustrate the point."

Steele smiled a little to hear that. *The benefits of modern technology.* She checked the bullets in her revolver.

"What sort of opposition can we expect?" she asked, looking back over her shoulder.

"Disorganized at best," Marceaux replied. "The men are probably drunk, but keep on your toes. If they're in league with pirates, they might have some real firepower on hand."

"Thankfully we have the element of surprise," Ray said.

The sound of thunder rippled through the sky, and the sounds of the jungle went quiet. It would be raining soon.

Steele cocked the hammer of her pistol. "Then let's get to it before it starts showering."

"Afraid a little rain will ruin your hair?" Ray asked with a playful grin.

Cheeky.

Steele smiled back. "Nonsense, Ray. I'm afraid it'll ruin your nice suit." She gave his cravat a sharp tug to emphasize the point.

Marceaux cleared his throat. "On my word." He counted to three on his free hand. "Go!"

Following Marceaux's lead, Steele broke from cover and dashed across the clearing. Ray followed close behind her, with the two policemen taking up the rear. They moved in a staggered formation, using the building's own camouflage to block the view of them from the windows.

Steele reached the cabin a step behind Marceaux and pressed up against the wall to avoid being seen. She glanced through the window and caught a momentary glimpse of armed men sitting about on mattresses and crates in the squalor of the main room. They were all quite probably drunk. Easy targets if they were caught off guard.

"Four of them," Steele whispered to Marceaux.

The inspector nodded his understanding and moved up to the rear door of the cabin. He looked back at Steele and the others to be certain they were ready. Steele raised her revolver as the first drops of rain began falling.

Do it.

Marceaux kicked the door open and rushed inside, shotgun braced against his shoulder. Steele was right behind him, with Ray and the policemen following her in turn. The rear entrance led directly into the main room of the cabin, which ran the entire length of the building. It was strewn about with rubbish, loose ammunition, and assorted weapons. Steele only narrowly avoided slipping on an empty beer bottle as she charged in. The entire place was hot and stuffy, and it smelled of sweat and stale alcohol. No question that it was a gang's hideout.

The men in the room leapt to their feet at the sight of Steele and her companions. They were half-drunk, and they fumbled in reaching for their weapons. One man drew a large revolver from the waistband of his trousers. Steele shot him twice in the chest and moved on. She was nearly deafened when Marceaux fired both barrels of his shotgun into the remaining men, knocking them down in a bloody heap.

Steele clutched her ringing ear with one hand. The room spun a little, and for a moment all she could hear was the metallic pattering of raindrops on the corrugated iron roof above her. Through the daze, she saw more men dash in from the adjoining rooms at the back of the building, armed with pistols and knives.

Bugger all!

She kept her body low and fired into the new batch of gangsters, killing one of them. Two more went down from the combined shooting of Ray and the policemen. Screaming obscenities, the gangsters returned fire. Bullets peppered the walls and furniture, sending splinters everywhere. One of the policemen was caught three times in the chest and went down in a bloody heap. Steele felt something hot and painful tug against her leg. She stumbled midstep and narrowly missed being hit as a bullet shot past her temple.

Staying out in the open was going to get her killed. Steele rolled over the top of a pile of crates and dove for cover. She hit the ground with a painful thump. More bullets followed her, passing just over her head. A moment later, she saw Ray vault over the crates and land beside her. He flashed her a toothy grin.

"Enough excitement for you?" he asked, dumping the spent cartridges from his revolver.

Steele replied with a noncommittal shrug.

"Eh," she said. "Not enough aeroplanes if you ask me."

She looked down at where she had been shot and spotted a pair of holes in the side of her uniform bloomers. The bullet had gone cleanly through, only narrowly missing her leg. A very near thing indeed. Steele sighed. The Group Captain would be hopping mad about it: he hated it when his pilots got their uniforms damaged off-duty.

With the firefight still raging, Steele reached over the top of the crates and fired a few shots blindly in the direction of the gangsters. Did she hit anything? It was hard to tell who was screaming amid the gunfire. As she reloaded, Steele looked over at Marceaux, who crouched behind a stack of mattresses a few paces away, gripping his shotgun with both hands.

"Inspector!" Steele shouted at him. She motioned toward her ear once she had his attention. "Mind where you're shooting next time! You nearly blew my head off!"

"I think you'll find that I saved your life back there!" Marceaux called back.

"I think you'll find you're wrong!" Steele said.

Marceaux grunted in a particularly noncommittal way. Shouldering his shotgun, he bounded to his feet and opened fire on the gangsters. Steele straightened up and peered over her cover to see the result. The first shot hit a gangster midway across the room, killing him outright, and wounded his nearest companion in the spray of buckshot.

Before Marceaux could fire again, a bullet from one of the surviving gangsters hit him in the arm. Marceaux cried out in pain and fell to the floor, clutching his shoulder. The shotgun dropped from his fingers and landed pointing toward Steele and Ray.

No!

In the few seconds she had available, Steele pushed Ray behind her to shield him. She winced for a moment, expecting the shotgun to go off. Thankfully, it did not. Steele exhaled. She was used to the rush of adrenaline but not while on the ground.

"I'm going for the shotgun," Steele said to Ray, handing his her revolver.

"You're *what?*"

Not bothering to reply, Steele darted from cover and ran the few paces to where Marceaux lay. More bullets flew all around her, twice Steele felt certain that she had been shot. She landed behind the stack of mattresses with her heart beating like mad, and she lay still for a few moments trying to steady herself.

Marceaux groaned at the sight of her.

"Hello there, inspector," Steele said. "How's the arm?"

Marceaux groaned again.

Steele patted him on the leg and grabbed the shotgun. She looked back at Ray as she loaded the empty barrel, slowly mouthing the words "on three." Ray nodded his understanding, although he looked furious with her for having exposed herself to enemy fire a moment ago. Steele simply flashed Ray a smile and counted down on her hand.

Three. Two. One. Go.

Standing, Steele raised the shotgun and fired off both barrels into the remaining gangsters. The noise of the weapon was tremendous, louder than what she was used to. Nearby, Ray and the remaining police constable followed her example, and they fired away with the three revolvers between them, filling the air with bullets.

Only one man survived the torrent of metal, and Steele could see that he was badly wounded. The gangster stared wide-eyed at his dying comrades and then bolted for one of the back rooms. It was futile to give chase, and Steele knew it. There was no telling what sort of a trap he might lead them into. Instead, she reached down and grabbed two shells that Marceaux held out to her. The inspector was clearly in pain, but he seemed determined to keep himself useful.

"Stop!" Steele heard Ray shout.

Steele paused mid-reload and looked behind her. She saw the remaining policeman run from cover and give chase to the fleeing gangster. Steele exchanged looks with Ray and rushed to stop him but it was too late. As the policeman ran into the doorway, the unmistakable clatter of a machine gun sounded from the room beyond. The policeman threw out his arms as if to shield himself a moment before the spray of bullets killed him.

Just on the policeman's heels, Steele and Ray dove apart, each finding cover on one side of the door. Steele leaned out to look into the room. She spotted a hand cranked agar machine gun in the far corner of the room, operated by a grizzled-looking man with a beard. The wounded gangster cowered at the man's side, and Steele could see a marked difference between them. The machine gunner had the look of a mercenary, not a drunk thug. But what was a professional doing in the hideout of some two-bit gang? And how had they gotten their hands on that kind of firepower?

As Steele's mind churned over these questions, the machine gunner spotted her and opened fire. Steele jerked back just in time, scarcely a moment before the edge of the door frame blew apart in a spray of splinters.

"Far corner, left side," she gasped at Ray, struggling to breathe after the shock of her narrow brush with death.

Ray nodded his understanding and reached beneath his coat. He removed an elongated metal sphere about the size of a kumquat and inserted what looked like a pencil into it. Steele flashed Ray a curious look but said nothing.

Striking the pencil end hard against the wall, Ray tossed the sphere into the room in the direction of the machine gun and then readied his revolver. After a moment's pause, there came the sound of a small explosion from the room and a man's cry.

Grenades, Ray? You think of everything, don't you?

Steele rushed through the doorway and saw the machine gunner lying dead on the ground. Ray's grenade had gone off almost directly at his feet. On the opposite side of the room, a flight of rickety wooden stairs led down into an earthen basement, and Steele could hear a man shouting from below.

"—raid on the house! Cancel the shipment!"

Steele exchanged looks with Ray and raced for the stairs. Whoever was in the basement, he was in communication with the outside. This was their chance to get some real answers, and Steele was not about to miss such an opportunity.

The basement she entered ran most of the length of the cabin. It was scarcely a glorified pit dug into the earth, and it smelled terribly of wet soil and moldering wood. At least some effort had been made to shore up the walls with logs and boards. They were probably the only things keeping the basement from collapsing beneath the building on top of it. A raised floor made from rough wooden planks sat a few feet above the bare earth, and Steele was thankful for it. She could hear water and muck sloshing around in the darkness below her feet.

There were heaps of contraband and stolen goods piled all over the room, and Steele saw a long table fitted out with aethercasting equipment positioned to one side of the basement. Wires ran up along the wall and disappeared into the floors above, no doubt continuing to the roof where they met the aerials. A grizzled and weatherworn man in patched clothes and a leather overcoat stood at the table, shouting into the microphone. Steele could tell at a glance that he was a Badlander

"This signal is no longer secure!" he cried.

The man looked over his shoulder and saw Steele as she raced into the basement, with Ray half a step behind her.

"The woman is *alive!*" the man shouted and threw the microphone away.

Having sent his last signal, he grabbed a hammer from the table and began to smash the aethercast machine.

"Stop him!" Steele cried. If he destroyed the aethercaster, they would have no way of knowing what frequency he had been using or who he had been talking to.

At her side, Ray drew his shock stick and raced forward like a sprinter. As Ray dove in, the Badlander yanked his arm back from a swing with unexpected agility and smashed Ray on the side of the head with his elbow. Ray tumbled backward, the shock stick flying from his hand.

Steele felt her heart stop for a second as she grabbed for the weapon. With unexpected dexterity, she snatched the stick out of the air, almost grabbing it by the live end in her effort to catch it before it hit the ground. The Badlander snarled and shouted something in an unfamiliar language. He lashed out at her, and Steele dove under his arm. Steele bobbed to the side as she came up again, evading a second blow by the Badlander. The man was fast, and Steele did not relish the thought of a prolonged fight: she knew the Badlander would probably win.

Stepping around the man's unguarded side, Steele shoved the stick against his neck as she had seen Ray do in the past. There was a jolt of electricity and a cracking sound. The Badlander's eyes rolled back into his head, his body shook, and he collapsed, unconscious.

Steele stood still for a few moments, breathing heavily. She looked at the smashed aethercast machine and sighed. It was damaged beyond repair. There was no way of knowing who the Badlander had been in communication with or even how often the machine had been used. She looked down at Ray where he lay on the floor and saw that he was very much conscious, with his eyes shut to block out the pain of his injury.

"How's your day going Ray?" she asked.

"Ugh . . ." came the groaned response.

"The aethercaster's been smashed into a thousand pieces," Steele added.

"I know how it feels."

SIX

"I'll ask you *one more time* . . ." Inspector Marceaux growled, as he leaned across the interrogation room table supported by one hand. His wounded arm had been cleaned, dressed and neatly placed into a sling.

Across the table, the Badlander who had been operating the aethercast machine sat handcuffed and glowered at the inspector, saying nothing.

"Where did you get the machine gun and the aethercaster?" Marceaux demanded. "Who do you work for?"

He was met with silence.

"You'd better start giving me answers before I lose my patience!" Marceaux growled. "What about the woman? I *know* you sent those men to kill her. Why?"

More silence.

"I could hang you right now in your cell, and no one would so much as blink! What do you say to that?"

The pirate's expression remained calm and disgruntled, but he replied with a question:

"How's the shoulder?"

Marceaux snarled in anger and backhanded the man savagely before resuming his parade of unanswered questions.

* * * *

At a window looking into the interrogation room, Ray watched the process with a placid but not altogether pleased expression. At least one thing was certain: the Badlander was a pirate. Ray had seen the tattoos himself. That made things all the more difficult. A gang was one thing, but a gang working for pirates was quite another. It meant better organization and military-grade supplies.

Ray glanced down the hallway and saw Steele walking in his direction, carrying a cup of tea. He studied her for a moment, out of habit. She was such a lovely young woman; it was a shame that she had been dragged into some pirate's intrigue. How typically foreign of the Badlanders to attack a pilot while she was on the ground. Even the brute Mercians had better manners than that.

"How goes the interrogation?" Steele asked as she joined him.

Ray watched Marceaux strike the pirate again before he responded:

"Slowly."

Steele sipped her tea. "Have we learned anything?"

"He says his name is Thomas, but I don't believe a word of it."

"Why not?"

Ray shrugged. "He looks more like a 'Jack' to me."

He and Steele watched the interrogation in silence for a time.

"This is going to take a while," Steele said at length.

"He'll crack," Ray replied.

Eventually. Everyone cracked eventually. But the pirate Thomas was showing an impressive degree of courage. It was a performance worthy of an SSB field agent.

"I'll admit Marceaux isn't showing his usual finesse at the moment."

"His arm probably hurts," Steele said. She took another drink, strangely calm about the slow going. "'Thomas' or whoever he is won't be talking any time soon."

"What makes you so sure?"

"I know pirates, Ray," Steele said. "Real ones. Not common thugs with a skull and crossbones and a gun to make up for their shortcomings; no, the real scum of the skies like this guy. The kind of men who'd rob widows and orphans, then sell them into slavery for some extra drinking money."

Steele watched Thomas as he continued to goad Marceaux in spite of the physical violence the inspector inflicted upon him.

"Whoever sent him here is worse than anything we can threaten him with," she said. "Pirate lords know how to instill loyalty."

Ray looked at her, his curiosity piqued.

"How's that?" he asked.

"Through fear," Steele said before turning away from the window and walking back down the hallway.

Ray followed her and together they returned to the lobby of the police station. After the events of the day, he was reluctant to let her out of his sight.

"Back to the drawing board then," he said.

"Whoever sent those men after me knows I'm still alive," Steele said.

That was probably true.

"And they'll assume you still have the card." Ray frowned, deeply troubled by this. "Even if I took it away from you, you'd still be in danger."

"Don't mind me," Steele replied, tossing him a smirk. "I make a good decoy."

Truer words . . . Ray thought.

"I'm not a believer in the live bait theory of strategy, thank you," he said, opening the door for Steele. "It often goes wrong."

"You're such a gentleman, Ray," Steele said. "You know how to make a girl feel special . . . like there's someone out there who doesn't want her to die a horrible death."

"Imagine that."

The two of them shared a smile in the street outside the police station. For a moment, Ray enjoyed the pleasant illusion that Steele's life was not in danger; that they were simply two people out for an evening in town. Espionage was nothing new to him, but the thought of Steele being dragged into it made him shiver. He knew she could handle danger, but assassination and intrigue were nowhere near her field of experience.

"Then what do you propose?" Steele asked.

"Propose?"

Steele nodded. "What do we do now?"

We?

Ray took a breath, his moment of calm broken.

"That depends," he said. "Can you get leave from your duties for a few days?"

Steele considered this. "I'm sure I can arrange *something*. The Group Captain owes me a few dozen favors, and Bazaine can handle the squadron with no trouble. Why?"

"Good!" Ray said, clapping his hands. "Then pack your bags. We're going to Vihara."

At least this way he could make sure Steele had protection. It was much more subtle than forcing a security detail on her.

* * * *

As they walked off in the direction of the SSB office, neither of them noticed the curious bird that watched them from its perch on the roof of the police station. The bird studied them through its photo lens eyes until they had passed out of sight. Then it sat still for a short while, only moving to commence those most basic of erratic movements necessary to complete the illusion that it was a living creature rather than a machine. The analytical engine inside its body whirred for several minutes, determining what its next course of action ought to be. Then, its calculations done, the bird took to the air.

* * * *

In his cell, the pirate called Thomas sat against one wall and whistled an eerily cheerful Badlands tune. He was bruised and bloodied from his interrogation by the inspector, but he had refused to give up any information about his employer. That was something to be proud of. The spineless men of the east might be broken by threats and torture, but not a true-blue Badlander like him.

His stubbornness was the result of a life filled with hardship and discomfort, punctuated by luxuries and pleasures earned through hard work, taken from the weak, or gifted as a reward by his lord. And besides, whatever the men of the Commonwealth could do to him, it paled in comparison to what his master was capable of doing.

There was a flutter of wings at the cell's only window, and Thomas looked up. One of the master's machine birds was waiting at the window, its metal claws rotated sideways to find purchase on the bars. The bird peered at Thomas for a moment, but despite the bruises on his face, it confirmed his identity and nodded.

Thomas stood and approached. The machine tilted its head, and then a voice issued out from a hidden speaker in its chest.

"'We're going to Vihara,'" the recorded voice of the Mahari bureaucrat said.

Thomas nodded. This was a good sign. He still had a chance to complete his task and prove that he was worthy of survival. To return to his master empty-handed would mean death; to return victorious would mean reward, luxury, and another step toward perfection.

"Follow them to their destination," Thomas said. "When I arrive in Vihara, come to me and show me where to find them."

The bird waited for a moment as the statement was recorded and processed. Its glassy eyes stared blankly ahead, and Thomas heard the sounds of gears and machine works turning inside its metal body. Then it suddenly took to wing and disappeared into the night.

Thomas lowered himself from the window and huddled in the corner. He had been waiting for just such a confirmation of where the woman would be. Once he made his escape, the alarm would be sounded, and he would have to act quickly—in this case, finding transportation to Singhkhand.

Reaching one hand up to his eye, he slid his fingers around the edge of the prosthetic and yanked it out. The sensation was painful, but Thomas no longer noticed the discomfort. Gripping the ivory ball, he clenched it in the palm of his hand, releasing a long stiletto blade from the iris. Working quickly, he used the blade to turn the lock on the cell door, then crept into the corridor.

A single policeman sat at a table near the iron gate that barred the way into the police station proper. He had his back to Thomas, reading a newspaper. It was most obliging of him.

Thomas slipped behind him and, without a second's hesitation, snapped his neck. Then he stripped the body of its uniform, changed into it, and set the policeman's helmet on his head. That ought to conceal his features.

Without a glance back, he opened the door, walked through the half deserted police station, and passed into the Kilkala night. His mind already whirled with the next stage of his bloody business.

SEVEN

The following afternoon found Steele seated in a comfortable and richly upholstered railway compartment on the Vihara Express, staring out of the window as the vast Singhkhand jungle shot past her in a verdant blur. Ray sat next to her, reading a newspaper and occasionally exchanging pleasantries with a young academic couple seated across from them. There was a lovely atmosphere of leisure and gentility in the compartment, and Steele was having none of it.

Instead, preferring to be antisocial under the circumstances, she limited her interaction to studying herself and her companions reflected in the window glass. She and Ray were traveling incognito, which might have been exciting if Ray had not been so insistent upon the need for disguise. She had no complaints about the blue and green day dress she wore in place of her uniform—in fact, she thought it looked rather fetching—but the absurdly—sized hat that Ray had made her wear proved to be no end of trouble. It was cumbersome and hot, and most irritating of all, the feathers on it kept finding their way into her face.

At least Ray had done his bit as well. He had changed his suit from a somber bureaucratic uniform to a pleasant three-piece ensemble in seersucker, with a white straw homburg on his head, and Steele had to confess that it suited him marvelously. And their disguises did the trick; together they looked like any pair of professionals from the city of Singhpur off to enjoy a weekend excursion away from the metropolis.

Steele listened half-heartedly as Ray and the academics spoke at length about the marvels of modern science and the great possibilities of electricity for creating weapons of war and home appliances. That was typical of academics: wanting to replace anything and everything practical with something new and unreliable. One of academics—a Ms. Das of Melmoth University—insisted that within ten years every aeroplane in the Commonwealth would fly by means of an electrical motor. The thought of it made Steele shiver, and not in a good way. Surely electricity would never produce enough power to keep a plane aloft; even if it could, it would never match the speeds attained by the Kumar-Kent steam engine in her Kestrel.

Steele was so transfixed by the horrible notion that someone might try to replace her plane's engine that she almost missed the transition from science to sport. Soon Ray began speaking emphatically about cricket, and Steele knew that the floodgates were open. This only encouraged the second academic—a Sabai gentleman named Abera—to expound on the great many benefits of boules. Suddenly Steele found herself back at home on Saba, listening to her mother and father arguing about who would come in first that season, New London, Melmoth or Mekel, Saba. Steele was suddenly reminded of why she made a point not to follow sports.

She did not begrudge Ray and the academics their enjoyment of the trip, but the cheerful conversation did little to alleviate the stress of waiting for some unnamed assassin to appear from nowhere and try to kill her. She almost wished one would: at least an attempt on her life would relieve the tension of waiting.

When a porter brought refreshments and Ray and the academics began to have an "indoor picnic" as they chose to name it, Steele found that she had just about had enough. Excusing herself from the compartment, she went for a walk toward the rear of the train, passing more and more compartments filled with more and more people having a wonderful journey, not at all troubled by the possibility of being killed at any given moment.

Reaching the end of the train, Steele let herself out the rear door of the last car. She stood on the platform for a while and watched as the train tracks and the poles of the telegraph vanished away into the distance in a never-ending line, like a ball of thread constantly unwinding. This far out of the capital, the Singhkhand jungle blanketed everything in sight save for a dozen or so feet along either side of the tracks.

The mass of greenery was perversely fascinating to Steele. It was too enclosed, too overgrown, too uncivilized to exist, and yet here it was, a primeval contrast to the metropolitan spires of Singhpur only a few miles away.

Even with all the exotic wonders of the far-off world, home still had mysteries of its own.

Steele had not noticed she was drifting off into a reverie until it was abruptly broken by a furious fluttering of wings. A large bird that might have been an eagle or a small vulture came to land on the railing nearby, and it studied Steele intently, its head cocked to one side.

How strange, Steele thought, approaching the bird cautiously. *Shouldn't it be afraid of me?*

But there was something odd about the bird, which Steele noticed as she drew closer. The feathers seemed little more than a veneer. Beneath the feathers, the bird's body seemed skeletal, but there was no hint of bone. And the eyes, as they looked up at her, were round, glassy, and unblinking. The bird tilted its head with a jerky movement. Suddenly Steele heard a soft whirring sound, like the gears of a calculating machine in the midst of doing figures. The bird opened its beak to squawk, but the sound was hollow and dead.

What the duce?

Steele slowly reached out to touch the creature—indeed, to grab and inspect it by force, if necessary. The bird looked up at her but made no move to flee.

Suddenly, Steele heard a scraping noise on the roof above her. She had barely enough time to crane her neck around and see a shadow fall across her before something gripped her collar. It was a trap!

She was hoisted into the air and felt her lower back strike the overhanging lip of the train car's roof. She cried out in pain and thrashed violently, half trying to gain a handhold, half trying to grab whatever had taken hold of her. One hand closed around the object gripping her collar and found it to be a person's wrist shrouded in a coat and a glove.

Ambushed. . . .

She was slammed hard against the metal roof of the car and left to lie there for a moment, struggling to catch her breath. Well, she had gotten what she wanted—another attempt on her life—though she hadn't expected it to involve the rooftop of a moving train.

Groaning in pain, Steele rolled onto her side and looked up at her assailant. She saw the pirate Thomas standing a few paces away, cracking his knuckles. He was dressed in a policeman's uniform, now stained with sweat and soot from the plumes of smoke that rose from the train's engine and flowed backward into them.

Thomas? What the devil's he doing here? How did he escape?

For that matter, how had he found her?

The bird. . . .

"Give me the box, girl!" Thomas said, approaching with an outstretched arm. "Tell me where it is, and I promise you a quick and painless death."

Like Hell I will.

Steele pulled herself up onto one knee, coughing as the acrid smoke flowing into her face stung her eyes and throat. She needed a weapon, and her service revolver was packed in her luggage. "To avoid suspicion," Ray had said. A fat lot of good it was doing now.

Steele began fussing over her garments, as if adjusting them for the sake of decorum. Thomas laughed at the sight and made some not particularly clever comment about Commonwealth women and their preening. *Laugh all you want*, Steele thought, as one hand found the pocket pistol concealed in her vest.

"What if I don't tell you?" Steele asked.

Thomas sneered.

"Then I'll ask you again," he said. "And again, and again, one extremity at a time, until you die. And if you die without telling me, I will ask you friend next . . . one extremity at a time."

Steele grinned. "I'm sure he'd like the chance to see you try, Tommy boy. But I'll have to disappoint him."

She drew her pistol in a flash, leveling it at Thomas with all the speed she could muster. Steele would be the first to admit that she was not the world's fastest draw, but she knew her business and had seen her fair share of firefights.

But Thomas had clearly seen his share as well. As Steele drew, he leapt forward with a fanatical roar, body tucked into a ball to present as small a target as possible. Steele swore inwardly as she tried to aim. The movement of the train sped her toward Thomas, and she had only time to fire off a single half-aimed shot before they collided, and she was flung onto her back. The impact hurt like Hell.

Steele kept her wits about her and tried to aim again. Thomas intercepted her and grabbed her wrist in an inhumanly strong grip. He tore the pistol from Steele's grasp and gave her a savage kick to the ribs. As Steele lay on the rooftop, clutching her chest and seeing stars, Thomas shuffled back a few paces and tossed the pistol into the brush alongside the train. It had vanished from sight even before it hit the ground.

Steele slowly raised her head, her body aching from the impact. "You're going to pay for that," she growled. "That pistol belonged to a friend."

"Oops!" Thomas laughed, spreading his arms. "I'll have to 'pologize later." He took a step toward her. "And as for you—"

Steele crawled back onto her feet and cracked her neck. It still hurt like Hell, but she would be damned if she was going to let a *Badlander* get the better of her.

"What about me?" she asked.

Thomas looked a little surprised at Steele's tenacity.

"Ain't got your gun, ain't got your machine, and you're still rearin' to go? Not what I'd expect from one of you city-bred Commoners."

Commoners. Steele hated the term. But what could one expect from the likes of an ill-mannered Badlander?

Steele dropped into a fighting stance and raised her fists.

"Commoner, eh?" she said. "Hold on to your hat, Tommy boy, because this Commoner's about to beat you from one end of the train to the other."

Thomas snarled at her. "Try it, missy."

Steele reached up to her hat and removed the long hatpin that secured it in place. Holding the pin outstretched in one hand and the hat close to her like a shield in the other, she slowly advanced toward Thomas.

Thomas snickered as Steele approached him armed only with a woman's accessory. He was in for a surprise. As Steele came within range, Thomas lashed out with the back of his hand. Steele saw the blow coming and ducked beneath it. It was a near thing. Had the blow landed, it probably would have knocked her senseless.

Springing back up, Steele thrust the hatpin into the underside of Thomas's arm, puncturing the thick fabric of the coat and drawing blood. Thomas grunted in pain and stumbled back a few paces. Steele smiled. The stab of a hatpin was like the sting of a bee: not fatal, but remarkably painful.

Steele drew back and waited for Thomas's next action. As Thomas worked to regain his balance, she dove in again and gave him a vicious stab to the side. Thomas roared in pain and lashed out at her, and Steele ducked away again. She smiled, pleased that Thomas was learning just how much he had underestimated her.

Emboldened by her successful strikes, Steele pressed the attack, thrusting with the pin and waving the hat to keep Thomas disoriented and on the retreat.

"Who sent you to kill me?" she demanded. "Who?"

Thomas continued to withdraw, grunting in pain as the pin continued to sting him. He lashed out at Steele with his fists, but she kept the broad-brimmed hat waving back and forth in front of his face to disorient him.

Finally, Steele's patience left her, and she gave Thomas a vicious kick to his wounded side, her skirt flaring out with a whooshing noise from the speed of the strike. Thomas flinched in pain and gasped for air, but he did not lose his balance. It had been a miscalculation for Steele. Before she could recover from the attack, Thomas grabbed her ankle. Steele had just enough time to curse her mistake before Thomas lunged forward and backhanded her across the temple.

The blow was like the kick of a mule, and Steele blacked out for a moment. When she came to again, she was lying on the roof of the train and could not remember having fallen.

Stay awake!

Steele's eyes snapped open again in time to see Thomas looming over her, a revolver in his hand.

"Where's the damn box?" Thomas demanded.

Steele barely heard the question over the noise of the train and the ringing in her ears. She had to overpower Thomas if she was going to get out of this alive. That meant taking him by surprise, and there was only one tactic that Steele could think of that she knew Thomas would not see coming.

As Thomas leaned down, hand reaching for Steele's throat, she flung her hat in his face. It struck Thomas, blinding him for a moment before the wind caught it and whipped it off into the distance behind the train. Good riddance to it. But at least the hat had served some useful purpose before meeting its untimely end.

Taking advantage of the distraction, Steele rolled onto her feet and struck Thomas in the shoulder with the hatpin. Thomas hissed in pain but did not drop his gun. It mattered little. Though Steele's head swam and her vision blurred, she found the coordination to lash out with another kick, which caught Thomas just above the knee on his inside leg. Unbalanced, probably confused, and already struggling to ride the rapidly moving train, Thomas slipped and struck the rooftop chest-first. The pirate's hands grabbed frantically for something to hold, but to no avail. As Steele watched, Thomas slid off the roof and was flung out into open air with a scream.

Dizzy and overcome by the heat, Steele collapsed onto the rooftop once again. She reached one hand up to the side of her head and came away with blood.

That's not good, she thought, although the realization was slow in coming. She was confused and disoriented from the repeated blows, all the more so now that the adrenaline was beginning to drain away.

She studied the crimson stain on her palm for a few moments before her senses returned to her. When she stood, she saw no sign of Thomas anywhere in the distance behind the train. There was nothing in view but the endless jungle stretching off in all directions.

The train shook and Steele stumbled a bit. Her body trembled as the competing forces of exhaustion and adrenaline tried to win control of her body. She fell to her knees and sat for a while on the hot metal roof, gasping for air. She had nearly been killed by Thomas, and she knew it. A fight to the death was a fight to the death, regardless of one's experience.

Coughing at the thick smoke of the train, Steele crawled to the rear of the car and slowly lowered herself down from the roof. She took a few moments to straighten her clothes and to brush her tangled hair out of her face. She was still a bloody mess, but at least she had made an effort to appear decent. Surely that counted for something.

Steele walked back to the compartment with her head held high. When she arrived, bloody, hatless, and soot-stained, the two academics suddenly broke off their conversation in mid-sentence and gasped in shock. They had probably never seen the aftermath of a fight up close before. Ray's eyes widened at the sight of Steele, and he sprang to his feet.

"What happened?" he asked, reaching to take her by the arm.

It was nice of Ray to try and steady her, but Steele's head was throbbing, and she was in no mood to be fussed over.

"Just getting some air," she said, gently pushing Ray's hand away. "Now I think I'll freshen up."

She stumbled along the corridor to a mahogany-paneled washroom with elegant brass furnishings and all but collapsed against the wall. The pain and exhaustion from the fight were getting to her, which annoyed her more than anything. Filling the washbasin with water from the tap, she began scrubbing her face, as much to feel the chill against her skin as to clean it.

Presently she heard a knock against the doorframe, and she turned to see Ray leaning into the room.

"Are you all right?" he asked. He had one of his especially charming expressions of concern.

Steele turned toward him and reached for a hand towel. She wobbled a little bit as her head took on the feeling of air, but she kept her feet.

"Of course I am," she said. "What sort of question is that?"

"The sort of question one asks when one sees someone covered in soot and bleeding from the head," Ray replied.

Steele felt her temple. "It's a flesh wound. I'll be fine."

"Steele—" Ray began.

"I was attacked by our old friend Thomas," Steele said, dabbing her face dry with the towel. It came away with fresh blood on it.

"Thomas who?" Ray asked. Then his eyes narrowed. "You mean *the pirate?*"

"In the flesh," Steele said. "Took me by surprise and tried to beat the location of the box out of me."

"What happened?"

Steele shrugged. "I threw him off the top of the train, of course. Mind you, I lost the hat you gave me. And the pocket pistol. That was a damn shame. The pistol," she clarified, "not the hat. The hat was absurd."

Ray leaned out into the corridor and looked in either direction. How good of him to make certain they were not being watched. Looking back at Steele, he asked:

"How did Thomas get from Kilkala to Singhkhand?"

Steele tossed the bloody hand towel into the washbasin and leaned against the wall.

"He must have stowed away on a ship of some kind," she said. "Maybe the overnight mail. If he'd stolen an aeroplane, it would have been reported, which I imagine your SSB chums would have mentioned when you checked in at Singhpur last night."

"They didn't do a very good job of telling me he'd escaped in the first place," Ray said.

He looked angry. It was touching.

"The UCTC's always bloody close-lipped about problems," Ray added. "I doubt they've even reported that he's missing."

Not report an escaped criminal? What an appalling notion!

"Why not?" Steele asked.

"The Company probably thinks he's still on Kilkala," Ray said. "They'll try to capture him on their own and pretend it never happened. Escaped prisoners who try to assassinate Air Force officers are the sort of things that get corporate privileges revoked, and the UCTC doesn't want that."

I'll bet they don't, Steele thought. She had seen the sort of luxury those corporate privileges bought.

Steele finished washing off the worst of the soot and blood and began dabbing her face dry with another towel. Her head still throbbed from the injuries, but at least the worst of the mess was gone.

"How marvelous for them," she said. "They get to keep their private eyot, and I get to have a brush with death. Everyone's happy!"

"What hap—"

Ray caught himself as a conductor meandered along toward them. Ray touched the brim of his hat politely as the workingman bowed his head in proper deference to a professional. When the conductor had passed, Ray resumed speaking.

"What happened to Thomas?"

"Poor fellow fell off the train," Steele replied, giving her hair a few brushes to remove the worst effects of the wind. "Tragedy of the century."

"Is he dead?"

"Probably at the speed we're going, but I couldn't confirm the kill."

Like any good fighter pilot, Steele never assumed that someone was dead. She had been shot out of the sky more than once, only to survive and be back on patrol the next day. Without a body, death was never a guarantee.

"That's why I like you," Ray said. "You don't make assumptions."

Steele flashed him a smile. "I thought it was my winning personality."

"That as well."

Ray offered Steele his arm, which she took. Though she would never admit it openly, it was nice to have someone to lean on once in a while.

"Shall we return to our newfound friends and our indoor picnic?" Ray asked.

Not that! Anything but that!

Steele made a pained face.

"I think I'd rather be fighting for dear life on the roof of the train."

EIGHT

Located deep within the Singhkhand jungle, Vihara was a pleasant little university town carved from the vast and overpowering forest. Between the towering trees and the slow-paced academic atmosphere, it immediately made Steele uncomfortable. How could anyone stand to live in such a claustrophobic place?

Upon arrival at the town's only sizable hotel, Steele took the opportunity to change out of her traveling clothes and into something not accented with blood and soot. She was not a believer in *avant-garde* fashion statements. After freshening up properly and enjoying an early dinner at the hotel, Steele walked with Ray to the nearby university.

The campus was effectively a perfect square, bounded on all sides by an ancient stone wall and centered on a great tiered tower that rose from an even more massive building. It was a remarkably pretty sight, Steele had to admit, although she immediately knew that she was not welcome. Vihara University was the domain of the academic class, and professionals like her and Ray were interlopers.

As they walked across the university grounds, arm in arm, Ray took the opportunity to play tour guide, pointing at various points of interest as he spoke.

"You may not be aware," he said, "but the Vihara complex is one of the oldest structures in the Commonwealth."

"Really?" Steele asked.

"Oh yes. It dates back hundreds of years before the Great Upheaval when it was constructed as a temple by my ancestors. Then, when order was restored after the time of chaos, it became the home of the philosopher-priests of Singhkhand. And now it's a university." Ray smiled. "A rather fitting continuation of its long history as a haven for truth and knowledge, I feel."

Steele looked about at the intricately sculpted stonework that surrounded them. The outer wall was lined with more stone buildings and covered walkways that connected to one another by modern wooden staircases that had been constructed to carefully mimic the design of the ancient stonework.

"Why are there so many wooden buildings cluttering up the place?" she asked. "They can't be original."

"Indeed not," Ray agreed with a laugh. "The original temple complex is reserved exclusively for places of learning. The main temple, for example, is home to the university library." He motioned with his walking stick to indicate the central building. "While offices and dormitories are necessary for an institution of this kind, the administration didn't think them quite the sort of thing that ought to be occupying a historical landmark, so they had new structures put up to house them."

"It's beautiful, Ray," Steele said with a smile. After a pause, she added, "I hate it."

"Not quite the response I expected," Ray said.

Steele sighed. "Oh, I don't hate *it*. I hate that it's a university. If it was a public park or something I'd be overjoyed, but it's not. It's the private world of the *effendis*, and ordinary people like you and me don't belong here."

"Nonsense," Ray said.

He waved his hand out in a broad arc that encompassed the central lawn, where students in seersucker suits and summer dresses sat around on blankets and chairs, reading and sipping lemonade, debating among themselves, or playing *boules*. The young academics were too busy with their own private conversations and studies to pay any notice to the strangers who had penetrated their private world.

"You see," Ray continued. "No one minds. We fit right in. Dress right and mind your manners, and the *effendis* think you're one of the academic elite, just like them."

Steele smiled at him but she shook her head.

"We're professionals, Ray. We get our education at academies or technical colleges, not universities. We'll never become professors, advance the frontiers of science, or go into politics. Those daft young people out there on the lawn have their heads in the clouds, and they'll never have to come down. And all because some test score on a piece of paper says that they're better than us."

"That's as may be," Ray said, "but the Commonwealth couldn't survive without us. The academics make the laws and manage the bureaucracy, but the humble public servants like myself are the ones who keep everything running."

Steele nudged him sharply and smirked. "'Humble' my eye."

"And don't forget your important role in things, my good Wing Commander," Ray added as they circled around the library building. "Not a single one of these promising young scholars will ever be a war hero. They'll never know the thrill of a dogfight. And when the pirate hordes mass in the west, or Mercia threatens in the east, who do they turn to to save them?"

"Some hotshot air commodore with a pay grade I can't even begin to image," Steele answered smugly.

"Quiet you," Ray said, laughing. "Come along, this is the place."

Ray led her to a wooden faculty building with a wide verandah and overhanging eaves. Like the others of its kind, it had been meticulously constructed to follow the same architectural and aesthetic design as the university stonework. Most of the building's windows were covered by delicate latticework screens that obscured any view of the interior. Steele paused at the bottom of the verandah steps and looked up at them, puzzled.

"All right, Ray," she said, as she resumed walking, "explain the window screens to me. I saw the same sort of thing when I visited Aksum University back home on Saba once. Do all the universities have them?"

"As I understand it, yes," Ray replied as they entered the building and headed for the stairs. The air inside was much cooler than without thanks to mechanical fans that extended from the ceiling. "Obviously they help keep the sun out, but apparently they're also used to prevent students from seeing whether their professors are in their offices or not."

"Whatever for?"

Ray lowered his voice. "Well, the dirty little secret about Commonwealth academics is that they have notoriously bad punctuality. If the students can't see whether their professors have left for classes yet, they have to arrive on time or risk a reprimand."

"Why should that be a problem?" Steele asked.

"Well, as my friend Djebar explains it, professors are even less punctual than students."

What?

Steele paused at the foot of the stairs and blinked a few times. She had been raised to think of academics as a cut above the rest of the Commonwealth population. But if they couldn't even keep track of time. . . .

After a few moments of consideration, she shook her head and followed Ray up toward the second floor.

"Ray, you realize that you're destroying my whole faith in the upper echelons of our society. I thought academics were supposed to be 'better' than us ordinary people."

"Nonsense, Steele," Ray replied. "We all have our part to play in maintaining an orderly civilization. The academic class does very important work, but they're no more vital than the rest of us. And regardless, to hear Djebar talk about it, they're about as disorganized a group as one could hope to find. Always getting distracted by something or other."

"So they really are a lot of absent-minded professors?" Steele asked.

A student bearing an armload of books appeared on the landing above them and rushed past them toward the ground floor, heedless of their presence. Steele only narrowly managed to sidestep a collision. Why couldn't young people learn to watch where they were going?

As Steele angrily brushed out her skirt and adjusted her collar, Ray pointed in the direction of the departing student.

"Exhibit A, Your Worship," he said, as if speaking to a judge.

"It's a bloody marvel they ever graduate," Steele said. Or that they weren't run over by automobiles while crossing the street. They certainly wouldn't notice when something was coming.

Ray laughed. "Well, they don't, in a manner of speaking."

"Come again?"

"It's not like a technical college, where you pass or you fail," Ray said. "When academics complete their five years of study, they take a series of tests designed to identify their areas of aptitude. If they score high enough in a particular field, then they go on to become researchers or professors. If they show general aptitude with a very high intelligence, they go into politics. But even academics who score poorly have a place in the world. What do you think the civil service is for?"

"A dumping ground for failed academics?" Steele asked.

"Bingo."

That came as no surprise. Steele had dealt with government bureaucrats far too many times in the past.

"Professional public servants like myself could easily run the government," Ray said, "but if we did, there would be no place to send all those fine young men and women who can't do anything else."

"Instead you get to be in the Special Survey Bureau," Steele said. "Isn't that fun?"

"Better than the post office."

That was probably true.

Steele followed Ray to an office just above the staircase and waited as he knocked on the door. After a few moments she heard a muffled "Come in!"

* * * *

The office proved to be a cozy haven of intellectual study that smelled pleasantly of sandalwood mixed with the musty scent of old books. Bookshelves lined either wall, and a sturdy desk sat in front of the windows at the far end. Behind the desk sat a middle-aged Beylikite with gradually whitening gray hair and a neatly trimmed beard. He wore circular reading glasses and a rumpled academic gown over his pale gray suit. He looked up as Steele entered, and his face lit up with a smile at the sight of Ray.

"Mr. Ray!" the Beylikite gentleman exclaimed, rising from his chair. "My word, what a delight it is to see you again."

"Hello Djebar," Ray replied, sporting an equally broad smile.

Rather than bowing to one another in the conventional greeting, Ray and Djebar shook hands. It was a clear indication of close friendship.

"And who is your lovely lady friend?" Djebar asked, indicating Steele.

Steele smiled back, uncertain of how one was expected to address an academic. Surely there was some complex ritual that members of the middle class were barred from ever learning. Steele concluded that it probably involved a secret handshake.

"Professor Djebar," Ray said, "it is my great pleasure to introduce you to Wing Commander Steele of the Commonwealth Air Force. Wing Commander, Professor Djebar of Vihara University."

"Namaste *effendi*," Steele said, calling Djebar by the respectful title commonly afforded members of the academic class. She was determined to make a good impression.

Djebar returned the greeting, smiling. Suddenly Steele wondered if she had been too formal.

"Come, come, sit," Djebar said, and quickly set about clearing stacks of books from two of the chairs in his office. It seemed that there was little in the office that did not serve as an improvised bookshelf.

"Now then," Djebar continued, "to what do I owe this pleasure? If I recall, Ray, you tantalized me with hints of some mysterious language you wanted my opinion on."

"Quite so, and I do not intend to disappoint," Ray said. "Steele, will you do the honors?"

'Honors,' he says, Steele thought. *Like I'm planting a tree or something.*

She reached into her vest pocket and drew out a piece of paper onto which she had meticulously sketched the symbols with every attention to detail she could manage. She passed the paper to Djebar, who adjusted his spectacles and began to study it.

"We were wondering if you'd ever seen this language before," she said. "It's rather obscure."

"Ho ho!" Djebar cried. "A mystery is it? I simply adore obscure languages, especially over a glass of raki."

He removed a bottle of the popular anise-flavored spirit from his desk and fumbled around for a few glasses. As he poured the drinks for them, he added,

"Many great things have been accomplished by the careful combination of keen minds and ardent spirits."

"Yes," Ray agreed. "And so have many dreadful things as well."

Djebar chuckled. "We'll leave such nonsense and *shenanigans* to impetuous students, shall we?"

* * * *

Afternoon faded into evening as Steele watched Professor Djebar pour over old tomes filled to brimming with obscure languages now either known only by a pocket community on some far-off eyot or lost to history altogether. The first challenge, Djebar explained, was in finding the alphabet associated with the strange characters. Only then could he even think about attempting a translation. While Djebar had given Steele cause for hope at the outset, the alphabet proved to be elusive.

In the meantime, Steele, Ray, and the professor chatted pleasantly. Djebar did most of the talking as he worked, catching up on current events and reminiscing about old times with Ray. Some of the stories were remarkable, and Steele felt certain she would never look at Ray the same way again, especially after one tale involving a quantity of stolen butter and a policeman's helmet. Apparently, for all his sturdy middle class upbringing, Ray spent an unhealthy amount of time among wastrel academics.

The raki was taken in moderation, mixed with liberal quantities of water to dilute the powerful alcohol, but it left Steele feeling pleasantly numb. After all the stress and frustration of the past two days, strong drink was a welcome relief.

At long last, Djebar sighed and removed his spectacles.

"Well, that settles it," he said. "This set of symbols is not used by *any* living culture in the Known World. Not even one of the eyot clans from the Badlands."

Djebar did not sound hopeful.

"What does that mean?" Steele asked.

"Well . . ." Djebar stroked his beard for a few moments. "I suppose it could be a code of some sort, but that's more Ray's field than mine. Or it may simply be an alphabet that has not been used in the past century, in which case, I will *eventually* be able to find it; it will simply require a greater investment of time than one pleasant evening."

Ray set his glass down and stood. Steele quickly followed his lead.

"Then I suppose we had best leave you to it," Ray said.

"Yes, alas." Djebar smiled. "Good evening to you both. Miss Steele, it was a pleasure to meet you."

Steele and Ray exchanged parting bows with Djebar and withdrew from the office. Steele felt a weight of disappointment upon her shoulders as they descended the stairs and walked out onto the grounds. It had been a bad day, and Djebar's inability to provide a quick answer was not a good way for it to end.

Though it was night, the activity on the campus had barely receded. Gas lights, torches and even the sparks of arc lamps lit the grounds with a sort of pale majesty, not unlike the light of the moon had it existed at the beck and call of human science. Students were still about, stargazing in the night, holding debates by firelight or simply enjoying the cool breezes that had finally come to Singhkhand at the very end of the day.

"What now?" Steele asked, as she and Ray walked back toward the hotel.

Ray thought for a few moments. His expression was displeased. He had probably expected Djebar's expertise to provide the answer for them.

"That depends," he said at length. "I had hoped Djebar would recognize the symbols. Mind you, he might still be able to find their meaning, given time."

"Might." Steele thought. *"Given time."*

She sighed. "Don't tell me we've come all this way to wait on some academic's research. No offense to your friend, but *effendis* take a long time to produce anything useful. Look at Parliament: case in point."

"Well, we can't all have the celerity of a fighter pilot, now can we?" Ray said.

There was that usual Ray charm winning through in spite of the setback. Steele smiled.

"Flatterer," she said.

They walked along Vihara's High Street. The night was pleasant, and Steele smelled the scent of tropical flowers drifting through town on the nocturnal breeze. Vihara was rather a nice place, she concluded, in spite of the trees and the academics. A pity her life was in danger; it was a lovely place for a holiday.

Still feeling warm and pleasant from the raki, Steele took Ray's arm and leaned her head against his shoulder as they walked the remaining distance to the hotel. Ray glanced at her and smiled, but said nothing.

* * * *

As they arrived, Steele disengaged herself from Ray and spoke again.

"But really, what's the next move?" she asked. "Because left to my own devices, I'll go back on patrol."

"Well, we can't have that when your life is in danger, now can we?" Ray said. As they climbed the stairs, he added, "Besides, I'm not out of aces up my sleeve yet."

Good old Ray; down but never out.

"Oh?" Steele asked as they reached their rooms on the next floor. "What exciting adventure do I have to look forward to now? A visit to the postal office perhaps?"

"Hush," Ray said, chuckling. "Go get some rest. Tomorrow we try contact number two."

"And who is that?"

Ray grinned. "It's a surprise."

"Oh lucky me," Steele said, stopping at her room and reaching for her key. "I'll surely dream of sugarplums tonight."

"Whatever keeps you safely in bed and out of trouble." Ray walked to his room, which was adjacent. "Good night, Steele."

"'Night." Steele smiled warmly at him with a mischievous glint in her eye. "Sweet dreams."

Steele shut the door behind her and turned the bolt. The room was small but comfortable, with a box-spring bed at one end, a table with a mirror to the side, and a standing wardrobe for hanging clothes. A set of windowed doors opened out onto a balcony overlooking a side road—though they were locked, of course—and a soft evening breeze drifted in through a window left slightly ajar. The breeze brought with it the heady night scents of the jungle or, perhaps more likely, of the flower gardens at the university. It reminded her of the recent stroll down the High Street.

Crossing the room, she sat on the bed and fell backward with a sigh. It had been an extremely long two days, and there seemed little respite in sight. She was used to working herself to exhaustion, but only under the restorative effects of excitement and adrenaline. The long, anxious waiting game that Ray seemed to enjoy so much was extremely unpleasant for her, nor did she share his taste for these elaborate and dangerous puzzles. She had no doubt that, concern for her safety aside, Ray was having the time of his life searching for an answer to the mystery of the punch card. Had he been the one hunted, Ray would probably have enjoyed it all the more, playing a game of cat and mouse with the unseen fiend orchestrating the hunt. Ray was such a curious man, but then again he was both a spy and a bureaucrat, which clearly meant that he was more than a little mad.

Determined to get some sleep while the buzz of the raki was still with her, Steele unlaced her boots and tossed them to one side, followed by her stockings. Standing, she unbuttoned her vest and blouse and left them draped over a chair before laying her skirt out on the sofa. She had brought a nightdress but by now had neither the patience nor the energy to change into it. Instead, she resolved to sleep in her camisole and bloomers, and even toyed with the idea of giving Ray a start when he called on her the next morning. She always enjoyed taking his sensibilities by surprise.

Steele walked back toward the bed. As she did so, she felt a slight breeze rush past her. She looked toward the balcony doors and saw that they were open. Suddenly the comfortable numbness of the raki was gone.

Oh Hell. Not now!

A floorboard creaked behind her. Steele spun about and saw Thomas, very much alive although sporting numerous cuts and bruises, as he walked toward her with his hands outstretched. He clearly meant to strangle her. Steele froze for a moment at the sight of him.

He's alive! Steele thought. But she had suspected as much. The real shock was in finding him here, in her bedroom, when she was exhausted and unarmed.

Thomas smiled at Steele and slowly raised a finger to his lips. Whether he thought this might actually silence her was unknown, for in the next moment he lunged for her throat.

"Oh Hell—" Steele managed before Thomas's grasp cut her off.

Exerting every ounce of control and leverage at his disposal, Thomas forced Steele down upon the bed, his hands choking the breath from her. Steele's head swam, her vision blurred, and her limbs became numb. Her brain was in agony and struggled to think. But she would not die here, not like this.

Working more on reaction than thought, Steele pulled her hands together over her chest and punched upward between Thomas's arms. The sharp force of the blow broke the pirate's grasp for a moment, just long enough for Steele to smash her forehead into the bridge of his nose. Thomas cried out in pain and fell backward.

That'll teach you!

Steele broke away from Thomas and gave him a sound jab to the jaw. Bleeding and confused, Thomas lashed out with his fist and caught Steele in the stomach. The blow knocked the wind out of her and she doubled over. As she struggled to regain her breath, Thomas grabbed her by the shoulders and shook her violently. This confused Steele: did he think that by roughing her up a bit, he could make her give in? If so, he was an idiot. She was not some Badlander saloon girl he could slap around a few times and have his way with.

Intending to make this point clear to him, Steele punched Thomas in the ribs twice and followed up with a jab to the gut. Thomas made a gurgling noise and doubled over, gasping for breath. But to Steele's annoyance, the pain only made Thomas's grip tighter. She slammed her knee into Thomas's torso, which finally gave him the hint to let go.

With a roar, Thomas flung her against the nearby wall. Steele landed with a crash and then tumbled forward over the sofa, dazed and disoriented.

* * * *

In the adjacent room, Ray had just sat down to enjoy a nightcap and an improving book when the wall beside him fairly shook with a forceful impact. Startled, he looked in the direction of the noise, just in time to hear the sounds of further violence from the other side of the wall. He was on his feet in a flash, with only one thing on his mind.

"Steele?" he called, and then pressed his ear up against the wall. He was rewarded with more noises. "*Steele!*"

* * * *

Back in the other room, Steele slowly raised her head as the blood pounded in her ears. She lay half sprawled over the back of the sofa, her hair in a wild tangle about her face and her body aching from the impact of the landing. Forcing herself to move, she looked up in time to see Thomas draw a knife and rush at her with murder in his eyes.

Steele resolved to put a gun in her stocking the next time she traveled. Assuming she survived this trip.

She darted out from behind the sofa, using it as a barrier. Thomas stumbled over the furniture, turned and charged again. Steele fell back a step and threw up her arm to block the blow, catching Thomas just beneath the wrist. She kept her other arm free just in case Thomas retaliated with a punch, but the pirate was more tactical this time. He lashed out with his feet and swept Steele's legs out from beneath her. She hit the floor with a thud.

So much for a quiet evening.

Rolling onto her back, Steele looked up in time to see Thomas drop onto her, knife raised to strike. His expression was triumphant, but he wasn't getting her that easily. She grabbed his wrists and threw every last ounce of strength into holding back the blows. Above her, Thomas's face contorted as he tried again and again to stab her.

Steele heard loud banging from the door, followed by Ray's frantic voice shouting her name. She and Thomas both glanced toward it for a moment then resumed their struggling. Unable to make any headway, Thomas snarled and clenched his eye. It was a particularly odd thing to do, Steele thought. There was a strange, all but imperceptible movement at the iris. Thomas drew his head back and then thrust it downward.

Steele yanked herself sideways just in time to evade the head-butt. Thomas's face almost touched the floor, such was the force of the attack, and he paused for no apparent reason at the end of his strike. Steele did not understand but was not about to question her good luck. Bringing up her arm, she elbowed Thomas savagely in the temple and then broke free.

Steele got to her feet just as Ray burst into the room. He was in his shirtsleeves, an informality that Steele had rarely seen before. The sight would have amused her under less dangerous circumstances.

"Steele, are you all right?" Ray demanded. "What's going on in here?"

"Thomas showed up again," Steele said. "Guess what he's after."

Nearby, Thomas drew himself into a crouch and yanked something away from the floor. As he stood, Steele saw that one eye was missing—or rather, that Thomas now held it in his hand, like the grip of a dagger. A long stiletto blade extended from the prosthetic eye's pupil.

"Something tells me it's not a nightcap," Ray said.

Steele glanced toward where her revolver lay among her luggage. Thomas was between her and it. This was going to get interesting.

"Make a run for the door," Ray told her.

Steele smirked. "I'm not in the mood for running."

"You never are."

Exchanging nods with Ray, Steele darted forward and lashed out in Thomas's direction. Thomas snarled and stabbed at her but

Ray moved in on his flank, dividing his attention between them. Steele circled Thomas, keeping just out of reach of his blade. Ray followed her lead on Thomas's other side, forcing the pirate to constantly turn in either direction to avoid being caught from behind by one or the other.

As Thomas turned his attention toward Ray, Steele darted past and dove for her pistol. Thomas turned to pursue, but Ray leapt upon him and dragged him backward. Snarling like an animal, Thomas slashed his blade across Ray's belly, tearing open his waistcoat and shirt. Ray fell backward and Thomas held him down, one hand gripping the man's throat, as he hovered above Ray with the blade poised to strike a fatal blow.

Steele grabbed her revolver and spun around in time to see Ray in peril.

No!

Without hesitation, she took aim and shot Thomas through the head. The pirate went limp and collapsed.

Ray quickly shoved the body away. He stood and brushed himself off, breathing heavily.

"Ray!" Steele cried, rushing to him. "Are you all right?"

She grabbed Ray and began feeling about his chest for the wound. Ray laughed and hugged her tightly for a moment. When he let go, Steele looked down at herself, expecting to be covered in blood. She saw none.

Ray patted his stomach and pulled away a torn strip of fabric on his waistcoat, revealing layered strips of flexible steel sewn inside.

"Right as rain," he said. "I always wear an armored vest, just like Mother used to say."

"Oh." Steele looked at Ray for a few moments. He had scared her half to death. Regaining her calm, she shrugged. "Well good, no harm done then."

She looked down at Thomas's dead body and sighed. Now he could never be made to reveal his secrets.

"I think he's dead," she said.

"You see," Ray told her, "this is the problem with your tactic of shooting first and asking questions later."

Steele eyed him. "Next time a man tries to kill you with a knife, I'll hit him on the nose with a rolled-up newspaper, shall I?"

"Well, it would be more civilized that way. And save on the cleaning."

Steele sighed. Now her only remaining lead was dead. Better him than Ray, but still. . . .

"This is a disaster," she said. "Two dead ends in one day, one of them literally!"

Ray shook his head and put a hand on her shoulder.

"We aren't finished yet," he said. "Get some sleep while I sort out the mess with the body. You can have my room. Tomorrow we'll take the morning train back to Singhpur and find you some civvies."

Civvies?

Steele looked at him.

"Why do I need civvies?" she asked.

"Because we're going to the Badlands."

The Badlands? That was a terrible idea. The Badlands meant more pirates and more danger. And more excitement. And enemies you could fight in the open, on your terms, instead of in bedrooms while tipsy.

And aeroplanes.

Steele's face lit up with a tremendous smile.

"You know what I like about you, Ray? You know just what a girl wants to hear."

"One tries," Ray said, not very modestly. He eyed Steele out of the corner of his eye for a moment and smirked. "Nice *unmentionables*, by the way."

In reply, Steele swatted him.

NINE

By the time Steele arrived at the Singhpur Sky-Yards around noon the following day, she had been made unidentifiable as her former self. With great reluctance, she had abandoned her flying uniform for a civilian pilot's clothing, incorporating broad denim trousers in a blue and white stripe, a worn shirt, and a man's vest, all topped with a knee-length leather pilot's coat and warm scarf of a hideously bright orange. It was not a look that she found even remotely enjoyable. Worse, her rather distinctive blond hair had been dyed a dirty light brown—at Ray's insistence; the man knew how to be persuasive when he put his mind to it. With a little smoke and engine grease on her face, she would be unrecognizable, save by someone who knew her well.

Ray met her at the airfield, looking rather please with himself. He had traded his respectable suits for a thoroughly un-Ray ensemble of drab checked trousers of red and brown and a sturdy leather duster. He had a bandoleer of bullets slung across his chest and a revolver and a machete hanging from his belt. Steele whistled in disbelief at the sight of him; it was a remarkable transformation. Not a bad one either.

As Steele approached, she spotted the aeroplane that Ray had secured for them. The moment she saw it, she took a profound dislike to it. It was a biplane about two-dozen feet long and constructed of wood and canvas. Its flanks were stained with oil and soot, and it looked patched-together and barely airworthy. The vehicle was a civilian explorer craft, not intended for military use, but some damned fool had bolted a mitrailleuse volley gun just ahead of the pilot's seat, and another sat on a swivel mount behind the passenger.

Steele stood with her arms folded and her mouth set in a frown as she studied the contraption in silence. A hot, dry breeze whipped across the open flats around the airfield and blew past Steele. For a moment she was reminded of her birthplace in arid Saba. The sensation calmed her, but it could not appease her professional distain for the machine.

"A United Aeroworks Kingfisher," she said to Ray. "We're taking a United Aeroworks *Kingfisher!*"

"I take it you don't approve?" Ray asked. He did not seem particularly concerned.

Steele glared at him. How could he ask such a thing?

"Of course I don't approve! Every fiber of my being is offended just contemplating it!"

Steele walked toward the aeroplane and began pointing toward all the things that troubled her.

"It has *half* the acceleration of my Kestrel, *a third* of the climb, the maneuverability isn't even worth comparison, and don't get me started on the exposed cockpit! And what are these mitrailleuses doing bolted to this thing? Where are the machine guns? We need *real* firepower if we're going into the Badlands. We'd be better off throwing rocks!"

Ray walked up behind her and laid a hand on her shoulder, offering her his most reassuring smile. "You just need to get used to it."

Steele glared at him. *"Get used to it," he says. Like it's an uncomfortable sweater.*

"I don't," she said.

"Think it over for a few minutes. You might change your mind."

"I won't," Steele replied, pushing Ray's hand away.

"You never know until you try."

Steele turned toward him in exasperation. "Ray, this thing is a *rustbucket!*"

They would be lucky if it held together for five minutes, let alone the entire day.

"Which makes it all the better for our purposes," Ray said. "Remember, we're traveling incognito. If we fly around the Badlands in a Commonwealth fighter, we may as well paint a giant target on ourselves and await the inevitable. Whereas the Kingfisher—" he indicated the biplane in a single great sweep of his hand, as if revealing something majestic, "—is one of the most prolific aircraft on the frontier."

"Prolific." Like it's a selling point. Steele shook her head at him. Ray understood nothing about aeroplanes.

"I know it is," she said. "I'm used to shooting them down all the time. It's not supposed to be a fighter, Ray. Pirates only use it as one when they're poor or desperate."

"It's got great fuel efficiency," Ray countered.

Steele stood and looked at Ray for a few moments. Although he still smiled at her with all his usual charm and diplomacy, Steele could see the stubbornness in his eyes. He really was dead set on it, wasn't he?

"I don't have any choice, do I?" she asked.

Ray put his hands on her shoulders and gave her a frank look.

"Steele, I *know* you want to find the person who is hunting you and do a little hunting in retaliation. But the only way we can do that is by infiltrating the Badlands by stealth and blending in. You know that as well as I do."

He was right about that. Part of it, anyway. Steele wanted nothing more than to hunt down the person who had sent the assassins after her and have a proper face-to-face confrontation. But she refused to believe that she had to do it in a *United Aerowork's Kingfisher!*

"Otherwise," Ray said, "you can sit the investigation out. I'm sure your Group Captain would be happy to give you a month's holiday out in the Beyliks. Something nice and isolated, like skiing in Devraz. Wouldn't you like that?"

Steele's eyes went wide for a moment.

Not that! Anything but that!

She hated mandatory leave, she hated peace and quiet, and she hated the cold. A holiday in Devraz would be a horrible concoction of all of them.

"Fine," she said, forcing a smile. "We'll do it your way until the shooting starts."

"And then?" Ray asked.

Steele's smile became far more sincere. "Then we do things *my way.*"

If she was stuck flying the blasted crate, at least she was going to have some fun with it.

Steele climbed into the pilot's seat and switched on the aeroplane's flash boiler. While the engine raised steam, she watched Ray stow their supplies and ammunition in the cargo compartment behind the passenger's seat. He was looking very pleased with himself at having won the argument. He was in for a surprise.

As Ray climbed into the back, Steele pulled her goggles down over her eyes and leaned over to him.

"Hold on tight, Ray!" she shouted. "These things tend to *rattle!*"

"Rattle?" Ray asked, strapping himself in. "What do you mean rat—"

He was cut off by a rush of air as Steele released the brake, and the aeroplane shot off down the runway. The machine did indeed "rattle", shaking tremendously as its powerful engine and increasing speed sent ripples of movement along its frame. The Kingfisher was designed to withstand a surprising amount of vibration without suffering damage, but its structure did little to absorb the shocks. Steele had flown the model a few times in the past, and she was quite familiar with the sensation. Ray was not.

Steele did a couple of loops once they had risen high enough in the air, just to emphasize the point. In the back, Ray leaned against his seat, one hand on his forehead, looking a little sick. As they leveled off in the sky above Singhkhand, Steele leaned back and shouted to him:

"How are you holding up there, Ray?"

"You did that deliberately!" Ray called back.

Steele had to keep her face forward to hide her broad grin.

"Don't be silly, Ray! I had to check the handling! You never know how these old crates fly until you do a few turns with them!"

Steele glanced back to see Ray's reaction. Ray had his hands over his eyes.

"I think you had an ulterior motive!" he said.

"Maybe!" Steele chuckled and gave Ray a firm pat on the shoulder. "But if you want, I can land, and we can get into a *proper* aeroplane!"

Ray cleared his throat with a cough. "I'm not done yet, Steele! Don't forget, I'm a cartographer! This thing is just a minor annoyance!"

Good old Ray, never one to admit defeat. It made Steele smile again, this time more kindly.

"Suit yourself!" she said. "Where are we going?"

"Turtle Island!" Ray called back. "Now if you'll excuse me, I'm going to sit here with my eyes closed for a while!"

* * * *

"Ah, Turtle Island!" Ray exclaimed as they landed at their destination. "A consummate free port's free port."

Steele sighed. Ray had recovered from his earlier discomfort, and now he was game as ever.

"Don't make it sound so romantic!" Steele called back. "It's a lawless haven for freebooters, smugglers, privateers, and any other sort of criminal you can name!"

"Does that include jaywalkers?" Ray asked.

"Quiet, you!"

Steele pulled off the runway and taxied the biplane to an empty space along the side of the airfield. Killing the engine, she climbed down and gave the free port an appraising look. She had seen Turtle Island several times in the past, and each time it displeased her.

As Ray said, it was a free port's free port, the sort of place people went when they were on the run from the law or they wanted a place to buy and sell illegal goods. The fleets of the pirate lords had little direct contact with the free ports, but they swarmed with mercenaries, privateers, and small-time freebooters, all on the lookout for easy money.

Steele could see the dangers inherent in the Badlands reflected in the port's erratic architecture. Parts of the town were sturdy and fortified, built of heavy stone or brick with wooden barricades and blockhouses in raised vantage points. But the settlement surrounding these strong points was something akin to a massive shantytown built on the scale of a small city, with narrow back alleys, grimy streets, and tiered walkways placed directly on top of the buildings below them. Steele hated it already. It was the sort of place where people got killed for taking a wrong turn or walking past a window at the wrong moment.

Ray joined her on the ground and whistled to a group of armed men who lounged around on crates nearby. One of them stood and slowly walked over, chewing a wad of tobacco in his mouth. He smelled horribly of beer and unwashed sweat, and Steele had to force herself not to react to the stench.

"Yeah?" he asked. "Whatcha want?"

Ray squared off in front of him, his stance and clothing making him look like any other Mahari mercenary gone native in the Badlands. Steele was impressed at the sudden transformation, though she realized that Ray probably played that role several times a month on visits to the region.

"You boys with Fletcher?" Ray asked.

The man laughed at this and then spat on the ground. "'Course we are. Wouldn't let us hang about here otherwise."

Ray pulled a pair of bank chips out of his pocket and passed them to the man.

"No one touches the Kingfisher," he said. "Savvy?"

Steele watched Ray in fascination. He even sounded like a Badlander, accent and all.

"Aye," the man replied, and he spat again.

Ray grabbed Steele by the waist and gave her a tight, overly familiar squeeze.

"C'mon, dolly," he said, "I need a drink."

Steele threw her arm around Ray's shoulders and allowed herself to be led off by him. As they passed out of earshot from the airfield guards, she leaned close and growled in his ear:

"Don't you 'dolly' me, mister. I know what that's short for."

"I'm just playing the part my dear," Ray said. "If you don't like it, hit me. It's what a Badlander would do."

Steele made a face at the suggestion. It was tempting, but it would attract unwanted attention. Things were not so equal in the Badlands as they were in the Commonwealth. True, there were plenty of assertive women out on the frontier, but they tended to get noticed. And that was the last thing Steele needed with a price on her head. Better to play the gangster's moll for the time being.

"This had better work," she said.

She accompanied Ray up the broad, dirty main street that ran all the way from the airfield up to the top of the turtle shell-shaped hill that gave the eyot its name. Steele looked about as unobtrusively as she could, taking in the sights. All the streets of the port were filled with people arguing, trading, drinking and fighting, and the central roadway was by far the worst of them all.

Thankfully, none of the locals paid her or Ray any mind, save for a few quick glances or the odd black marketeer offering them some "choice merchandise." Once, however, a pickpocket tried his luck with Ray's wallet, but when he caught the man in the middle of the act, Ray merely gave him a firm kick, told him to "clear off", and then sent him packing. Steele was shocked at first, but as she thought about it, Ray's actions made sense. In a Commonwealth city, the first thing to do would be to call the police, but in the Badlands there was no one to call.

At the top of the hill, Steele found the closest thing Turtle Island had to a "town hall." It proved to be a massive, fortified drinking hall, part saloon and part redoubt that no doubt served as the core of the port's defenses during raids. Like the towers, blockhouses, and walls, the drinking hall bristled with machine guns and anti-aircraft weaponry, all obtained from the thriving black market.

"Nice place," Steele said. She glanced back over her shoulder at the port. "Maybe I'll buy a bungalow here and retire."

"Aren't we cocky today?" Ray laughed. "Don't get overconfident. This place is thick with the sort of people who want you dead."

Good old Ray, always finding the downside.

Steele took Ray by the arm and leaned her head on his shoulder for a moment. "How lucky I am to have my very own bodyguard."

"Don't even start," Ray said.

Steele followed Ray into the hall. The main taproom was reminiscent of an old-fashioned tavern or pub built on an impossibly large scale. Steele was almost overwhelmed by the sight of it, and she spent a few moments staring around like a tourist, marveling that something so tremendous—the size of a modern hotel lobby—could have been built by *Badlanders* using wood instead of steel and concrete.

Bars lined either side of the room, and the center was filled with tables and chairs occupied almost to capacity by the rowdy patrons. Everything was made of aged wood so old and worn it resembled black glass in the dim kerosene lamplight. Balconies and walkways ringed the ceiling, accessing bedrooms for drunks, travelers, and prostitutes and their customers. Steele was glad they weren't planning on spending the night. It was the sort of place where one caught diseases just by looking at the linens.

"Well isn't this a charming little teahouse," she said.

"Don't knock it," Ray said. "This is where I hope to find some answers. Now wait here and try to stay out of trouble. There's someone I need to see."

Steele sighed in resignation, folded her arms, and leaned against the bar. The last thing she wanted was more waiting.

"Don't be too long," she said. "I may get bored."

Ray shook his head. "Steady on. You'll give me a heart attack saying things like that."

Steele winked at him.

"Hurry back soon."

Ray patted Steele on the shoulder and disappeared into the mass of people and pipe smoke. Steele tried to follow him with her eyes, but the slippery spy was too good at his work, and he had vanished by the time he had passed the second row of tables. Sighing again, this time more deeply, Steele turned and knocked her knuckles against the bar. At least she could get a drink while she was here.

"Bartender! Palm wine, and make sure it's heavy on the lime!"

Having ordered, she turned back to face the room and did her best to resist the urge to start shooting.

* * * *

Weaving in and out of the crowd, Ray made his way toward the back of the drinking hall where a raised platform offered a commanding view of the room. The centerpiece of the platform was a high-backed leather armchair occupied by a somewhat paunchy man with graying temples and a broad, waxed moustache, who sat gazing out across the rowdy drinking hall like a king surveying his domain. He was dressed like a gentleman in a frock coat of green with plaid trousers and a waistcoat to match, and he smoked an expensive cigar as if it were a cheap cigarette.

Typical of Fletcher, Ray thought.

The platform was surrounded by bodyguards armed with short-barreled revolving carbines, heavy sidearms, and hardened leather body armor. As Ray approached, one of them held out his hand and motioned for Ray to back off.

"I'm here to see Mr. Fletcher," Ray said, politely but forcefully.

"Do you have an appointment?"

From the bodyguard's tone, it was clear that he found this to be highly unlikely.

"No," Ray said, "but he's expecting me. By now, he should always be expecting me."

At this, the man on the platform looked up from his smoke and peered at Ray. After a moment he chuckled and beckoned for Ray to join him.

"Well, well, well. . . . Amartya Ray. Come, have a seat."

Ray stepped around the bodyguard and climbed the stairs onto the platform. One of the attendants quickly pulled another chair up to Fletcher's table for Ray to sit on. For all his many faults, Fletcher at least knew how to treat a guest.

"Cigar?" Fletcher asked, offering the box.

Ray was not in the mood for smoking, especially after seeing how Fletcher treated the expensive cigars. It rather put him off, like watching someone guzzle fine wine.

"No, thank you," he said, sitting.

"Suit yourself." Fletcher selected a fresh cigar for himself and stubbed out his old one. "Now then, what brings you to my humble establishment?"

As if he doesn't know, Ray thought. Fletcher knew his business, and he probably already knew Ray's.

"Information, what else?" Ray said, placing a stack of metal bank chips on the table and sliding it halfway toward Fletcher. "At the regular price, of course."

Fletcher set his cigar on a gilded holder over his ashtray and folded his hands. "Your money is always welcome here, Ray. What are you after?"

"I want to know who hit the airship *Fortuna* two days ago."

Ray spotted a familiar look in Fletcher's eyes. The man already knew what he was after. Fletcher had an uncanny ability to antici- pate what his clients wanted to know. It was why he was still in business.

"Ha!" Fletcher laughed aloud. "No you don't," he said. "You want to know who's after 'Lucky Lizzy' Steele." There was a pause as Fletcher waited for an indication of Ray's reaction, which never came. "Drink?"

Ray could hardly refuse, having already rejected the cigar; and besides, Fletcher was not likely to poison one of his best customers. But one could never be too sure.

"Whatever you're having," he said. To a Badlander, the words had a literal meaning.

Ray leaned back in his chair as an attendant poured him a glass of whisky from Fletcher's own bottle. He took a sip and found the drink to be sharp and invigorating. Fletcher had good taste, even if he had a poor way of showing it.

"What makes you think I want to know about Elizabeth Steele?" Ray asked, setting his glass down.

Fletcher smirked. "Because she's a valuable Commonwealth asset and that sort of thing is rather your line of work, isn't it?"

Ray kept his expression ambiguous, but he smiled in reply.

"And also," Fletcher continued, "because a certain *someone* just happened to take an interest in her after the *Fortuna* raid I happen to know she repelled."

Now that was interesting information.

"Very well then, who's after Steele?" Ray asked.

Fletcher took a sip from his own glass and shook his head. "You don't want to know, my friend. This is out of your league."

"Last time I checked," Ray said, "I'm the paying customer. Tell me what I want to know, *old chum*, or I'll take my money to someone else with better business sense."

To emphasize the point, he reached out and placed his hand back on the stack of chips.

Fletcher grimaced and held up his hands. "Fine, fine, have it your way. But don't say I didn't warn you."

Fletcher took a long draw on his cigar before continuing. When he spoke, there was a dark tone to his voice, one betraying more than a hint of fear:

"His name is Burkhalter, and he's one of the most dangerous men alive."

"Burkhalter, eh?"

Ray kept his expression placid, but his mind whirred as he tried to place the name. It sounded *very* familiar.

"He's a heretic from the Kingdom of St. Corbin," Fletcher said. "About ten years ago, he sided with a group of religious radicals against the orthodox government. They lost, and Burkhalter found himself on the wrong side of a religious schism. Faced with certain death, he fled with his followers into a self-imposed exile in the Badlands.

"Now he controls one of the most powerful pirate fleets in the world, and one of the most ruthless. Every day, cruel men flock to his banner in the hope of obtaining wealth, power, and mechanical perfection."

"Mechanical perfection?" Ray asked. He did not like the sound of it.

"When he fled into the Badlands, Burkhalter brought with him the techniques of St. Corbin's prosthetic limbs. As his soldiers prove themselves and rise in rank, he gifts them with greater and great augmentation until there's little left to mark them as human. His lieutenants are rumored to have barely a scrap of their original selves left."

Ray frowned.

The followers of *Sankt Korbinian*—translated as "Saint Corbin" in the Commonwealth—were a fastidious and devout people who resided in a "Holy Kingdom" far to the south, beyond gilded Tali. Ray had visited St. Corbin once as part of a diplomatic mission, and it had not been a pleasant experience. The Corbinites were obsessed with cleanliness and assumed that everyone not of their faith was the potential carrier of disease or spiritual corruption. Most only left their enclaves to spread the holy word either by religious mission or by crusade. But they were talented engineers who had mastered a method of creating mechanical automata and even fully functioning prosthetic limbs. Ray had seen a demonstration of the Holy Kingdom's heavily augmented warrior-knights, and their prowess was formidable. If such a technology had been released into the Badlands, it could dramatically upset the balance of power in the region.

"And you say this Burkhalter wants Steele dead?" Ray asked, careful not to fall silent as he mulled over the threat that had just been placed before him.

"*Every* pirate wants Lucky Lizzy dead," Fletcher replied. "But Burkhalter's the one you've come to me about."

"How do you know?"

"Because he put out a bounty on her head *yesterday*. I just got word of it this morning, and now here you are asking me about it." Fletcher smiled and spread his hands, symbolizing the *fait accompli*.

Ray kept his expression guarded. The timing of the bounty could not be a coincidence, and a pirate lord might have the far-reaching influence necessary to call upon the services of a Kilkala gang on short notice.

"Interesting," he said.

Fletcher laughed. "More than interesting, my good Ray. *Peculiar*. He's offering a fortune, and the terms of the bounty stipulate the return of Steele's head *and* of all her personal possessions." He leaned forward and fixed Ray with a pointed look. "Now why do you suppose that is?"

"I couldn't say," Ray said, and took another sip of his whisky.

Fletcher's expression changed from one of devious disinterest to one bordering on concern.

"Ray, listen to me," he said. "Burkhalter isn't some run of the mill warlord. He's a proper pirate lord in every sense of the word. His fleet is large enough to rival the dynasties of Blücher, Tecumseh, Pryce, and Ney, and he's as ruthless as they come. And worse, the stories say that the infernal Corbinite technology he uses has made him immortal and impervious to harm."

"Surely you don't believe such superstition."

"No," Fletcher said, his expression grave, "but I can read between the lines. The old pirate lords don't like upstarts coming in and threatening their power. You remember what happened when Lord Mirambo came here from Tali? Ney is *still* sending assassins to try to kill him, and that's after a conventional, twenty-year rise to power. Burkhalter's been in the Badlands for barely a decade, and already he's a major player. The other lords don't like that. It frightens them. I don't want to think how many attempts on his life there have been, and he's shrugged them all off like they were nothing. Burkhalter is dangerous, Ray, and you *don't* want to get anywhere near him."

Fletcher was right: anyone who could go from being a newly arrived immigrant in the Badlands to a major warlord in ten years was not someone to be trifled with. Ray was troubled by the warning, but he betrayed no outward sign of it. He was not about to give up just because of a little danger, certainly not while Steele's life was at risk.

Instead, he placed a second stack of bank chips on the table next to the first.

"Just tell me where I can find him."

* * * *

By the time Ray returned to Steele, a bar fight was raging along that side of the drinking hall.

It had begun innocently enough, over a simple misunderstanding. One of the local toughs, upon seeing Steele on her own and just on the verge of finishing her drink, and being of a generous nature, had insisted, quite fervently, upon buying her another. Though Steele had modestly refused the offer, the ruffian had pushed the point with increasing vigor until finally she consented to a refill of her glass, which she then proceeded to enjoy while paying the ruffian little attention. The ruffian, intent upon making Steele feel welcome in the unfamiliar establishment, proceeded to give her a long, reassuring pat on the backside. Steele, understanding the kind and charitable spirit in which this action was taken, consented to let the ruffian fondle the point of her fist with the side of his face.

The ruffian toppled over sideways, struck the bar with a loud thud and lay there, dazed, as he tried to understand why he had been punched. His drinking companions, for reasons unfathomable to the average mind, mistook Steele's affectionate exchange for an outbreak of violence and rushed in eagerly to defend the honor of their half-conscious friend. Steele reassured them of her friendly intentions with a series of gentle pats, administered to their heads and stomachs by her fists, elbows, boots, and knees. In due course, all of the drunken pirates in the area had begun to follow her example. By the time Ray arrived, the pirates had lost all track of how the fight had started, and those that made the mistake of attacking Steele did so without the realization that she had kicked off the whole imbroglio.

"There you are!" Ray cried, bounding out of the crowd and landing beside her. "I thought I told you to stay out of trouble!"

How typical of him to think she was the cause of the disturbance. It didn't matter that she actually *was* responsible; principles were at stake.

Steele put her hands on her hips and gave Ray a hurt look. "There's a fight going on, so you automatically assume it was *my* fault?"

"I—" Ray began.

Steele interrupted him. "How are we supposed to build any trust in this relationship if you blame me for every little disruption to public order that happens to break out?"

"Now see here—"

Ray's reply was interrupted again as a one of the many barroom toughs burst out of the mob. The ruffian looked around for someone to hit, spotted Steele, and took a swing at her.

Lovely! They just keep coming. Must be my winning personality. . . .

Bending at the waist, Steele ducked beneath the blow and then dropped into a crouch. The ruffian stumbled as his swing missed and teetered off balance. Steele was about to spring up and attack when Ray dove in and knocked the ruffian out with a solid double jab. Steele held her crouch and looked up at him, startled by how quickly he had taken advantage of her opening. She had to admit, Ray was proving to be the sort of chap a girl could take places.

Steele took the hand that Ray offered her, and stood. Smiling at him, she dusted off her hands and gave him a wink.

"Why, hello there," she said. "Come here often?"

"You know how it is," Ray said. "Come for the drinks, stay for the fistfights."

Another man tumbled past them, narrowly missing Ray with his flailing arms.

"Speaking of," he added, "we should—"

"Go," Steele finished for him.

Grabbing his hand, she raced through an opening in the crowd and made for the door. Ducking past swinging fists and thrown drinking mugs, she darted through the brawl and out into the street with Ray close behind her.

"Well that was a bit of fun," she said, ruffling her hair.

"I can tell you've been having a good time of it," Ray answered. "You've such a pleasant glow about you."

Steele took his arm with a smile. "Why thank you, Ray. What a lovely thing to say."

"Even though I *know* that bar fight was your fault."

"Oh, hush," Steele said.

And so, arm in arm, they walked back toward the airfield as the bar fight spilled out of the drinking hall and into the streets of Turtle Island.

"Any luck with your friend?" Steele asked as they walked. Hopefully, the trip had been worth the trouble.

"Possibly," Ray said. "I'll know for sure when we check out the coordinates he gave me."

"Can you trust him?" she asked.

"In principle? Of course not," Ray replied, echoing Steele's own instincts. "Fletcher's an old smuggler, and he got that way by being as devious as they come. But he knows I'm a good customer, and he won't do anything to risk the money I bring in."

Ray seemed confident, but Steele wasn't so sure. She did not like trusting bought friendships. It was too easy to be outbid.

"I hope you're right," she said.

Ray grinned. "So do I."

TEN

It took Steele a little over two hours of flying time to reach the co-ordinates that Fletcher had given Ray, although she was careful to avoid a direct route. She knew the Badlands well. Ambush points were plentiful amid the rubble-strewn skies, and experienced pilots knew how to identify dangerous areas and steer clear of them. Those who didn't often found themselves the victims of pirates lurking just out of sight along the major flight paths.

Pirate hunters, on the other hand, made a habit of strafing hiding points to spook anyone lurking nearby into fleeing. It was much the same principle as using beaters to drive out game for a hunt. It took Steele a great deal of concentration to avoid falling back on old habits and go hunting for pirates amid the floating rocks. In the Kingfisher, she wouldn't stand a chance.

The location of Burkhalter's fleet was clear enough for Steele to see, even from several miles out. The eyots and fragmented rocks floating through the sky gradually took on a purposeful layout, as if some of them had been dragged into position by airships. Steele saw outposts, landing strips, and ambush points with increasing regularity and it soon became clear that they had arrived at the outskirts of an entire skirmish screen. If Burkhalter was like most other pirate lords she had encountered, the defenses would be laid out in a series of rings that formed a sphere around the fleet's head-quarters. Fighters and armed airships patrolled the area in small groups, each keeping to its own private territory but clearly serving the purposes of a greater whole.

It took Steele only a few moments to identify a weak point in the defense network, and she carefully slipped in beneath one of the fortified eyots. She had led small raids on pirates in the past, and then with more fighters to worry about being detected. A single nondescript biplane would attract little attention even if it was seen at a distance. This realization made Steele scowl for a moment. Ray had been right , not that she would admit it to him.

The noise of the patrols masked the sound of her engine as she passed the pirates just out of eyeshot. Beyond the defenses, the region was further fortified and patrolled but with far less intensity. It took some careful flying on Steele's part, aided by some very active observation from Ray, but she got them past the pirate skirmishers undetected.

Further in from the picket lines, she encountered what in a more civilized land might be classified as civilians: freighters, construction teams, and supply ships, all working to keep the logistical side of Burkhalter's empire functioning so that the soldiers and pirate crews could engage in their business of war and pillage. Most of the laborers were slaves, people taken by Burkhalter's pirates as yet another form of plunder and forced to work or die.

Steele felt the overwhelming urge to intervene, to attack the soldiers guarding the slaves and urge the prisoners to flee for freedom. But without a proper squadron complete with airship support, the slaves would never make it past the pirate lines. Steele gritted her teeth and focused her thoughts on finding Burkhalter.

The majority of the region was wilderness, which came as no surprise to Steele. For a pirate lord driven by a lust for plunder and the control of trade routes, prestige came from the amount of territory controlled, not settled. Steele doubted if the concept of "settlement" even occurred to someone like Burkhalter.

Much of the airspace was empty, dotted here and there with airbases for raiding parties or strongholds to defend the region in the event of attack. Steele was quite experienced with operating in pirate-controlled skies, and she wove her way around these hard points with ease.

As the biplane drew toward the heart of Burkhalter's territory, Steele began to sense that something was wrong. The biplane crested over a small eyot, and suddenly the sky was filled with a vast armada of aircraft. Taken by surprise, Steele banked sharply away. As she skirted the massive fleet, she struggled to take in the scale of it all. It seemed to go on forever.

She saw row upon row of armed airships clustered into semi-coherent squadrons, arrayed in such quantities that, from below, they almost blotted out the sun. Fighter aircraft darted about the fleet, patrolling for hostile forces as the larger airships were loaded with ammunition and supplies. Steele felt her breath catch in her throat. Only once before had she seen such a massing of pirate ships, and the memory of it set her heart racing.

Turning in the air, she dove toward a nearby eyot that sported a healthy collection of trees and brush and was long enough to accommodate landing. Making ground, she and Ray pushed the biplane beneath some trees and covered it in camouflage netting. No point in giving their presence away.

Steele grabbed a pair of binoculars and walked to the edge of the eyot, awed by the size of the fleet. Ray joined her, carrying a small box camera and a case of surveying equipment. Without a word, he began studying the fleet, taking pictures and scribbling notes in a small journal. Steele glanced at Ray but said nothing. Best to let him do his work.

As Steele watched the pirate fleet in all its perverse glory, she felt a shiver of dread pass along her back. She could see Burkhalter's capital ships lurking at the heart of the fleet, dirigible aircraft so large that they required multiple envelopes to support their armored hulls. These flanked a final terrible vessel: a virtual floating fortress with steel-encased flanks and half a dozen decks bristling with guns that hung from a network of armor-plated gas bags. Massive propellers extended from the keel of the command ship, augmenting the balloon support with whatever upward momentum they could muster. Steele knew at a glance that this was Burkhalter's headquarters.

Bloody thing could probably take on a wing of warships by itself.

The ensigns, banners, and even the hulls of the pirate aircraft were all emblazoned with the symbol of a skull backed by a stylized gearwheel. Corbinite machinery and the Badlander death's head united.

Cold mechanical precision and bloodthirsty ruthlessness in one, Steele thought. *Burkhalter's private metaphor for himself.*

"This is bad," she said, her voice so numb it sounded calm and matter-of-fact. "This is very, very bad."

"There are so many of them," Ray said, looking up from his work with wide-eyes. "I've never seen anything like this!"

"I have!" Steele said. "Back when I was just a flight lieutenant, fresh out of the academy. You remember the Monroe Incident?"

Ray inhaled sharply at the mention of the name. "Monroe. . . . I've heard the stories."

"Whatever you heard, it was worse."

Steele gazed off in the direction of Burkhalter's fleet, a sick sensation forming in her stomach. Monroe was not a pleasant memory to dig up. She had spent a lot of time forgetting.

"Lord Monroe's raiders had begun hitting shipping along the border harder than anything we'd seen before. From Kilkala to Singhkhand, even all the way up to the Beyliks in the north. Turns out he'd amassed a fleet like the one you're looking at here."

She fell silent for a moment. Monroe's fleet had been *smaller* than the one before her now.

"Naturally we sent an intervention to deal with it. Three whole air groups went into the Badlands to show Monroe a little gunboat diplomacy. We had no idea what we were up against."

"But we won, didn't we?" Ray asked.

That was the funny thing about winning. Victories were rarely total, and sometimes they were barely a step above defeat.

"Oh yes, we won," Steele said. "After days of fighting, we finally smashed Monroe's fleet into oblivion. But our casualties were horrendous. We lost so many aircraft, so many people, it took the Air Force *four years* to fully recover. If we'd been attacked during that time, we'd have been overrun. We were *lucky* with Monroe. We might not be so lucky a second time."

Steele gritted her teeth. *And I'll be damned if I stand by and let that happen again.*

"This is bigger than you or me or the punch card now," Ray said. "We have to warn London."

"Agreed."

Steele's trained eye noticed something peculiar in the flight patterns of the pirate fighters out on patrol. The planes had shifted from their previous routes and now were zeroing in on the eyot in a series of broad spirals.

They know we're here. . . .

One of the pickets must have spotted the Kingfisher and reported it. Burkhalter's security was more efficient than Steele had expected.

"Ray, we need to get moving," she said. "We've got fighters incoming."

"Just a moment!" Ray was still snapping photographs and scribbling frantically in his notebook, seeming to record every last nuance about the fleet that came to mind. At least he was being thorough.

Steele looked back toward the approaching fighters. They were single-seat triplanes armed with agar guns: military grade equipment, not modified civilian machines. Either Burkhalter had a lot of money for black market purchases, or his fleet enjoyed some kind of cottage industry.

The fighters swept in closer, weaving in both above and below the level of the eyot as they scoured the area for their quarry. At least that meant the pirates didn't yet have a fix on them. There was still a chance to get the plane back into the air before they were discovered. And that, Steele knew, was an opportunity they couldn't miss. If they were caught on the ground, they'd be in the soup before they'd even started.

"No time for moments; we have to go *now!*" Steele shouted, shaking Ray.

With a roar of engines and a rush of air, one of the triplanes shot up past them from beneath the eyot. The pilot craned his neck this way and that, and finally caught a fleeting glimpse of them just before he shot out of view behind a floating cluster of rock.

"Time to go!" Ray agreed, shoving his equipment back into the leather case.

Steele ran back to the Kingfisher as the pirate fighter turned in the air and came back to find them. Ray was right behind her. Together they yanked the camouflage netting away.

Looking over her shoulder, Steele saw the fighter open fire at a distance. Too far away for accurate shooting: an amateur mistake. Twin lines of gunfire darted across the eyot ahead of the Kingfisher, as Steele had predicted. But the pirate was coming in fast, and he wouldn't be out of accurate shooting range for long.

"Ray, keep him off me!" Steele shouted as she swung into the pilot's seat.

"Roger!"

Ray climbed in behind her and readied the rear mitrailleuse. As the triplane came around for another pass at them, he fired all twenty-five barrels at it. Steele glanced back to see the result. It was the first time she had seen him using heavy weaponry. She hoped to be pleasantly surprised.

The shots peppered the fighter's hull but did nothing to stop it.

Ah well, can't have everything.

Steele kept her head down as the pirate returned fire. Most of the shots missed, except for a few that tore holes in the canvas of the Kingfisher's upper wing. The pirate's aim was improving.

Behind her, Ray ejected his gun's empty ammo block with the pull of a lever and slammed a new one into place. As the pirate swept past overhead, he adjusted his aim and fired again, emptying the mitrailleuse into the pirate's engine. The triplane's motor smoked, sputtered and finally seized, and the machine vanished behind the lip of the eyot.

Steele blinked. Perhaps she had judged too soon.

"What are you shooting with?" she demanded, astonished at the effectiveness of the burst.

"Sabot rounds with armor-piercing flechettes!" Ray shouted back.

Steele grinned. "You spoil me!"

She took off from the eyot and immediately began to climb. Between the gunfire and the smoke from the fighter, the rest of the pirates would be on them soon. Using the cover of floating rocks and smaller eyots, Steele evaded detection by the fighters that dove in to investigate the disturbance. A few hundred feet above the crash, she leveled out and began the long dash for the border of Burkhalter's territory.

Midway to the picket lines, a shadow fell across the plane for a brief moment. Steele's aviator instincts took over before she consciously realized what had happened, and she turned sharply down and to the right. A moment later, a hail of gunfire filled the air across her flank. Steele looked up and saw a pirate triplane diving toward her with guns blazing.

Damn it! So much for an easy escape.

"We've been spotted!" she shouted.

"On it!" Ray said, bringing his mitrailleuse to bear. "Just get us out of here!"

Steele wove in and out of the sky-borne rubble as the pirate fighter gave chase, trading shots with Ray between the rocks. She saw three more fighters take off from a nearby airfield and join in pursuit, peppering the air with gunfire. Steele twisted the King-fisher this way and that, evading the machine gun fire as best she could. It was difficult flying, made all the worse by the biplane's terrible handling. Steele enjoyed a challenge, but this was border-ing on the absurd.

As she approached the picket lines, five new fighters swept in from her flank. Steele recognized the tactic; they were trying to force her to turn away from their attack and back toward the pursuing pirates. Well, they were in for a surprise.

Steele spotted an anti-aircraft gun emplacement on a nearby eyot. She dove beneath the eyot before the weapon could fire and came up again on the other side with the pirate fighters close on her tail. Bullets tore the canvas of the Kingfisher's wings and flank as Steele continued her evasive maneuvers, all the while swearing furiously. The biplane held, but it would not be able to withstand the assault forever.

Nor, Steele knew, could it outmaneuver the pirate fighters, not like her Kestrel could have, at least. The triplanes behind her enjoyed better turning, handling, and lift than the ungainly King-fisher. Climbing for higher altitudes or diving to escape—tempting though they were—would only play into the pirates' hands. The two advantages that Steele had were her plane's ever so slightly higher cruising speed and better fuel efficiency. The triplanes were ambush fighters, designed for the ferocious close-quarters tactics of the Badlands. They were not meant for long chases. If she could just keep ahead of them for long enough, she and Ray could make good their escape.

Still, Steele reflected, as the pirate fighters peppered the air around her with bursts of gunfire, keeping ahead of the planes was one thing; keeping ahead of their bullets was quite another.

Behind her, Ray kept up his return fire, shooting at the pirate fighters in short bursts to conserve his limited ammunition. Steele was relieved that her earlier assumptions were unfounded. Ray was a spy, not a soldier, but he knew his way around a machine gun. Throughout the chase he had managed to bring down two fighters and force a third to withdraw, its fuselage riddled with holes and its engine smoking.

"I'm out!" he suddenly exclaimed.

Steele made an exasperated noise that was largely lost to the rushing wind.

I knew things were going too well!

"Ray, do me a favor!" she shouted.

"What?"

"Next time you surprise me with a new aeroplane, make sure it has machine guns with *ammunition belts!*"

She shoved two of her own ammunition blocks into Ray's hands and then turned back to her controls. The Kingfisher had reached the outer ring of fortifications, which were definitely on full alert by now. The anti-aircraft guns began firing, filling the air with smoke and shrapnel.

The sight and noise of the familiar "archie"—Air Force slang for anti-aircraft fire—made Steele feel a bit calmer. There was no point to fearing the archie: either it would hit you, or it wouldn't. As the thunder of the shell bursts and the rush of the wind overwhelmed Steele's senses, she relaxed into a meditative state, reacting to the fighting around her without bothering to think about it.

Behind her, the pirates were busy over-thinking things. One of the triplanes chased Steele directly into a shell burst, which tore the wings along its right side to pieces. Steele glanced back in time to see the fighter tumble from the sky in flames. She smiled a little, enjoying the heady sensation of adrenaline. Finally, she was back in her element.

With the remaining mass of triplanes behind her, Steele dove in toward the nearest pirate fortress. Turning the biplane onto its side, she swept along the fort's brick wall just beneath the guns. Two of the triplanes kept close on her tail while the rest broke off. She knew they would be back once they had circled the obstacle by a safer route. A third biplane tried to follow as well, but its pilot dove in too sharply. It clipped the side of the building, spun out of control, and crashed.

As Steele cleared the fortress eyot, two more fighters appeared in the sky in front of her, sweeping in from either side to cut her off. She had to find some way to lose her pursuers before every pirate aeroplane in the area was on her tail.

Banking sideways, Steele ducked between the newcomers' lines of fire and shot a burst from the forward mounted mitrailleuse into the cockpit of one of them. The pilot, riddled with steel flechettes, slumped forward in his seat, pitching his plane down into oblivion. The second advancing triplane tried and failed to turn after Steele. It collided with one of the pursuing fighters in a burst of splinters.

A moment later, Steele shot past the picket line and out into the open Badlands. She glanced over her shoulder: only three fighters still behind her. A significant improvement, but they weren't in the clear just yet.

The pirates were flying full-throttle in a bid to overtake her, and the strain showed. Their engines were smoking from the tremendous heat, and one had even begun venting steam in a sizzling cloud. A moment later, that same fighter's engine erupted in flames that washed back over the windshield. Then the steam pressure in the engine failed, and the plane tumbled downward, fire streaming from its burning frame.

Bloody fool, Steele thought, watching the triplane fall from the sky. *Always know your machine's limits!*

Going down in flames was a terrible way to die. The pirate probably deserved it, but Steele would have preferred to shoot him down fair and square. Letting an enemy burn out his engine felt a little like cheating.

The remaining two triplanes were closing in fast, still trading bursts of fire with Ray. His shots punctured holes in the wings and fuselages of the two fighters, but their pilots were skilled enough to make themselves difficult targets. Worse still, they were keeping pace with Steele, and their engines, though overworked, were holding.

"They're still on us, Ray!" Steele shouted. "What are you doing back there? Playing tiddlywinks with them?"

"Do forgive me for *only* shooting down *three planes!*" Ray said. "Clearly I'm off my game today!"

Steele hid a smile.

"Never mind," she said. "I'll handle this! You just sit back and have yourself a little nap while I finish the real business of saving our lives!"

Steele dove sharply, inviting the triplanes to follow her, which they did with all haste. Their machine guns spat bullets all around her, tearing holes in the Kingfisher's flanks. As they gained on her, Steele twisted upward again in a seemingly futile attempt to flee. The pirates did likewise, hurrying to catch up as Steele forced every last bit of speed from her engine.

Steele looked back and saw the pirates in hot pursuit. She smiled. *Thanks for being so obliging, boys.*

As the pirates turned upward, she dove once again, this time coming at them head-on. Bullets whipped around her, tearing through her wings, but still she attacked with her lips drawn back in a maniacal grin.

She zeroed in on one of the fighters and opened fire with the mitrailleuse. All twenty-five barrels volleyed into the triplane and tore its propeller and nose to pieces. The plane glided past Steele and fell out of sight.

The remaining pirate made a tight turn and dove at Steele just as she finished leveling out. Steele cursed the poor handling of her sluggish machine. In her Kestrel, she could have matched the pirate turn for turn. Her top wing was torn to pieces by the machine gun fire, and she was hit by a shower of splinters.

Steele wiped her face and watched the triplane swing around for another pass. He'd had his chance to kill her, and he'd bungled it up. Steele was in no mood to give him another try.

Twisting the Kingfisher around as sharply as it could manage, she slipped beneath the triplane and came up on its tail. Ahead of her, she saw the pirate look about frantically, trying to spot her. Steele loaded a fresh ammo block into her mitrailleuse but held her fire as she closed the distance between them. She would only get one chance like this.

The pirate turned in his seat and looked back at her. Steele was near enough to see the expression of dread on the man's face. She flashed the pirate a smile that she dearly hoped he saw and opened fire. All twenty-five barrels of the weapon volleyed and shot the pirate and his aeroplane to pieces.

In the rear seat, Ray let out a cheer at their narrow escape and gave Steele's shoulders a firm shake. Steele smiled back at him, but she could already feel that something was amiss with the biplane from the way it shook and shuddered.

"What's wrong?" Ray asked. He must have noticed her expression.

"The engine's ruptured!" Steele called back. "We'll start losing pressure any minute now, assuming we don't burst into flames first!"

"*What?*"

Poor Ray. Steele sometimes forgot that non-pilots were prone to panicking when aeroplane engines stopped working.

Thick, oily smoke began pouring out of the engine as the lubrication grease caught fire. A moment later, clouds of steam began pouring out from a ruptured pipe. Well, that was that. The only thing left to do was to try to make a controlled crash landing somewhere.

Steele wrestled with the controls as she looked around for an eyot to land on. There were plenty of rock fragments, but few large enough for a forced landing and none with any signs of habitation or the resources necessary for survival. If she and Ray were to be stranded somewhere, they would need to last long enough to send a signal for help or be picked up by a passing airship willing to risk taking on strangers in the Badlands. That could take days, or even weeks. Unless an eyot had its own food and water, they would be dead before they could be rescued. Having just survived a dogfight in a *Kingfisher* of all things, she was in no mood to be done in by starvation.

Steele's eye caught a glimpse of an airship's envelope rising from among the pine trees of a forested eyot half a mile away. It would be a difficult flight—or rather a glorified glide—but the distance might give her time to slow the plane's descent enough to survive the crash with only minor injuries. The presence of an airship was a good sign; even if it was hostile, it was still better than nothing at all. A camp of pirates would have access to something useful: an aethercaster, another aircraft they could steal, or even simply food and weaponry.

"We're going down!" she said. "I'm going to try to put us down on that eyot over there! Hang on tight; this is going to get rough!"

She road the wind as best she could, blinded by flames and choked by smoke as her engine continued to rupture under the strain. Before long the propeller had stopped turning altogether. Pieces of the biplane disintegrated around her as the force of the winds overpowered wood and canvas already weakened by bullet holes.

Suddenly the eyot was beneath her. The tropical forest rose into the plane's path even faster than Steele had anticipated. She managed to keep the Kingfisher steady until it hit the trees, at which point she lost all control. The aeroplane smashed through the foliage like a shell shot from an artillery piece. Steele's face was stung by leaves and branches, and she threw up her hands to protect herself.

Finally, the plane struck something solid enough to halt its fall. Steele was flung forward against the controls. Her head struck the edge of the cockpit, and in an instant she was in darkness.

ELEVEN

Steele woke with a start.

She had been slumped against the front lip of the cockpit, and she bolted away from it as she opened her eyes. She was confused for a moment. Where was she? How had she come to be there? Her heart pounded as she looked around at the bush and foliage that surrounded her. The nose and propeller of the plane was tangled in it.

Where was her pistol?

Steele grabbed blindly for the top of her boot and drew her revolver. Moving hurt like Hell, but she couldn't shake the certainty that she was about to be attacked at any moment.

I'm panicking, she thought. *The plane crashed and I'm bloody well panicking.*

Steele took a few deep breaths and slowly felt the spike of adrenaline subside. As she began to calm down, she began to notice a sharp ache just above her collarbone. The pain had been there all along, but in the post-crash panic she had ignored it. Now, with the adrenaline gone, it made her gasp with each breath.

She pulled down her collar and felt around her neck. Her fingers located a splinter of wood and yanked it out. It appeared to be a fragment of the propeller. Or was it part of the wing?

Blasted wooden planes. Always breaking to pieces on a girl.

She turned around and saw Ray in his seat behind her, unconscious. At least they were both alive. Steele leaned across and slapped his cheek to bring him around. Ray awoke with a start and grabbed for the knife strapped to his torso. Taken by surprise, Steele darted back and threw up her hands. Ray stopped in mid-draw and exhaled.

"Oh, it's you," he said.

"Happy to see you too, Ray," Steele said.

Ray rubbed his head. "What happened?" he asked.

What a silly question.

"We crashed," Steele said.

"Yes, I *had* noticed."

Steele climbed out of the plane and helped Ray to the ground. Ray moved gingerly from the battering he had suffered in the crash, but he got down without complaint.

"I don't suppose there's any point in asking if you can get the plane flying again," he said, surveying the damage.

Steele laughed. "About a pirate's chance in Belgaet," she replied, stating a Commonwealth adage that referenced the Air Force's impregnable fortress shipyard. "The only way we're getting off this eyot is with a new aircraft."

Ray opened the cargo compartment and began pulling out tools and supplies.

"Then we'd best get moving," he said. "I saw signs of activity on the far end of the eyot when we were going down."

"Why do you think I picked this place?" Steele asked with a smug grin. "The romantic scenery?"

They set off through the undergrowth.

* * * *

It took over an hour of brisk walking to cross to the far end of the eyot where the airship had been spotted, and Steele felt her body complain every step of the way. Walking away from a crash was one thing; forced marching was quite another. At least the thick vegetation of the tropical forest made for pleasant scenery, and the local animals—whatever they might be—kept their distance.

Steele found the encampment in a low bowl of open land that offered ample space for the airship to be moored close to the ground. Keeping to the foliage and shadows, Steele crept around the fringes of the clearing with Ray until they found an ideal observation point. Lying down amid the brush, Steele accepted a pair of binoculars from Ray, and together they began a proper assessment of the camp and whatever threat it might pose.

The clearing's primary business appeared to be digging. Broad pits had been carved out of the soil in a methodical manner, leaving the dirt piled up in great mounds out of the way of the holes and the nearby tents. Steele saw a number of men and a few women working in the pits with hand tools and light machinery. The excavators were dark-skinned, like the Sabai, but they were all too short and too broad to be people of the Commonwealth.

"Talians, you think?" Steele asked. She had met a few Talians in the past, mostly merchants and tourists. They were a decent lot, very gregarious. It was certainly better than being marooned with pirates.

"Probably," Ray said. "The clothing looks right, and they have Talian builds. They're certainly industrious enough. I'm fairly sure they aren't Badlanders."

"No," Steele said. "*Those* are Badlanders."

She pointed toward a group of weathered-looking men and women in shabby clothes who sat around the camp in clusters, smoking, drinking, and cleaning the numerous weapons they carried.

Ray nodded. "Definitely Badlanders."

It begged the question, what were Badlanders and Talians doing in such close proximity? The two groups seemed to get along. As she watched, Steele saw several of the Badlanders wander over to the excavation pits and exchange words with the Talians, and both groups could be seen eating together near the cook tent.

"Well, the Talians aren't prisoners," Steele said. "That's a good sign, I suppose."

"On the contrary," Ray said, "it looks like they're running the show."

He pointed toward a hill at the center of the camp. Steele raised her binoculars and took a better look and saw three Talians speaking together in the shelter of an open-walled tent. Two of the Talians carried clipboards and were probably foremen overseeing the diggers. The third was a plump woman in an expensive robe of blue, white, and yellow. She had the bearing of an executive, and she was clearly in charge.

As Steele watched, a dark-haired Badlander dressed in a blue pea coat approached the tent. The wealthy Talian gave her a sign of greeting, and the two began speaking.

"Well I'll be . . ." Steele murmured. "Sarah Wren."

"A friend of yours?" Ray asked.

"She's a mercenary," Steele said. "A privateer."

A glorified pirate for hire.

"We've crossed paths before," Steele continued, "and she's got a warrant out for her arrest. If circumstances were different, I'd be down there tying her up right now."

Beside her, Ray smirked behind his field glasses. "Now that's something I'd pay to see."

"Quiet you," Steele said.

Suddenly she heard the sound of a firearm being cocked behind her, and she froze.

"Well how'd you do?" asked an unreasonably amiable voice. The accent was Commonwealth, but it was affected with an unmistakable Badlander twang.

Steele slowly looked behind her. She saw a tall, lean man standing over her and Ray with a scoped lever-action rifle braced against his shoulder. The man had a firm chin and well-groomed mutton chops, a long leather duster, and a battered hat. He wore the same rugged field clothes as the Badlanders in the camp and had the surly expression to match. From his stance and confidence, Steele could see that he could and would shoot his prisoners before they could try anything.

Well that's torn it.

"And what do we have here?" the Badlander asked. "Looks like a couple of interlopers to me."

"We're just here for the bird watching," Steele said.

"Bird watching?" The Badlander did not sound convinced. No surprise there.

"Specifically, the Lesser Crested Cormorant," Ray said. "Have you seen any about?"

Steele glanced at him. *There's thinking on your feet, Ray,* she thought, and sighed.

"Nope," the Badlander said, "but I'm proud to say I've come across a couple of sneaking rats, and I mean to add 'em to my collection. Now on your feet, and I advise you to keep your hands where I can see them or else something unfortunate might happen."

"There are two of us," Ray said, "and you've only got one shot before you have to chamber a new round. What's stopping us from rushing you?"

The Badlander grinned. "I'm the quickest lever-man around, partner. I can put lead into both of you before you see me reload."

"Why should we believe you?" Steele asked, watching for any signs of hesitation or doubt. There were none.

"Because I'm 'Gentleman' Jack Wolfe," the Badlander replied. "'Gentleman' on account of I used to be one. You may have heard of me."

Jack Wolfe? Steele froze. She should have recognized him from the wanted posters. Everyone in the Commonwealth had heard of Jack Wolfe. *Jack Wolfe, formerly Captain in the Moorlands Regiment. Jack Wolfe, third best sharpshooter in the Army. Jack Wolfe, deserter, murderer, and highwayman!*

Here he was, right in front of her, and there was nothing she could do about it.

Wolfe laughed at Steele's expression. "So you *have* heard of me."

"Of course I have," Steele said. "Though you really shouldn't act so proud of yourself. You have a dishonorable discharge under your belt, Wolfe. *For murder.* In case you've forgotten, that's a *bad* thing."

Wolfe grinned from behind his rifle's sights. "Don't forget gambling debts and public drunkenness."

Cocky bastard.

"I think murder overshadows both those charges," Steele said.

"Those constables had it coming," Wolfe replied. "They shouldn't have tried to arrest me when I was having such a damn fine time on leave!" He expression hardened. "Now I think the Cap'n would like to make your acquaintance. Get walking."

* * * *

They were quick-marched down the hill into the camp with Wolfe walking behind them, ready to shoot. Steele had no illusions about his ability to gun them both down if they attempted to run. The man's reputation in marksmanship had been confirmed during his Army service, and his speed of reloading was a legend upon which his highwayman's reputation had been built. Even if they could overpower him, one of them would be shot and left easy pickings for the other Badlanders nearby. For the time being, compliance was the only viable option.

The mercenaries and the diggers looked up from their work in interest as Steele passed them, and a few of the ones enjoying a break began to crowd in to see what was going on. The Badlanders kept their hands on their guns, as suspicious as Wolfe. Steele and

Ray were marched to the central tent, where Wren and the Talian woman were speaking.

As Steele neared the tent, she saw that it had a third occupant: a broad-shouldered Talian man with a stubborn expression and a thick jaw to match. His face and bald head were marked heavily with old scars, and his body was encased in a sturdy suit of plated armor. His left hand rested against the top of a massive body shield that stood by his side.

He's a Gao, Steele thought, recognizing the insignia on the shield. Whoever the head woman was, she could afford the best of the best as a bodyguard.

The bodyguard noticed their approach and took a half step closer to his employer. One hand readied his shield, while the other rested on the grip of a massive revolver hanging from his belt. He studied Steele with a long stare, sizing her up like a strategist examining a battlefield map.

Wren noticed them as well and dropped one hand to a volcanic pistol resting on her hip. She moved to meet them, walking with the arrogant stride that Steele knew well. Not that Steele could blame her for that. It was difficult being a woman in the Badlands. The only way to get respect was going about like you owned the place.

"Well now, Jack," Wren said, "what's this you've brought me? I didn't know it was my birthday."

Wolfe gave a smart salute. At least that much of his Army training hadn't been lost, Steele thought. What a pity his combat skills had been retained as well.

"Just a couple of interlopers, Cap'n," Wolfe said. "I thought I'd best bring them along for you and Miss Molekane to interrogate."

The Talian woman smiled at Wolfe. "How thoughtful of you, Mr. Wolfe," she said. She turned toward Steele and Ray. "Now then, who can you two be, and what can you be doing here at my excavation?"

Ray took a step forward, keeping his hands visible. "We're just travelers passing through, ma'am, honestly. Our aeroplane had engine problems, and we crashed on the eyot."

"Why were you spying?" Wolfe growled.

"We weren't," Ray said, edging away from the man and his bared teeth. "But as you can imagine, here in the Badlands a fellow doesn't present himself to a lot of armed strangers until he's had time to measure them up."

"I reckon that's true," interrupted Wren, as she sidled up to Ray and gave him an appraising look. Smiling, she patted him on the cheek. "You strike me as a smart enough man to look before you leap." She then turned to Steele, her smile becoming even more pronounced and more than a little severe. "But I'll be *damned* if I ever believe that Lucky Lizzy Steele showed up on my doorstep because of a little 'engine trouble.'" She folded her arms and looked Steele in the face, matching the unwavering glare that Steele gave her. "Because *that* is just too rich to be believed."

Of all the people to recognize me. . . .

Molekane tapped her fingertips together for attention. Though the sound was soft, the precision of it was enough to silence the rest of them and draw all eyes toward her.

"I am led to believe that you ladies know one another," she said.

Wren turned away and pointed her thumb at Steele.

"Miss Molekane," she said, "allow me to introduce you to Wing Commander Steele of the Commonwealth Air Force. Though what she's doing here in *normal clothes* like the rest of us is beyond me."

"So you are Commonwealth soldiers, then?" Molekane asked, looking at Steele.

Steele was at a loss for words. She merely gritted her teeth and forced a smile as she searched for something not terribly incriminating to say. At her side, Ray quickly stepped forward and bowed his head politely. He kept his hands open and where everyone could see them.

"She is, madam," he said. "I'm just a cartographer. Amartya Ray of the Commonwealth Special Survey Bureau, at your service."

Molekane gave him a cautious look. "And what, exactly, has brought you to my doorstep, Mr. Ray?"

"Reconnaissance," Ray replied. "I came out here to map the region and identify any hostile forces. Wing Commander Steele was assigned as my pilot. Unfortunately, the hostile forces found us and we were shot down. I assure you, we had no intention of disturbing your work—whatever it is—nor did we have any knowledge that you were here."

Steele marveled at how easily Ray could tell the truth dishonestly. It must have been his bureaucrat's training.

"Ah." Molekane smiled. "'Hostile forces.' That would be Lord Burkhalter's pirates no doubt. He holds sway over this region of the Badlands."

"You are familiar with Lord Burkhalter?" Steele asked.

"Of course," Molekane said. "My excavation remains free from interference at his good will, purchased, I might add, at a rather steep price."

"Excavation?" Ray asked.

Steele saw Ray's eyebrow raise slightly. For some reason he found the word particularly interesting.

"I am an archaeologist, Mr. Ray," Molekane said. "Unfortunately, what I hope will be one of the greatest finds of our generation rests within the domain of a pirate lord. So, I did what any self-respecting woman of Tali would do."

"Which was?"

Molekane's grin was sincere and proud. "I rented it from him."

You what? Steele's eyes widened.

"You can't possibly believe that he'll leave you in peace!" she exclaimed, with visions of a massacre floating in her head.

"Of course I can," Molekane replied, looking a little offended. "I have him under contract, and that is something Talians take very seriously. While a run of the mill band of thieves might break their word, one does not become a pirate lord without walking a very fine line. If Burkhalter were to break his contract and attack me, word would get back to Tali, and even members of the criminal classes would begin to question his validity as a trading partner."

Steele considered this. At least Molekane had given the matter a lot of thought, although Steele's instincts bristled at the thought of civilians trusting their lives to the honesty of a pirate lord.

"Then what are Wren's hoodlums for?" she asked.

"*Hoodlums!*" Wren exclaimed.

Molekane's smile became rather sly as she replied, "Well, one can never be *too* cautious."

Steele sighed in relief. Molekane had put *a lot* of thought into it, and she clearly didn't trust Burkhalter one bit. The arrangement was probably one of those 'necessary evils' that Steele—like most Commonwealth officers—profoundly disliked.

"You need not fear for the safety of my camp," Molekane said. "I know that the bribe I paid Lord Burkhalter will induce some lethargy. Hopefully, his greed will remain sated until my work is completed. And if not, a show of force and another bribe will likely do the trick."

Molekane snapped her fingers, and one of the mess tent workers hurried over and presented her with a cup of chilled coffee.

"The real question," she said, "is whether I can trust *you*. And that is something I have not yet decided."

"For whatever it may be worth," Steele said, "I give you my word as an officer that we have no intention of interfering with your work. All we want is to get out of the Badlands and back to Commonwealth airspace. Once we're gone, you'll never hear from us again."

Molekane sipped her coffee as she considered this. "I know that Londoners are said to be honest to a fault—unless one asks a Mercian, who will tell you that the Commonwealth, like Tentetsu, is perfidy personified—but I did not become a successful businesswoman by believing national stereotypes. Unfortunately, you have no one to vouch for you, and that makes my decision much more difficult."

"I can vouch for them," said Wren.

What? Steele slowly turned her head and stared at Wren. *What the hell is she playing at?*

"*You* will vouch for them?" Molekane asked.

"If Lizzy Steele gives her word, she keeps it." Wren gave Steele a meaningful smirk. "Three years ago, she swore to me that she'd see me behind bars, and she's never given me a moment's peace ever since."

That was true, and Steele still meant to see it done.

"Her dedication aside. . ." Molekane said.

"She's honest, ma'am," Wren said. "I'd trust her with my life if I had a reason to."

Molekane turned back to Steele with a bemused expression. "Your enemy defends you as if she were your friend, Miss Steele. What a remarkable turn of events for you." She looked at her bodyguard. "And what do you think, Mwai? Am I in danger from these two strangers?"

The bodyguard gave Steele and Ray an appraising look and replied, "No, not more than usual."

"'Not more than usual,'" Molekane murmured, sounding amused. "What a wonderful way you have of putting things, Mwai." She took another sip of her coffee and spoke to Steele. "Mmm, Cook has done a remarkable job with today's brew. You and your associate should have a seat and join me for a cup. We can discuss what is to be done with you."

"I'm not really—" Steele began, confused at Molekane's strange and abrupt invitation.

"It would be our pleasure," Ray interrupted, taking Steele by the arm and leading her to one of the empty chairs.

Steele gave him a curious look. "I though you hated coffee," she whispered.

"I do," Ray said, "but she's offering us hospitality. If we accept, we're under her protection so long as we mind our manners and don't betray her trust."

"You're like a walking guidebook, you know that?"

"Cartographer," Ray said.

Steele took her place at the table next to Ray Wren and Wolfe sat opposite, flanking Molekane. Mwai stood at Molekane's elbow, looking both alert and relaxed. The message was clear: if Steele had any ulterior intentions toward Molekane, she would have to get through the three of them. It was a good thing she had no intention of doing so.

More chilled coffee was brought from the mess tent, and soon those seated were all drinking away. Through the shared refreshment, the tension of recent events begin to ebb away.

"Very well," Molekane said at length, "I have decided what is to be done with you. I shall keep you as my guests. You shall share my food and enjoy my hospitality. I am expecting a supply ship from Tali later in the week. Once it arrives, I will arrange for you to be returned to the nearest friendly port and from there back to your Commonwealth. In exchange, I expect you to mind your manners and leave my employees unmolested. It will do me no good if someone attempts to arrest Captain Wren and her soldiers."

"You have our word that we'll do no such thing," Ray said.

Steele felt him prod her with his foot.

"No such thing," she said, eyeing him.

In reality, she wanted little more than to call for an airship squadron and have Wren and Wolfe arrested once and for all. Each of them would be a nice feather in her cap, and there was also the basic principle of letting criminals like them go free. But there were much bigger priorities on hand than a privateer and a murderer.

"Good," Molekane said. "Then it is settled."

Ray cleared his throat softly but forcefully, as only a bureaucrat could manage.

"We are most grateful for your generosity and kindness, Ms. Molekane," he said, "but the most ideal turn of events would be for us to return immediately. Our information regarding local distribution of pirate forces is of the utmost importance, and it may very well save lives. And what is more, if we do not return, the worst may be expected, and a rescue party could be sent into the Badlands to find us. I would not want those men and women sent into danger unnecessarily."

"A commendable thought," Molekane said. "What alternative do you propose?"

"Is there a spare aircraft that we could borrow? I would be more than happy to pay for it, of course."

"I fear not. Captain Wren's airship is our only craft capable of long-distance travel, and I have neither the authority nor the wish to give it to you."

"Of course not," Ray said.

Not that we could hope to make use of it, just the two of us, Steele thought. Ray had no background in aviation that she knew of, and she certainly couldn't fly an airship all by herself.

"What about using your aethercaster to contact the nearest Commonwealth patrol?" Steele asked. "If they know where to find us, we could be retrieved immediately and leave you to your business."

Molekane shook her head. "Out of the question. I cannot have a Commonwealth warship flying to this eyot, drawing the attention of every pirate and freebooter in the area. And what is more, I have no wish to risk having Captain Wren and her crew arrested."

"We've already given our word that we would not let that happen," Ray said.

"*You* have, but if a Commonwealth force were to arrive, how can you promise me that they would hold to your oath as well? Surely you do not have such authority."

She was right, Steele knew. Any Air Force officer worth the title would arrest the Badlanders in a heartbeat.

She and Ray were silent for a few moments, exchanging looks. Ray's expression showed his thoughts: he was as displeased as she was. If they waited until the supply ship arrived, Burkhalter's fleet might be sent into battle before they could warn the Commonwealth.

Molekane smiled and set her empty cup down on the table. "Come now, do not be troubled. It will only be a matter of days. And surely, a week's delay in your report will not cause undue danger to your nation."

"So I hope with all my heart," Ray replied, before taking another very long drink of coffee.

TWELVE

Coffee was followed by a light meal of porridge blended with dried fruit. Steele ate hungrily. She had not eaten since breakfast, and between the dogfight, the crash, and the hard marching, she had exhausted whatever reserves of energy she had built up with her morning omelet.

At her side, Ray ate more slowly, but he gave clear signs that he was enjoying it. It was probably another matter of protocol. Molekane certainly seemed pleased with her role as the magnanimous host as she watched them eat.

"If I may ask, Ms. Molekane," Ray said at length, "what do you propose that Steele and I do to occupy ourselves while we wait for departure?"

It was a question that had been on Steele's mind as well, but she was unsure of whether it was polite to ask. They were now in the realm of diplomacy and foreign relations, and it was probably best to leave all that nonsense to Ray.

"You are free to do as you please, Mr. Ray," Molekane said, "provided it does not interfere with our work. I imagine you will want to prepare you maps and reports for when you return to the Commonwealth. I also have some books that may interest you, including a few of my own monographs on the subject of archaeology."

"That is most kind of you." Ray sounded rather excited at the prospect of Molekane's monographs. Steele knew that he had an obsession with "improving books" at bedtime. Steele preferred a little light music herself, but to each his own.

Molekane leaned forward. "Tell me, Mr. Ray, are you a draftsman as well as a cartographer?"

"I am, yes," Ray said. "Why?"

"My workers are currently searching for the entrance to some ruins buried beneath the soil of this eyot. We have already found promising signs, and I believe that they will locate an intact tunnel network any day now. My work would be greatly assisted if I had a second artist to map the layout of the rooms for me and to help catalogue the artifacts we find."

"I suppose it would keep me well occupied," Ray said. "It would be my pleasure. And I'm certain Steele would be happy to assist as well. She has a keen and ready eye."

"Then it is settled," Molekane said, pleased. "Now then, make yourselves at home in our little camp, and we will get you started on work tomorrow morning. In the meantime, you are probably tired from your journey. I will have some space prepared for you in one of the tents."

Ray bowed his head. "Your generosity is most appreciated, Ms. Molekane."

"We Talians are known for our hospitality. It would be wrong of me to disappoint."

"By your leave . . ." Ray said, half rising.

"Good afternoon, Mr. Ray," Molekane said, nodding her head.

Ray stood and bowed, first to Molekane, then to Wren and Wolfe. Steele, not at all used to diplomatic dealings with foreigners, quickly copied his movements. She followed him out of the tent and together they took a walk along the edge of the trees. Steele spotted some of the Badlander mercenaries watching them, but the soldiers made no move to follow.

"So what is the plan?" Steele asked, when she reasoned that they were out of earshot. When she was met with silence, she added, "You *must* have a plan."

Ray always had a plan. He was like clockwork in that regard.

"Betraying hospitality is a bad policy in general," Ray said, frowning, "and it can be fatal when dealing with a Talian. Did you see Molekane's bodyguard?"

Steele inhaled. How could she not?

"He's a member of the Gao Company," she said. "I could tell that much from his shield."

That was very serious, Steele knew. Gao was the top employer of bodyguards in the Known World for a very good reason. They were some of the toughest soldiers out there, and Steele had heard rumors about their sense of professional honor. Death before failure was the rule, not an ideal to aspire to; and Gao bodyguards were known to protect first and ask questions later.

"If we make any move that he regards as threatening to his employer, he'll break us in half."

"He could probably do it with his bare hands," Ray said. "And even if we got a lucky shot on him, Wren's mercenaries outnumber us more than ten to one."

Steele nodded in agreement. "Overpowering them is out of the question."

She paused on a low rise in the land and looked down into the camp. To one side of the hill were the tents, to the other the excavation pits. Wren's airship hung just above the ground at the far end, tethered by heavy ropes and metal anchors. Its envelope was kept low enough to the ground to be sheltered from the wind by the surrounding trees. The airship was compact with a detached crew compartment, a design common in the Badlands. Steele found the style to be terribly primitive, but it did the job.

Steele could see that the airship was equipped for combat, armed with a mismatched scattering of machine guns and light one and two pounder autocannons, nicknamed "pom-poms" for their characteristic firing sound. The hull was wood, covered in armor plating, and even the envelope was lined with metal scales to shield the fabric from tears, shrapnel, and bullets.

"If we could somehow pull off stealing it, could you fly that thing?" Ray asked.

Steele gave the airship an appraising look for a few moments. Then she shook her head. She could probably fly it, provided she remembered enough of her basic training—it had been years since she'd been behind the controls of anything larger than an aeroplane—but she would need at least one other person to manage the engines while she was busy at the helm. And come to think of it, she wasn't particularly comfortable with the idea of flying through the Badlands without someone manning the guns, and each of them required a two-member crew.

She sighed. "Out of the question."

"I'll put you down for a tentative no," Ray said. "Not that I would want to leave anyone stranded without transport in the Badlands anyway. What about a smaller craft?"

"I haven't seen any aeroplanes," Steele said, looking around the camp. There wasn't really enough open ground for a plane to land or take off, at least with the camp in the way. "Wren might have some powered gliders in the airship, but they're one person apiece, and I'm guessing you don't know how to use them."

"I do, actually," Ray replied, with a smug smile. "But I also know that they don't have the necessary range to get us to a friendly port."

Steele raised an eyebrow and gave him an approving look. "Well, well, well, Mr. Ray," she said, reaching out and adjusting Ray's collar, "aren't you a man of surprises?"

"I like to keep you ladies guessing," Ray replied.

Learn something new about you every day, Steele thought. It was actually becoming rather fun, waiting to see what new surprise Ray had in store. She would never have taken him for a field agent before this little adventure of theirs.

"If we can't fly out, we'll have to get help to come to us," Ray said. "What if we got a hold of their aethercast and sent a message to Rahul?"

Steele considered this. It was a decent idea, but. . . .

"It would take them hours to get to us," she said, "assuming we could even give them accurate coordinates. And I doubt very much that we could get the message out without being caught."

Ray frowned. "I'd prefer to avoid armed conflict, but London needs to be warned about Burkhalter."

"When Molekane catches us—" and she *would* catch them. "—she'll either kill us or imprison us. When reinforcements get here, it'll be a bloodbath. At best, they'll be arrested for assaulting citizens of the Commonwealth. If they resist, they'll be gunned down."

Shoot first, ask questions later: that was the rule in the Badlands.

"Agreed," Ray said. "We either need to convince Molekane to let us use that aethercaster, or I have to get access to it without arousing suspicions."

"Can you do it?" Steele asked.

Ray took a deep breath and looked over at the camp. Steele followed his gaze. She spotted the tent with the aethercaster on the side opposite the airship. It was easy enough to spot thanks to the tall aerials that extended past the canvas roof and into the air. She saw no one guarding the tent, but it was within easy view of the entire camp, and several of Wren's mercenaries sat nearby, cleaning their weapons.

"Getting in won't be the hard part," Ray replied, "but if someone's inside, they'll see me. And once I start broadcasting, if there's anyone at the ship's aethercaster . . ."

"They'll hear it," Steele finished for him. "Bugger all." She folded her arms and stood in thought. It was a bad situation, but there was only one course of action that really seemed likely to work.

"I think we need to be straight with Molekane," she said. "If we explain that we want to warn the Commonwealth about Burkhalter's fleet, she'll understand. She's a civilized woman, and Burkhalter represents as great a threat to Tali as he does to us."

Ray looked dubious. "Perhaps," he said, "provided she believes us. *And* provided she isn't in league with him."

"No, she isn't," Steele said. "I know Wren. She's a privateer, but she hates the pirate lords and everything they stand for. She wouldn't be working with Molekane if there was any real loyalty to Burkhalter."

"You really think you can pull this off?" Ray asked.

Steele took a deep breath and then exhaled.

"I hope so," she replied.

* * * *

Steele found Molekane in the main tent, examining a cluster of artifacts that had been laid out on the table. They were an odd assortment of goods dating back to a time before the Great Upheaval, and they told a fascinating tale of advanced and even modern technology. There were the rusted remains of metal cans, bits of porcelain crockery, eating utensils, bricks, and countless other objects of a less identifiable nature.

Molekane was busy cataloguing them all with a fascination that only an archaeologist could show toward old rubbish. Steele could scarcely comprehend her interest in most of it. As ever, Mwai stood nearby, eyes alert for anything untoward. He spotted Steele immediately and gave her and Ray a polite nod. There was that Gao professionalism again. Steele knew he didn't trust them, but he was still perfectly civil about it.

"Mr. Ray, Ms. Steele, what can I do for you?" Molekane asked without looking up.

Steele took a step forward and saw Mwai's hand drop to his hip, casually putting it close to his revolver. Well, she could hardly blame him for being cautious.

"We've come to request the use of your aethercast device to contact the Commonwealth," she said.

Molekane flashed her a curious look.

"Out of the question," she said, "as I have already explained. While I am willing to take you at your word—and having only just met you, I trust you understand how significant a show of trust that is—I cannot risk your relief force attempting to arrest my mercenaries. I know that they are criminals in the eyes of the Commonwealth, but under Talian law they are legal privateers, and what is more, without them my workers and I will be in gave danger should a band of pirates happen through the area. My contract with Lord Burkhalter stipulates that his men will not harm me, not that they will protect me from harm."

"We understand that," Ray said, advancing a pace to stand at Steele's side, "and we have no intention of giving our coordinates or requesting retrieval. All we want to do is to send our superiors the details of our scouting mission. They need to know about the distribution of pirate forces in the area *immediately*."

Steele could tell that Molekane did not share their sense of urgency. She continued making notes regarding the artifacts as she spoke:

"I cannot imagine that the balance of power in the region will change significantly over the course of a week. Surely your information will be just as useful to them when you are returned to your country by other means."

Now came the hard part: making the urgency clear to Molekane without it looking like scaremongering.

"Tell me, ma'am," Steele said, "when you arranged the contract with Lord Burkhalter, did you do it on his flagship or in his fortress?"

"Neither," Molekane said. "I never dealt with him directly myself. It was all managed through an intermediary, as I understand is often the case with pirate lords."

That made sense. Pirate lords were paranoid about assassination attempts and rarely allowed anyone but their most trusted followers to come near them.

"Then you haven't seen the distribution of his fleet?" Steele asked.

"His fleet?" Molekane looked up at her in surprise. "Why should I care about his fleet?"

Steele exchanged a look with Ray.

"Burkhalter's fleet is massive," Ray said. "It's grown beyond any reasonable size for the territory he claims."

"It's reached boiling point," Steele said. "A pirate fleet as large as his must inevitably attack *something,* or else it will begin to disintegrate as its members go looking for plunder or turn on each other. Which means that soon, probably in a matter of days, Burkhalter is going to take his ships and start raiding. If we're lucky, he *might* target another pirate lord in a bid for territory, but I wouldn't risk money on that. I suspect he'll try to plunder the civilized lands to his east."

"And that," Ray said, "means either the Commonwealth or Tali. And while our priority is the protection of the Commonwealth, your homeland is very much in danger as well."

Steele jumped in again. "I know that if I were a greedy pirate lord with a massive battle fleet, I'd take my ships south and target Tali. Burkhalter's no fool. Most pirates raid our airspace because they want our technology, or they're after revenge for our punitive expeditions, but everyone knows that the real money's in Tali. Burkhalter's fleet could break its way past your patrols, assault the capital, and plunder the Bank of Tali."

"Preposterous!" Molekane protested, but it was clear to Steele that she entertained the very real possibility of it.

"It would be hard fighting," Ray agreed, "something that most pirates wouldn't dare risk, but Burkhalter is aggressive and ambitious. Think about it. He'd gain access to the largest depository of wealth in the Known World, and he'd be able to restock his supply of troops from all of the mercenary companies headquartered in Mjikuu, who I'm certain would rather throw in their lot with a victorious warlord than die to a man. And think about what it would mean for the rest of the world. The collapse of Tali would mean the destruction of international commerce. Trade coinage would suddenly be meaningless, and exchange rates would fluctuate like mad. It would be the perfect coup against the civilized world."

"Assuming he chose to do it," Molekane replied, "assuming he managed to pull it off, *and* assuming that you are telling the truth. Have you any proof that his fleet has grown to such a size?"

"I do," Ray said. "Photographs, if you have facilities for me to develop them."

"We have a photography tent. Come with me and I will introduce you to Ms. Akukweti, my photographer. She can handle the development. But believe me Mr. Ray, I hope with all my heart that you are lying."

Steele wished that they were.

Molekane motioned for Ray to follow her and then left the tent. Mwai fell in just behind her, keeping himself between her and Ray. Knowing that she would be of no use dealing with the development of the photographs, Steele departed the other way. She walked over toward the excavation pits and saw Molekane's workmen hard at work unearthing what appeared to be the foundations of an ancient building from beneath the soil and refuse that had piled up on top of it over the centuries.

She watched them for a while, marveling at the thought of what they might uncover. Glancing to the side, she saw Wren moving in her direction. Steele waited for Wren to arrive and offered her a polite nod.

"Wren," she said.

"*Captain* Wren," the privateer reminded her.

It was a typically Badlander misuse of vocabulary. They had a very peculiar approach to word usage, and they were notoriously arrogant about it. Like how they insisted on mispronouncing "aluminium."

"Captains are in the Army," Steele said. "*Group Captains* command airships."

Wren smirked. "Only in the Commonwealth would that sort of nonsense make sense."

There was a lengthy, somewhat awkward pause.

"Tell me, Wren, why did you vouch for us?" Steele finally asked. It had been bothering her ever since the meal. "You know I've been after you for years. I'd have thought this would be the ideal time to dispose of me once and for all."

And it would have been a typical Badlander tactic to do it.

Wren laughed. "For the same reason that you've sworn not to attack me and mine. What's the point if we're on the ground letting other people do the work for us? Besides," she added, more seriously, "what I said was true. You're honorable, and though you might not believe me, I respect that."

You're right, I don't believe you, Steele thought.

"You see me as a pirate for hire," Wren continued, "but out here in the Badlands I'm an officer and a lady, and I have standards of conduct that I hold myself to. I'm not one to lie about an enemy just to have her killed. There's no sport in it and no honor either."

"I'm grateful nonetheless," Steele said. But she wondered what Wren's real angle could be.

"Believe me, Steele," Wren said, "if the Commonwealth hired privateers, I'd be fighting with you, not against you. But you lot don't like mercenaries, and I need to make a living."

"You could always enlist," Steele said. She was only half joking. Wren had criminal inclinations, but she had skill. And, truth be told, Steele acknowledged that a privateer who followed the rules of cruiser warfare was far better than a pirate who saw murder and enslavement as a way of life. She meant to see Wren behind bars some day, but at least there was no need to hang the woman.

Wren grinned at the suggestion of enlistment.

"Too many regulations," she said. "I like being a free agent without a chain of command to tie me down. It's a good system, more efficient than what you lot are doing. You'll never pacify the Badlands if you insist on tying the hands of your officers."

Steele knew Wren was right about that—she'd seen the evidence of it firsthand—but she was not about to admit it.

An awkward silence followed when Steele did not reply. Steele felt as if she should say *something*, but she had no idea what to talk about. She and Wren were on opposite sides of whatever topic they had in common, and the last thing they needed now was an argument.

After a moment, Wren cleared her throat.

"Steele," she said, "I want to thank you. You gave your word that you wouldn't try to arrest me or my troops, and I appreciate that."

Steele shrugged and looked away, uncomfortable at being thanked by someone she intended to arrest or kill eventually.

"Don't. I could be lying."

"You're not," Wren said. "You don't lie. You'll use every dirty trick you can think of in the sky, but you don't lie face-to-face. And I respect that about you. If I'm going to be hunted by someone, I'd rather it be you than someone who can't keep her word."

"Well, I won't be arresting you any time soon, that much I know," Steele said, sighing.

"You sound disappointed."

"I am."

THIRTEEN

Molekane studied the photographs that Ray had presented her with a growing expression of dread and irritation. The evidence was clear to see. Lord Burkhalter's fleet was clearly sizable, possibly even on the scale the two Commonwealth agents claimed. She knew the habits of pirate lords well—with so much of her work taking place in the Badlands, it was a matter of necessity—and with such a fleet at his disposal, Burkhalter would certainly put it to use very soon.

If she allowed the Londoners to warn their people, that same fleet might be on her doorstep an hour later. Burkhalter was no fool, and he would certainly be monitoring aethercast traffic in his territory. But if she did nothing, she would be an accomplice to what was likely to become one of the bloodiest pirate raids in history.

Molekane looked at the photographs again and sighed. She was faced with the choice between honorable sacrifice and cowardly self-preservation, and she found neither of them to be particularly appealing.

Molekane set the prints down on the table and looked at Ray.

"I assume you were shot down by Burkhalter's men because of these photographs," she said.

"In part, yes," Ray answered. "I suspect they were more concerned about what we had seen than how we intended to convey news of it to others."

"Did any of them return to give your location to the fleet?"

"None," Ray said. "Steele shot them all down. Our crash was due to damages sustained during the firefight, but it happened after we emerged victorious."

That was good. At least there was nothing definite to link the Londoners to the eyot, although Burkhalter was likely to think of the excavation eventually.

"They will be out searching for you," Molekane said. "If we send a warning out, they will hear it and descend upon us like hyenas."

Molekane sighed. She knew the right course of action, and she had been raised a proper Talian woman. Sometimes sacrifices had to be made for the sake of the public good.

"Nevertheless, you *must* send it," she said. "I will not be a silent witness to a massacre."

"I can send it in code," Ray said, "and on a frequency they aren't likely to be monitoring. But as you say, it must be sent, whatever the risk to us."

Molekane considered this for a few moments, rightly displeased. She had ventured into the Badlands at great expense and personal risk for the sake of science and study, only to find her work derailed by politics. She was furious, though she showed little outward sign save for a clenching of her jaw.

"Very well," she said at length, pushing a pen and paper toward Ray. "In code then."

Molekane watched as Ray began writing, breaking the message down into short groups of four letters placed in columns. They seemed to have no discernable meaning, but Ray was clearly putting much thought into them. He wrote slowly and with great calculation, and every so often he would pause in thought as he worked out what the next sequence ought to be. In spite of herself, Molekane was fascinated by the display. The mental agility required to perform encryption in the midst of writing must have been tremendous.

Finally, Ray finished his work and scribbled an aethercast frequency on the top of the paper.

"It's done," he said. "Ready for transmission."

Molekane nodded.

"Mr. Kemboi!" she called, motioning toward the aethercast operator who waited nearby. She took the paper with Ray's message and passed it to him. "Transmit this on the indicated frequency. Do it once an hour throughout the night, but at irregular intervals."

Kemboi looked at the paper. "But it's gibberish—"

Molekane was in no mood for delays or arguments.

"Do it."

"Yes, ma'am," Kemboi said, ceasing his protestation and nodding in consent. Molekane had worked with him for two years now, and he knew better than to question her. Kemboi gave the message another curious look, mumbling something about Londoners and their codes, and departed for the communications tent.

"What do we do now?" Ray asked.

"We get a good night's sleep, of course," Molekane said with a slight smile, "and then tomorrow we carry on with the excavation."

It was necessary to keep the appearance of normalcy in case Burkhalter sent men to check on the camp. Molekane knew better than to risk arousing suspicion. Besides, she had come there at great expense to excavate pre-Upheaval ruins, and she meant to carry out her work, circumstances be damned.

Ray was quiet for a moment. Molekane could tell that something weighed upon his mind.

"Ms. Molekane," he said, "if Burkhalter's men do find the signal and track it back here, it will certainly be in your best interest to pretend that we have covertly infiltrated your camp and used your aethercaster without your knowledge. By that point the message will already have been received by the Commonwealth authorities, and our capture will be unable to prevent the arrival of reinforcements in this region of the Badlands."

"Did you just suggest that I turn you over to a man who will torture and kill you?" Molekane asked.

Ray paused. "Let us say that I am acknowledging the course of action that is in your best interest to take and that I am assuring you I will understand and hold no ill will if and when you take it."

Molekane was genuinely offended for a moment. How dare he tell her to break her pledge of hospitality? But of course, Ray's suggestion was not malicious. He was a Londoner: they did not understand such things.

"For a man well-versed in the language and customs of Tali, you seem to have a very poor understanding of us," Molekane said. "I have given you my hospitality, Mr. Ray. I have no intention of rescinding it. Do you think me the kind of woman who will go back on my word simply because it becomes more convenient? For shame, Mr. Ray. For shame."

Ray folded his hands and bowed his head deeply to Molekane.

"I am eternally grateful for what you are doing for me and the Wing Commander, Ms. Molekane. I hope that I live long enough to repay you."

Molekane put the cap back on her pen and tucked it into her pocket.

"As do I, Mr. Ray," she said.

* * * *

Molekane rose early the next morning to oversee the final excavations. She had already alerted her workers and Wren's mercenaries to their situation, and the morning air was filled with tension. Molekane noticed a few sullen glances toward her guests as they left their tent, but it was kept controlled. Molekane's workers understood that Tali was in danger, and that the Londoners might offer a chance to save it, while the Badlanders seemed almost pleased at the prospect of combat. She knew that Wren's people hated the oppression of the pirate lords, and they seemed to be spoiling for a fight.

Well, they were likely to get one.

Molekane was joined by Wren just after breakfast and by Steele a few minutes later. The three women stood together for a while, watching as the workers finished the last of their unearthing. Many of the surrounding excavation pits had hit a flat expanse of cement and paving stones, something that suggested the remains of a roadway or perhaps a courtyard in some pre-Upheaval city. Only one hole had been dug beneath the pavement layer, and it entered into an old basement made of brick. Molekane had already ordered that this be the focus of the workers' efforts, and the direction had paid off. Just the previous day they had unearthed a heavy wooden door that had survived two centuries of burial intact.

With Steele at her side and Mwai behind her, Molekane climbed down into the pit as her photographer, Lukia Akukweti, finished taking a picture of the door. Akukweti was a striking woman, slightly taller than Molekane, with golden threads plaited into her long hair. They had worked together off and on for more years than either of them cared to count, and Molekane was pleased to have Akukweti with her during such an important find. Clear photographs were very important to modern archaeology, and good photographers were hard to come by.

Molekane gave the door her own examination, making certain that it did not have any important writing on it that might be damaged. Satisfied that it did not, she clapped her hands twice and motioned to the workers.

"Open it."

The workmen rushed in with crowbars and began prying. Both the lock and hinges of the door had rusted through, so they were broken easily by a mallet and chisel. Then, with a terrible groan, the door was wrenched from its frame and fell onto the ground in a cloud of dust. The space beyond was a yawning mouth of darkness, and from it issued the dank, stale smell of a place untouched for generations. It had the fitting stench of a tomb.

Molekane accepted a chemical lantern from one of her foremen and ignited it. The flame crackled and hissed as it gave off an eerie crimson light. The rest of the company were handed lanterns as well as they lined up outside the doorway. Molekane saw Wren and Ray appear on the ledge above. They were both armed. That was probably unnecessary, but one never knew for certain.

Wolfe was nowhere in sight, having returned to the forest to continue his habitual patrol. He was a curious man, but Molekane was glad to have him and his snipers in her employ.

Behind her, Molekane heard Ray exchange greetings and pleasantries with Akukweti. It pleased her that they seemed to have formed an accord while developing photographs the previous evening. It was best when one's associates got along. Things ran more smoothly that way.

Molekane smiled at her companions. The excitement of a new discovery always made her feel giddy, in spite of the past day's troubling revelations. There was truly nothing like work to take one's mind off of one's problems.

"Ladies and gentlemen," she said, "this is a great moment for modern scholarship. We are about to enter the untouched remains of a city lost to humanity during the Great Upheaval. This is a great honor for all of us. I would like to remind you that the artifacts we find here are very valuable and may be fragile. Be extremely careful about where you walk and what you touch. Now then, let us make history!"

So saying, she ducked into the doorway and flooded the chamber beyond in the crimson chemical glow of her lantern.

FOURTEEN

Steele had not known what to expect when she entered the ruins, but what she saw proved to be greater than anything she had imagined. Far from simply one or two rooms, the space inside the eyot proved to be an entire network of subterranean chambers that stretched onward far beyond the space of the camp. They were all built of brick or heavy stone, some with crumbling plaster caked upon the walls. Most had low arched ceilings. A few had wooden crossbeams to support them, and some of these had rotted through and collapsed, leaving their rooms filled with dirt and rubble.

Part of the network was intentional, made by doorways and corridors that connected the basements of what must have been a dozen buildings or more. But any openings that Steele saw were inadvertent: a broken wall here, missing bricks there, all conspiring to link the chambers in ways that their builders had never intended.

As Steele made her way through the basements with the excavators, she found the remains of a world lost to history. There were bits of rubbish, old tools, canned goods, and other items. A few rooms had been part of workshops; others had been used for storage. And there, bathed in the red glow of their lanterns, she found the dead.

Corpses littered many of the rooms, and she saw more than a few in the corridors as well. They were dressed in the tattered remains of pre-Upheaval clothing, and they were all hideous to behold. The sealed confines of their artificial tomb had protected them from rot and decomposition, leaving the bodies withered, discolored, and mummified. They lay, some in heaps where they had cowered together until inevitable death, others on their own, killed during the chaos of the event itself. The lucky ones had died in violence, crushed by falling debris. The rest had suffered the long agony of starvation, dehydration or suffocation. Most of the rooms had become sealed against the outside during the Upheaval, and the rats and other crawling things had died before they could make a meal of their human companions. It was dreadful to contemplate, but

Steele supposed that it did offer a great opportunity for scientific study.

The excavators fanned out and began examining the complex. Steele stuck close to Molekane, unsure of what she should be doing but fascinated at the sights before her. Molekane was methodical but quick, examining each room in turn as she moved along, while the excavators assisting her stayed behind to catalogue the find.

As always, Mwai remained at Molekane's elbow, even though they were unlikely to find anything that could threaten her in the tombs. Ray joined them, carefully mapping out the extent of the rooms and tunnels on a portable drafting board. Akukweti took pictures with a portable camera.

Steele drifted toward the rear of the advance team, feeling more than a little unnerved by the surroundings. She disliked enclosed spaces as a rule, except when they had the good sense to be man-made vehicles, and while she was no stranger to death, actual corpses were an uncommon sight for an aviator. Those dead that she had seen in the line of duty tended to be freshly killed, then whisked off to a proper cremation or burial at sky. Even the ossuaries kept by many families in the Commonwealth were far less unnerving than the bodies that filled the basement. There was something peaceful about bare bone that mummified flesh did not share.

About halfway across the complex, Steele caught a flicker of movement out of the corner of her eye. She turned toward it, only to find it gone. It was odd, but she quickly put it out of her mind. Probably a trick of the light caused by the flickering chemical lanterns.

A few minutes later, it happened again. Certain that she had seen something, Steele spun around only to face an empty hallway. Molekane and the rest of the company had already moved into the adjoining room, but now Steele's curiosity was peaked. Drawing her revolver, she slowly advanced along the brick passageway, holding her lantern out ahead of her. The crimson shadows flickered ominously, but no real movement presented itself.

The passageway ended in a sturdy metal door. Against it lay the body of a man—now only identifiable as such by the remains of his clothing. He appeared to have been in the process of trying to force the door when he had succumbed. But chilling as the sight was, nothing at the end of the passageway seemed capable of producing the movement that Steele swore she had seen.

This was why Steele hated confined spaces. One's eyes were always playing tricks on a person.

Turning back, she almost jumped in fright at the sight of a small figure standing in the center of the hallway, just at the edge of the lantern's light. It was undoubtedly a child, a girl if the rags were any indication. There was something unnatural about the little figure. She seemed radiant, like someone bathed in the light of a sun that could not possibly be shining so deep underground.

Where did she come from? Steele wondered to herself. *No, this can't be right. I'm seeing things.*

Steele rubbed her eyes with the back of her hand. Opening them again, she saw with a start that the girl had approached by several paces and now stood only half the distance away from her. At the closer range, Steele could see that the girl's angelic face was distorted by a curious expression, half sneer and half snarl.

Steele watched the girl in silence. She ought to call to the others, but somehow she couldn't seem to make a sound. Something wrong was happening. But so long as she kept her eyes fixed on the little girl, the ghostly figure remained perfectly still like a painting or a statue. Whenever her gaze shifted away, even for a moment, the little girl moved a little closer.

Got to keep my eyes open, Steele thought. The very thought made her blink.

When she opened her eyes again, the girl was directly in front of her, looking up at her with pleading eyes and that horrible expression. The girl reached out and brushed her hand, like a child wanting her mother to comfort her. The touch stung like lightning. Steele hissed in pain and dropped her revolver. It struck the ground with a dull noise.

Steele recoiled and thrust the lantern—now her only weapon—toward the girl to keep her at bay. The girl's mouth opened in a silent howl, and she darted forward. Steele bolted to the side and turned in time to see the girl fall onto the body at the base of the door and vanish from sight.

Not a moment to waste.

Steele snatched up her revolver from the floor and turned about in place, looking every which way in case the child returned. Where the devil had the little girl gone? In each direction, Steele was met by the flickering crimson shadows of the chemical lantern.

Vanished? But that's impossible! Steele felt her heart pounding. What was going on?

She heard a cracking noise behind her and turned toward it. She saw the mummified corpse slowly pick itself up from the base of the door, its joints snapping and popping beneath the withered flesh. Steele backed away a few paces in shock, struggling to come to terms with what she was seeing.

The corpse had no such hesitation. With a curious light burning in the hollows of its eyes, it took a few halting steps toward her. Steele finally regained her senses and raised her revolver. She fired two shots directly into the corpse's body. It jerked from the impact but kept coming.

Steele backed away further and fired again, this time at the corpse's head. One shot went wide and pinged against the wall. The others hit home into the corpse's face. It tumbled backward and lay on the floor, still twitching with an afterthought of life.

A moment later, Ray burst into the hallway, holding his revolver. Molekane and Mwai were close at his heels.

"Steele!" Ray shouted, rushing toward her. "What was that shot? What's happening?"

Steele turned toward him, automatically reloading her revolver. Her hands were shaking, but the movement helped calm her.

"It . . . it attacked me," she said, too confused by recent events to properly explain them.

"Why are you discharging a weapon in here?" Molekane demanded. "You might damage something!"

"The corpse attacked me," Steele said, finally finding her voice. As she spoke, she realized how mad it sounded.

"The *corpse* attacked you?" Molekane looked shocked at the very suggestion. "Of all the absurd . . . What do you mean it attacked you?"

Steele spread her arms indignantly. How many things could that sort of statement mean?

"I mean that it attacked me!" she said angrily. "There was a little girl standing in the hallway. Then she ran to the body, she disappeared, and it got up and came at me."

It wasn't *that* difficult to understand. Far-fetched, maybe, but not difficult.

"A little girl?" Ray asked. "Steele, you're not making sense."

"None of it *made* any sense!" Steele said. "She looked odd, like . . . like—"

As Steele worked to find a fitting explanation, she chanced to look down the hallway. Standing some distance behind her companions were three more figures, two men and a woman. They looked like the little girl had looked, with a peculiar glow about them and expressions distorted monstrously. Steele's voice caught in her throat for a moment, and in that time one of the men and the woman turned silently and walked into the adjoining room. The remaining man kept his place, staring ominously at her.

"There!" Steele cried, pointing.

Her companions turned in place and froze at the sight, except for Mwai who immediately placed himself in front of Molekane and drew his heavy pistol.

"By my ancestors . . ." Molekane whispered.

"What *is* that?" Ray asked to no one in particular, drawing back and raising his weapon.

"It looks like a ghost," Steele said, also taking aim.

"How do you know what a ghost looks like?" Ray asked. "Have you ever seen one before?"

Steele looked at him. What sort of a question was that?

"No," she said, "but if you ask me, that's what a ghost would look like if I ever saw one."

Their exchange was interrupted by a scream from the nearby room. Steele exchanged glances with Ray and then looked back at the figure in the center of the hallway. It showed no signs of noticing the noise.

"Lukia!" Molekane cried and rushed toward the room, heedless of the specter.

Mwai was close on her heels and interposed himself between Molekane and the ghostly figure. It still showed no signs of interest, even as Steele and Ray ran past as well. Mwai slowly backed away into the room and then turned to rejoin Molekane.

Steele found Akukweti in the center of the room amid a heap of toppled barrels. Two of the mummified bodies that had lain on the floor nearby were now on their feet, looming over the Talian and clawing at her with their bony fingers. One of the corpses was hunched over, and it gnashed its teeth like a hungry animal as it strove to bite its victim. Steele saw Akukweti struggling against them, but the Talian was about to be overcome.

Heedless of her own danger, Molekane ran to the nearest corpse and grabbed it by the shoulders. Steele rushed to help her, Ray following close behind. Together, they managed to drag it away from Akukweti. Now interrupted from its task, the thing gnashed its teeth and twisted about, trying to decide which of them to feast upon instead.

Steele began shooting with her revolver. Ray quickly joined in. The corpse twisted and turned, seemingly refusing to die, until finally the weight of bullets in its head and torso sent it falling to the ground.

She turned to see Mwai grab the second corpse, wrapping one gloved hand around its throat to force its mouth shut. That was some good thinking on his part, Steele noted. The corpses seemed mostly intent on biting and chewing. The clawing fingers were almost an afterthought.

The corpse struggled violently. Using all of his tremendous strength, Mwai ripped it away from Akukweti and flung it aside. The body stumbled and then fell, only to rise again with shaky, confused movements. They were bloody tenacious. But, undaunted, Mwai raised his revolver and blew the corpse's head apart.

Steele rushed to Akukweti's side with Molekane. The photographer was wounded, her sleeves torn and her forearms scratched horribly from the teeth and fingers. She had protected most of her body with her bloody arms, but a few blows had gotten through and left marks on her face and abdomen.

"Come on," Molekane said, her tone brisk and businesslike, "on your feet Lukia."

Akukweti was breathing heavily, her eyes tearing in pain and fear. She was probably on the verge of screaming after the ordeal, but she kept control of herself. That was admirable, especially for a civilian. Steele gave her a forced smile.

"You're going to be ok," she said to Akukweti. "But we need to get you to the surface."

Akukweti nodded, biting her lip to keep from screaming. She shivered as Ray bound her arms with bandages from the medical kit Molekane carried. Then, with the worst of the bleeding halted, Steele helped the photographer stand and looked back toward the door.

She saw the third ghostly figure still standing in the hallway. It had turned without anyone noticing, and now it stared silently in her direction. Its gaze and twisted expression were hypnotic as it slowly, inexorably advanced into the room inch by inch while seeming never to move.

Behind the figure, shambling shapes advanced into the edge of the crimson light. More of the mummified bodies had come to life, and now they converged on the room with shuffling steps and horrid burning eyes.

Steele opened fire on the cadaverous mob, joined by Ray and Mwai. A few of the corpses fell here and there, but the rest came on heedless of the gunfire.

"We have to get out of here!" Steele shouted.

"How?" Ray demanded. "They've blocked the only door!"

"Here!" Molekane said.

Steele saw Molekane hurry to the nearest wall with Akukweti. Keeping her revolver trained on the mob, she withdrew to join them. Ray followed her, while Mwai kept firing at the corpses advancing through the door. His high caliber revolver was their only truly effective weapon against the walking dead. What took Steele two or three aimed shots to accomplish, Mwai's weapon managed with the force of a single bullet.

The section of the wall that Molekane had gone to was in poor condition. Much of it was crumbling, and several of the bricks had broken free and fallen onto the ground. Steele could see that it wouldn't take much to break through. It was their only way out.

Steele snatched up a length of metal pipe that lay nearby and tossed it to Ray. Ray nodded and gave the bricks a few experimental blows, but there was little result.

"I'm not strong enough," he said. "It'll take ages for me to force it."

Mwai fired his last shot into the mummies and hurried to join them.

"Give it to me," he said, holstering his revolver and holding out his hand.

Ray passed the bar to Mwai as Steele began shooting in the Talian's place. At least a dozen corpses had shambled into the room and were closing in on them with outstretched hands. This was very bad, Steele knew. She kept firing, but her lower caliber weapon could do little to slow the assault.

At the wall behind her, Mwai was bashing and prying the bricks with all the vigor he could manage. Mortar dust and dried clay filled the air in a cloud as the big Talian forced a hole large enough for a person to crawl through.

"Go! Now!" he shouted to Steele and rushed to replace her. He did not even bother to reload his revolver. Instead, he hefted the now bent pipe like a club as he took up the rear guard.

Steele was the first through the hole, which led into what had been the basement of an adjoining building. She saw more mummies inside, but thankfully they remained still as she approached. She helped Akukweti crawl through after her, followed by Molekane and Ray.

Peering back into the first room, Steele saw Mwai standing in the midst of the cadaverous mob. The bodyguard laid about himself with the pipe, his fist, and his feet, repelling the clawing hands and biting mouths that assailed him from all sides. He was in grave danger of being overcome. Steele could tell that only Mwai's great strength and conditioning prevented him from being dragged down, and only his sturdy armor kept the corpses from tearing his flesh with their fingers. Even so, the gnashing, grasping things drew blood even as Mwai struck them soundly with his improvised club.

"Mwai!" Steele shouted, waving at him. "Get out of there!"

If he didn't break away soon, he would be overwhelmed.

Mwai glanced back at her and saw that they had all made it through the opening. With a roar from his belly, he forced his way free from the corpses and ran for the hole in the wall. One corpse still clung to his arm and was dragged along. Mwai merely smashed it against the wall and threw it aside as its grip slackened from the force of the impact.

Steele looked about for something to block the hole. The corpses would follow them through if it remained open. She spotted the remains of a table laying on the ground. Its legs had broken, but the surface was still solid. She lifted the table onto its side as Mwai crawled into the room. Once he had cleared the opening, she shoved the table over to block it. A moment later, she heard the sounds of the corpses clawing at the table from the other side.

"That won't hold them for long," she said, "but at least it should give us a few minutes to breathe."

"Let us be doubly sure of that," Mwai said. "Come, help me reinforce the barrier."

Working together with Mwai and Ray, Steele moved several more pieces of rubble and furniture against the table to secure it in place. It was a good thing that they did so, for the table began shifting midway through the process, until they blocked it with heavier materials.

As they worked, Steele glanced over at Molekane and Akuk-weti. The photographer leaned back against the wall with her eyes closed, probably on the verge of unconsciousness. Molekane had opened her medical kit and was busy treating Akukweti's wounds.

"You must stay awake for me Lukia," Molekane said. "Can you do that?"

Akukweti nodded slowly and forced her eyes back open. "I will try, Nakaaya. I will try."

Molekane forced a smile. "Good. Now that we have some more time, let me deal with your injuries properly."

Steele was suddenly thankful at Molekane's foresight in bring-ing the medical kit. And poor Akukweti. Steele didn't relish the thought of being set upon by a horde of walking dead either, but at least she was used to people trying to kill her. Akukweti and Molekane were civilians. This was probably a new and terrible experience for them. Not that shambling corpses didn't have their own dreadful novelty for Steele.

She turned away from the barricade and dusted her hands off on her trousers.

"Just to be sure that I'm not completely mad, there really is a mob of walking corpses on the other side of that wall, isn't there?" she asked.

"Unless we're all collectively losing our minds, yes," Ray said, dabbing his face with a handkerchief. "A perfectly morbid way to start the day."

Nothing was making any sense. Ghosts weren't real, and the dead simply did not walk. Except, of course, that down here they were real and they certainly did walk. And bite.

Even so, there's no excuse for the dead not staying dead!

Steele crossed the room and knelt by Molekane.

"Ms. Molekane, have you *ever* encountered something like this on a dig before?" she asked.

Molekane was busy slathering Akukweti's wounds with anti-septic paste before she bandaged them, and she did not look up from her work as she replied:

"No, never, though a colleague of mine once told me a story such as this."

"Really?" Steele asked. So it wasn't an isolated incident after all.

"During an excavation near the border of Jianguo many years ago, my colleague opened a tomb-ruin, such as this one, where the dead rose and forced her workers to leave. She said that the spirits of the departed drove the bodies they had occupied in life like you or I might drive an automobile." Molekane sighed. "At the time I gave her words little attention. She always has had a remarkable sense of humor and I assumed it was a tall tale at my expense. I see now that she was more sincere than I gave her credit for."

"Ghosts," Steele said flatly. "Not the sort of thing a person normally believes." She sighed. "So much for a rational explanation to all things." That sort of superstitious nonsense was contrary to everything she had been raised to believe.

Ray looked up from his map of the tunnels. "Not necessarily," he said. "I seem to recall reading a rather interesting monograph on the subject about a year ago."

Steele looked at him. Of course he had. She doubted there was a single subject that the man *hadn't* read a monograph about.

"Oh yes?" she asked.

"Yes, by Maxwell Boyde. You've probably heard of him."

Steele thought for a moment. "Name sounds familiar, but I can't place it."

"Senior lecturer on aether physics at Melmoth University until he was dismissed two years ago for illegal experimentation."

Illegal experimentation? Steele blinked. *Well, that's academics for you. Closet skeletons aplenty.*

Aloud, she asked, "And this Boyde fellow wrote a monograph about ghosts?"

"Among other things," Ray said. "Boyde had a theory that because aether particles can transmit electrical signals and because our brains use electrical impulses—"

"They do?"

"Apparently," Ray said, before continuing on, "Boyde argued that you could store thoughts in a cloud of concentrated aether, and that ghosts, if they exist—"

"Which they do."

"Which they do," Ray agreed. "—are just memories of the dead trapped in clouds of aether, shaping their containers to look as they did in life."

The clawing noises at the barricade began to intensify suddenly and a banging sound joined in as well, causing the table and rubble to shake a little with each impact. Mwai looked in the barricade's direction with a nonchalant expression and began reloading his revolver.

"We should keep moving," he said.

"Agreed," Steele said. "Ms. Akukweti, can you walk?"

"I'll try," Akukweti replied, making soft noises of pain as Molekane helped her to her feet.

"Come, Lukia," Molekane said, "lean on me."

Steele took up a position by the door and waited for the others to assemble. Ray joined her, looking over his map intently. He was, no doubt, determining the fastest route back to the entrance.

"Tell me, Ray," Steele said, "did this Boyde fellow have an explanation for the *dead bodies trying to kill us?*"

"Well, the nervous system is just a complex electrical network. I suppose if a ghost entered a dead body, the electrical signals would re-enter the nervous system and control just as they did while the body was alive."

"That is an extremely eloquent argument in favor of superstitious nonsense," Steele said.

Ray grinned. "I hate to remind you, Steele, but that superstitious nonsense is on the other side of that wall, very clearly trying to kill us."

Well, he was right there. Outlandish theories aside, one couldn't argue with an army of the walking dead. As if to emphasize that point, the barrier shook again and several pieces of rubble tumbled away.

"Let's go," Steele said to Ray.

Ray took one last look at his map. "All right, follow me," he said.

Steele forced open the room's door and led the way into the next chamber. Ray followed, giving directions. Mwai took up the rear, keeping Molekane and Akukweti in the middle of a protective triangle. As they passed into the next room, the barrier against the wall was finally knocked aside, and the corpses began crawling in. A moment later, the bodies on the floor begin to rise in the same jerky, shambling manner and joined the others.

"Hurry!" Mwai shouted.

Leading the group, Steele rushed ahead half-blind, confused by the dim cast of the crimson lanterns that made every shadow seem to be a figure and every pile of debris appear like a corpse. She turned right at an intersection, only to find two more of the specters waiting for her with more corpses shambling along from that direction.

"Other way!" Steele shouted and motioned for the others to go left.

Mwai threw open the nearest door. Ray went in first, followed by Molekane and Akukweti. Steele followed and found herself in an old coal-caked boiler room. Mwai was right behind her, and he slammed the door shut just as the two cadaverous mobs met at the intersection.

Steele grabbed some pieces of fallen rubble and wedged them against the base of the door. Hopefully, that would secure it long enough for them to make good their escape.

"Ray, we need a way out of here!" she shouted.

Ray peered at the map and tried to reorient himself.

"This is a section we haven't visited yet," he said, "but if we can go about thirty feet ahead and ten to the right, we should hit the chamber just inside the entrance. It'll be touch and go, but it's the best I can do."

"No time to waste, then," Steele said.

The boiler room connected to the next part of the basement through a long arched tunnel made of brick. It was dark and narrow and filled with the bodies of people who had sought shelter there during the Upheaval. Steele took up the lead, holding her lantern out ahead of her. She picked her way around the bodies and tried not to think about them.

Midway along the tunnel, a curious sensation of dread came over her, and she turned in place to look back at her companions. There, in the darkness behind Mwai, stood the first ghostly figure that had heralded the coming of the risen mob. The figure watched Steele in silence, the light doing horrible things with its distorted expression.

Turn around! Steele cried silently, but yet again she found her voice stifled.

Mwai must have seen something in her expression, for he spun about and lashed out with the back of his hand at the unseen foe.

The blow slid through the specter's head as if it were vapor, and Mwai let out a cry of pain. He kept his stance and poise, but as he withdrew a few paces, he looked down at his hand and flexed his fingers only with a certain amount of effort. Steele knew exactly what he had felt.

The figure raised its arms toward the ceiling, and with echoing groans, the corpses in the hallway began to twitch.

Oh Hell . . . Steele thought. *Not again!*

"Run!" she shouted, her voice finally returning to her.

She opened fire upon the bodies, trying to knock them down before they could finish rising. Mwai joined her, blowing corpses apart with his higher caliber weapon. Ray hurried to Molekane's side, and the two of them helped Akukweti dash for the end of the tunnel.

"Go ahead!" Steele shouted to Mwai. "Make sure they aren't rushing into an ambush!"

Mwai nodded, fired two last shots into the corpses behind them, and rushed to the head of the group. Steele glanced over her shoulder and saw him smash a path through the bodies rising at the head of the tunnel. That would give the others a way out, if Steele could hold their pursuers at bay. Not that the corpses seemed to be much daunted by gunfire.

As the others cleared the tunnel, Steele turned and ran to join them, reloading as she did. Hands snatched at her feet and ankles, but each trip and stumble only drove her on faster. She burst out into the next room and spun about, taking up a rearguard position. Ray appeared at her side and they stood together, shooting into the shambling legion that filled the tunnel.

"I wish you'd be more careful," Ray said. "You could have been killed back there."

Steele laughed. "Tell me that in ten minutes, if we're both still breathing!"

Behind her, Mwai flung the nearest door open. A corpse loomed in the doorway, its jaws wide as if hungry, but Mwai merely barreled into it and smashed it against the wall.

"Time to go," Steele said, grabbing Ray by the arm and pulling him toward the exit.

Ray looked at his map again. "Left!" he shouted.

"You're taking us in circles, aren't you?" Steele said.

"Nonsense!"

They turned down an adjoining passage with clusters of risen corpses shuffling toward them from all directions. An empty path branched off to one side, and Steele made a dash for it. There were corpses there, lying on the ground, but none of them moved as she approached. She quickly motioned for the others to follow her.

Steele heard the sounds of gunfire from somewhere ahead and made in that direction. More specters loomed in the shadows, reaching out to brush her with a poisonous touch, but she charged on heedless of the danger. Gunfire meant people just as surely as it meant more of the corpses.

She finally reached the entry chamber with the others close behind her. She saw Wren standing in the center of the room, firing with both of her pistols into a crowd of corpses that had entered through a second doorway. Most of the workers had fled, and Wren was covering the retreat of those few who remained.

Wren kept the volcanic pistols spinning about her fingers, firing each time one came to eye level and reloading just as quickly. Steele had to admit, the woman was a damn fine shot. A regular Badlands gunslinger.

"There you are!" Wren shouted. "What in damnation's happening?"

"The dead are walking!" Steele said. "What does it look like?"

Wren flashed her a sick grin. "Leave it to you to raise the dead!" she said with a laugh.

FIFTEEN

Steele was the last to leave the tunnels, holding the rearguard with Wren until everyone else had escaped. She bolted out into the excavation pit and turned to face the door, ready to fire. Ray, Wren and Mwai stood at her side, aiming their weapons in the direction of the tunnels with similar intent.

She waited for a few long, tense moments, expecting the dead to shamble out through the doorway at any moment. Instead, there was silence. Why weren't they following? Did the dead really care for nothing but their final resting place?

Steele heard a cough from above them followed by a gruff Badlander voice:

"I hate to interrupt y'all when you're havin' such a fine time," said a man with a heavy accent indicative of the southern Badlands, "but I'ma gonna need y'all to come up here now before I lose my patience."

Steele turned and saw men standing on the lip of the pit above them. They were Badlanders if their clothes and weapons gave any indication, but they were not Wren's Badlanders. The speaker was a burly man with thickly matted blond hair and a sizable beard. He had a patch over his right eye, thick scars on that side of his face, and an arm that appeared strangely distorted beneath his heavy coat.

"C'mon," he said, motioning toward Steele and her companions. "Up y'all come."

Well, no point in arguing with the barrel of a gun.

Steele slowly climbed out of the pit with Molekane and the others. Akukweti was all but unconscious from fright and blood loss, so Mwai carried her in his arms with all the tenderness of a father holding a sleeping child. At the top of the pit, she saw Wren's mercenaries and the rest of the workers sitting around in a large cluster at the foot of the hill. They had all been disarmed and their weapons piled up out of reach. A dozen and a half other men in rugged clothing stood around them, holding them at gunpoint with rifles and shotguns. Many of the armed men wore armbands and patches emblazoned with Burkhalter's skull and gear emblem. The pirates had come for them after all.

Steele kept her head down and quietly complied as the pirates disarmed them and put them under guard with the other prisoners. It chafed to obey the orders of criminals but, so heavily outnumbered by the enemy, putting up a fight was unlikely to accomplish anything other than civilian casualties.

Steele sat with Ray at the edge of the cluster of prisoners, studying the movements of the pirates for any reasonable opening. The pirates were characteristically overconfident, swaggering about with the look of men who had never met a problem that couldn't be solved with a gun.

Looking back over the crowd of prisoners, she noticed that Wolfe and several of Wren's Badlanders were missing, doubtless still on patrol. Their homecoming would not be a happy one. And, as she looked over the cluster of prisoners, she realized that someone else was missing too.

"Where's Molekane?" Steele whispered to Ray, suddenly realizing that the woman was not with them.

Ray nodded in the direction of the lead pirate. Steele turned her head and saw Molekane standing in front of the man, glaring at him with a furious expression.

"Bloody hell, what is she doing?" Steele asked. Molekane was going to get herself killed.

Mwai's was watching his employer in desperation, clearly thinking the same thing. Steele could feel the tension radiating from his body. He was a bodyguard. His instinct was to protect his employer, by physical force if necessary; but if Mwai made any movement toward approaching Molekane, they might all be shot.

Steele looked back at Ray. The spy sat with a serene expression, hands folded in his lap. He smiled softly at her. Steele knew he was looking for an opening, just as she was. Hopefully, it would come before something happened to Molekane.

* * * *

Molekane shared none of Steele's concerns for her safety. Like any self-respecting leader, she had no time to worry about herself when her workers were in danger.

The lead pirate—the big bearded man who had greeted them in the excavation pit—had not yet noticed her presence. He was far too busy shouting orders at his men, ordering them to search the camp like they owned the place. It was beyond toleration.

"Stay where you are!" Molekane barked. Her tone was severe enough to make the pirates freeze in mid-step.

The lead pirate turned on Molekane. "What the Hell are you doin' standing?" he demanded. "And what d'ya mean by orderin' my men about—"

Molekane cut him off, in no mood to be spoken back to by such a ruffian.

"I can see by your emblem that you serve the Lord Burkhalter," she said. "In light of that, I am outraged at your intolerable behavior in my camp."

"Now listen, missy—" the pirate began.

"What is your name?" Molekane asked.

"Say what now?"

"What is your name?" she repeated.

The pirate grinned. "Aw, ya can call me Bill if ya like," he said. His face distorted in a snarl. "Now shut up and sit down. I don't know what you're used to back in 'civilization', but out here we've got ways of showin' a woman when she's gettin' uppity."

He brandished his hand. It glinted in the light, as if composed of polished metal. One of Lord Burkhalter's mechanical prosthetics no doubt.

Molekane retained her composure without flinching. Either Bill would strike her or he would not; either way, such a man did not deserve the pleasure of a reaction. Bill kept his hand raised menacingly, but it seemed to be an empty threat. From his expression, Molekane could see that he had expected the gesture to be enough. Perhaps the women of the Badlands could be cowed by such antics, Molekane thought, but never a Talian.

"You will not speak to me in that impudent manner," she said. "You call me 'uppity', Mr. Bill, but it is you who forget your place. Lord Burkhalter and I have an agreement, *under contract*."

She emphasized those final words. A contract was something that every Talian, whether law-abiding or criminal, took very seriously.

Bill scoffed and waved at his men to resume their search. "Yeah, well, some things're more important than the writin' on a piece of paper, missy. Now go sit down 'fore I lose my temper."

Such insolence. Molekane was astounded at the pirate's inability to understand his place. He actually believed himself to be in charge.

"No," Molekane said. "Now explain to me why you are here, in my camp, uninvited and in violation of your master's contract."

"Ha!" Bill laughed. "Ya got brass, missy." He grinned for a moment and then drew close to Molekane and snarled. "But don't think that's gonna get you anywhere with me. Ya got a crashed plane about a mile outta camp. Didja know that?"

The pirate's tremendous smell accomplished what his threats could not, and Molekane drew away slightly. Had Badlanders never heard of bathing? Or, at the very least, of perfume? Molekane knew the difficulties of grooming on the frontier, but even on the most trying of expeditions she always managed to maintain at least a basic level of hygiene.

"Mr. Bill," she said, "my excavation demands all of my waking attention. What should I care if some fool has crashed in the forest?"

"So you wouldn't know nothin' about that, eh?" Bill asked.

Molekane looked at him with utter distain. "It is none of your business what I would *know anything about.*"

How dare he presume such a thing? And with such terrible grammar.

"Just so happens the pilot of that plane was out spyin' on my Lord's private property," Bill said. "So tell me again, just what ain't my business?"

"The terms of the contract are clear, Mr. Bill," Molekane said. "Your master has leased me this eyot to do with as I please. *If* I find this pilot you want, you may rest assured that I will give all due consideration to whether I want to sell him back to you. But until my excavation is complete, you do not set foot on this eyot without a 'by your leave' and a good set of manners."

* * * *

Steele watched the exchange with wide eyes and an astonished expression.

"Is Molekane *insane?*" she asked softly.

"She's . . . brave," Wren said in the most diplomatic manner she could muster. "We Badlanders don't like being talked back to, and when a fellow's got a pirate lord backing him up, it only gets worse."

"I think it's quite inspiring," Ray said. "She's got real courage. An example to us all."

An example of how to get killed, Steele thought.

Mwai seemed to be only half listening to them as he kept his attention focused on Molekane. His hands were clenched in frustration as he silently mouthed the word "Stop!" over and over again as he tried to catch his employer's eye.

"She will be a *dead* inspiration if she is not careful," he whispered.

Steele nodded in agreement. He was right.

Ray nudged her.

"Company," he said.

Steele looked in the direction he indicated. Two of the pirates were busy circling the prisoners, checking each one in turn for concealed weapons. Steele quickly lowered her head and avoided looking in the pirates' direction, though she chanced a glance at them as she did so.

"Damn and blast," she said. "They must be looking for anyone who could be the downed pilot."

"One hesitates to be the bearer of bad news," Ray said, "but *you're* the downed pilot."

"And *you've* still got that SSB camera on you," Steele said. "I don't imagine they get too many of those in the Badlands."

Ray made a face. "Bugger."

"Bugger" was right. If the pirates searched them, they would probably be found out, not to mention what would happen if Steele's disguise failed to hold.

As the pirates came around, Steele hung her head unobtrusively and tried not to be noticed. It did not work. One of the pirates carried a metal rod in one hand, and he used it to force her face upward. He studied her for a moment while his companion began rifling through her pockets. The first pirate was about to move on when a look of curiosity crossed his face, and he peered at her again. Presently, recognition seemed to click in his head.

"Hang on a minute now . . ." he said. "Hey, Joey, take a look at this broad. You seein' what I'm seein'?"

The pirate identified as Joey released Steele's coat and shoved his face in front of hers, one eye bulging wide to get a better look. He smelled of tobacco and cheap beer, and Steele made a great effort to avoid gagging at the stench.

"What am I seein', Pablo?" Joey asked.

Pablo put his hands over Steele's forehead to cover her hair. "Just the face, forget the rest."

Steele forced herself not to react to the rough handling. She did her best to look like a sullen Badlander.

Joey narrowed his bulging eye, and the other one opened as if to compensate for it. "Well, I'll be damned. Goddamn Lucky Lizzy. . . ."

Steele felt sick to her stomach. Now they were in for it. Being found out as the pilot was bad enough, but being recognized as herself was probably a death sentence.

"Sir! Sir!" Pablo shouted in Bill's direction. He pulled Steele to her feet, grabbed her by the chin with one rough hand, and forced her to turn her face toward Bill. "Look what we got here!"

Bill spun around in irritation.

"What in Hell are you—"

He caught himself as he saw Steele's face. "Well I'll be damned," he said as he sauntered over toward them.

Bill pushed Joey and Pablo out of the way and gave Steele a looking over, forcing her to turn her face this way and that so he could see it from all angles. He was extra rough, probably trying to get some of his manliness back in the wake of Molekane's dismissive treatment. Well, what could one expect from a man who made a living off the suffering of others?

Satisfied, his mouth split open into a triumphant grin, like the cat that had caught the proverbial canary.

"If it ain't Lucky Lizzy Steele, right here in front'a me. Looks like today's *my* lucky day."

May as well deny it, Steele thought. *What do I have to lose?*

"I don't know whatcher talkin' about," she growled in the best Badlander accent she could manage. It was not her most impressive performance. "I ain't no Lizzy, and I damn sure ain't feelin' too lucky right 'bout now."

Bill laughed and said, "Spoken like a true Commoner. You funny-talk people just can't get your mouths 'round a real language, can ya?" He snapped his fingers. "Take 'er."

Pablo and Joey grabbed Steele by either arm and prepared to drag her away. Steele planted her feet firmly and squared her shoulders. If they were going to take her, they would have to wear themselves out doing it. Maybe she could cause enough of a distraction to give the others the break they had been looking for.

"Halt!" Molekane said.

Steele felt the pirates holding her freeze in place.

Bill wheeled around and stormed toward the Talian.

"Now ya listen here, missy," he snapped, "I ain't got no time for this. Lord Burkhalter wants this lady bad, so I'm takin' her. An' you'd best be thankful that I ain't shootin' ya just 'cause I can."

Molekane retained her obstinate expression. "If this woman is of value to your master, then I would be overjoyed to place her in his hands." She smiled. "You may depart at once and inform Lord Burkhalter that he may send an emissary to me at his earliest convenience so that we may discuss the terms of sale."

"Terms of sale—" Bill began.

"If she is so important to him, I am confident that he will be willing to provide me with a fair price. Now then, with our business concluded, I suggest that you and your men depart at once, before I lose my patience with you."

"Lose your patience?" Bill sputtered. "Lose *your* patience? Missy, have ya lost your mind? We're the ones with the guns here. Now you sit down an' shut your mouth 'fore I shut it for ya!"

"Very well then," Molekane said. "My patience has run out. Your actions are clearly in breach of your master's contract. I am afraid that I must now exercise my rights of ownership over this eyot by force."

So saying, Molekane raised one hand into the air. It was answered instantly by the sounds of gunfire. Steele snapped her head around in time to see four of the pirates fall dead. The others looked about frantically, aiming their weapons at an enemy they could not see. Steele could hardly blame them; she wanted to know who was doing the shooting as well. Had Wolfe's patrol come to their rescue?

There was another volley that cut down four more pirates. This proved too much for the pirates' nerve, and with cries for help they began fleeing the camp in all directions. Steele hoped that her captors might be so good as to follow suit, but they were not obliging. Deciding to play things safe, Joey grabbed a large hunting knife and raised it to Steele's throat.

"Nobody move!" he shouted. "I'll kill 'er!"

Steele sighed, now completely immobilized. Considering his jumpiness, Joey was liable to cut her throat any moment on impulse.

Oh for the love of—

Without warning, Ray sprang to his feet, drawing a pair of narrow blades from inside the lining of his coat. He lashed out with one hand, knocking the blade away for a moment as he put himself in front of the two men. Without breaking his momentum, he dove forward and stabbed each of them through the chest as near to the heart as he could manage. He grabbed Steele in his arms and pulled her away with him, in case his strikes had missed their targets.

They had not. The two pirates collapsed in a heap on the ground, dying before they could understand what had happened.

Steele was breathless from the speed of Ray's attack, but she found voice enough to laugh.

"Looks like you don't want to share me with anyone, Ray," she said.

"Quiet you," Ray said, breathing heavily.

He held her tightly. Steele did not object. She felt the blood pounding in her temples, and it was suddenly very welcome to have Ray to lean against.

Her moment of calm was broken as Mwai bolted to his feet and charged at Bill, roaring in fury. Steele turned and saw him send the pirate flying with a blow to the jaw and then place himself in front of Molekane.

Bill scrambled to his feet, blood streaming from his nose and staining his beard. For a moment he looked about to fight, until he caught sight of his men, either dead or fleeing for the woods, several more of whom were gunned down by the unseen shooters as they fled.

As he realized he was now completely outnumbered, Bill accepted that discretion was the better part of valor and bolted for the edge of camp. Steele watched as he drew a flare gun from inside his coat.

He was calling for help!

Steele broke away from Ray and ran after Bill, but she was too far away to stop him before he could fire. A flare shot into the sky and as it descended slowly toward the ground, the shape of an airship's envelope came into view over the trees. It was a small craft built in the standard two-piece design found in the Badlands, outfitted with weapons and armor but designed for skirmishes and for preying upon poorly armed victims. If Steele had had an aeroplane nearby, she could have shot it out of the sky without breaking a sweat. But on the ground and unarmed, none of them were a match for it.

Bill began shouting and waving his hands, and a rope ladder was dropped from the deck. Bill grabbed hold of it and started climbing with the urgency of a man fleeing for his life.

Steele reversed direction and began running back toward the center of the camp. The only hope of stopping the airship was the weaponry on Wren's own vessel.

"Airship!" she shouted at Wren, pointing at the pirate craft. "They're making a break for it!"

Wren snapped her head in the direction Steele indicated.

"Oh Hell's bells . . ." Wren said. Wasting no time, she ran for her own airship, shouting for her troops to join her. "Hurry!" she commanded. "We've got to stop them before they warn Burkhalter!"

But the pirates had anticipated her. As the smaller airship twisted around, it began firing upon Wren's craft with everything it had. Machine guns, a single pom-pom gun, and even the rifles and pistols of the crew were lent to the barrage. Under the concentrated close-range fire, the armor plates on the envelope gave way, and holes began to appear. In moments, Wren's airship was leaking gas in tremendous quantities.

Screaming obscenities and threats of murder, Wren jumped on one of her own pom-pom guns and began firing at the retreating pirate craft. A few shots hit home, blasting the hull and once even blowing a few of the pirates overboard, casting them down into the vast sky beneath them, but it was no use. The pirates drew further and further away, making good their escape as Wren's envelope slowly deflated and sagged against the nearby trees.

* * * *

They had tried to save the airship, of course, but by the time the crew managed to start patching the holes, the envelope was beyond saving. The airship sank to Earth and sat there listlessly. The loss of the airship meant that they were now stranded on the eyot, left to wait for Burkhalter's wrath to fall upon them.

Never one to waste time, Molekane called a meeting of her foremen and officers in the main tent. When they had all assembled, she began speaking with the force and direction of a military commander. She knew it was necessary to keep in control of things lest panic break out.

"Let us speak plainly," she said. "Burkhalter clearly has no intention of keeping our agreement. This is no great surprise, but it does change our position. Since the ship escaped, he will know that we fought back. We can expect him to attack in force within the next few hours. We must be ready for him when his soldiers arrive. Because of the damage to Captain Wren's airship, there can be no hope of escape. We must hold our ground until help arrives."

"What help?" Wren demanded. "The only thing coming to find us is the supply ship, and it's not due for days."

And the supply ship would be useless in a fight.

"No, but thankfully we have a Commonwealth officer in our midst." Molekane turned to Steele. "Wing Commander Steele, I need you to contact your nearest airbase and call for aid. My aethercast operator has our coordinates. If you call, will reinforcements come?"

"They should," Steele said. "Hopefully they already have forces on standby thanks to our warning yesterday. But if we send out a distress call, Burkhalter will know our situation, and he'll know that he's on the clock."

"Burkhalter's pirates didn't know about the message we had sent out," Ray said. "They came looking for the crash site. If we use that same frequency, it may slip past unnoticed."

"It's a long shot," Wren said.

"It's all we have."

"All right, I'm on it," Steele said and left the tent.

Molekane unfurled a large map of the eyot. "Even assuming help will be sent for us, we must last long enough for it to reach us. We need a plan of defense."

"We're completely grounded," Wren said, grimacing. "That means we have to protect ourselves from the ground rather than the air. Jack," she said, slapping Wolfe on the arm, "this is your area. Show me what I pay you for."

Wolfe made an irritated grumble.

"Thought I'd done that when my boys and I saved all your asses from Billy-boy half an hour ago."

"Sniping's in your job description," Wren replied. "So start earning some overtime."

"Alrighty."

Wolfe moved up to the table and peered at the map.

"We've got the advantage of tree cover most of the way around the camp," he said. "That'll make it harder for them to do strafing runs. The trick's going to be if they have bombers, but I'm not concerned."

"And why not?" Molekane asked. Bombers would seem to be the ideal way of dealing with them.

"No one uses them out here," Wren said with a laugh. "Even the pirate lords go light on ordnance unless they're targeting airships. Bombs and shells get pretty expensive when you're throwing them away at the ground. It's cheaper to swarm fortifications with infantry."

Molekane considered this for a moment and decided that it made sense. The vast population of the Badlands offered a tremendous resource for anyone willing to use cannon fodder, and she had seen that the pirate lords held no scruples about throwing away life.

"Speaking of fortifications . . ." she said.

"Yep, we want 'em," Wolfe said. "I'm no engineer, but I can draw up a workable plan. It'll give the diggers something to do."

That was good. Molekane's workers would need some activity to keep their minds off of the looming danger.

"We'll also want to get all of our heavy firepower into the entrenchments once they're dug," Wolfe continued. "That means taking the pom-poms and gatlings off the *Resolute*." He pointed at Wren's airship. "They'll have better sight lines that way, and we can use them against both aircraft and ground forces."

Wren sighed. "You always want to dismantle my airship."

"Don't blame me, Cap'n. I'm just doing what you pay me for." Wolfe looked over at Ray. "Mr. Ray, you said you were a surveyor, is that right?"

"I am," Ray replied.

"Well then, let's you and me take a turn around the camp and see what we can make of it."

Wolfe picked up the map from the table and folded it over so only the section around the camp was visible. As if an afterthought, he added,

"Oh, mind if I take this?"

SIXTEEN

Lord Burkhalter was not a man who tolerated failure with any degree of patience. As he stood on the upper deck of his flagship, he contemplated the prostrate form of his most recent disappointment and toyed idly with the idea of throwing the man overboard or having him drawn and quartered. A good execution did wonders for keeping the men in line, and it always made Burkhalter feel better. The mechanical bird resting on his shoulder clearly had similar thoughts inside its clockwork mind, for it studied the pleading pirate with a hunger that should have been unknown to a creature that did not eat. Burkhalter smiled a little behind his expressionless steel faceplate. He had programmed Adler well.

"Rise, Herr William," Burkhalter said, his voice heavy with a Corbinite accent. He had briefly tried to learn the Badlander accent many years before but had found it to be confused and unpleasant.

The pirate Bill scrambled to his feet and stood, head bowed, trying not to do anything that might reverse his sudden good fortune. This amused Burkhalter, at least to the extent that he remembered what amusement was. With each passing year and each successive augmentation, he found himself feeling less and less, and this gave him great satisfaction.

Big though Bill was, he was dwarfed by his lord. Concealed in a voluminous robe and cowl, Burkhalter stood easily seven feet tall. His unnatural body, where it could be seen beneath its shroud, was monstrous: an unholy construction of metal that was not quite a statue or a skeleton or a suit of armor, but an amalgamation of the three shaped in a parody of the human form. Whatever part of Burkhalter remained flesh and blood, it was hidden within the depths of its steel shell.

"You have greatly disappointed me, William," Burkhalter continued. "I have shown great faith in you, have I not?"

"Yes, lord," Bill answered.

"I gave you that arm to replace the imperfect one that you were born with. I did this because I had *faith* that you were capable of carrying out the tasks that I would set for you!" Burkhalter shouted. His calm voice suddenly changed and became shrill, making Bill cringe in fear. Abrupt changes in tone were wonderful for keeping the men off-guard. Burkhalter resumed his mellow voice as he continued, "I do hope that I have not misjudged you, William. I would not like to think that I must take my gifts back. . . ."

"N-no, lord!" Bill cried.

Bill's expression of fear gave Burkhalter great satisfaction. Burkhalter made a point of forcing his underlings to watch when he reclaimed prosthetics from those who had displeased him. Death from blood loss was the common result. It reminded them all that once they had accepted his gifts, they lived or died by his will.

Burkhalter took a step forward and wrapped one of his massive mechanical hands around the back of Bill's neck. He made certain that the grip of his fingers was strong but not yet painful. It was a practiced movement. The absence of discomfort made Bill quake all the more.

Meanwhile, Burkhalter's three lieutenants stood in a semicircle nearby, their bodies smaller copies of Burkhalter's massive, inhuman shape. Like him, they wore monastic robes to conceal their mechanical forms and masks forged to look like faces to conceal their true features. They had risen so high in Burkhalter's esteem that, like their master, it was impossible to tell what part of them remained human.

"William," Burkhalter said, patting Bill on the cheek, "I want you to know that I am not angry with you."

"No, lord?"

"No, not angry. *Disappointed.*"

Another calculated turn of phrase, and one that made Bill shiver with fear. Disappointment was always worse than anger.

"P-please, l-lord . . ."

Behind his mask, Burkhalter smiled, but the still expression on the faceplate gave no indication of this.

"William, I have decided to be generous," he said.

Such words would do little to calm Bill. Generosity might mean a quick death rather than a slow and painful one as easily as it might mean survival or forgiveness.

"G-generous?" Bill asked.

"*Ja*, generous," Burkhalter said. "Most generous. You should say your prayers of thanks tonight."

Burkhalter released Bill, dropping him onto the deck. He had made his point, and touching the man's dirty *flesh* was a defilement of the machine that he could not tolerate for long.

"You say that you found the woman Steele among Molekane's people?" Burkhalter asked.

"I did, lord," Bill said.

"*Sehr gut.* I will give you a chance to redeem yourself, to earn your salvation. You will join the squadron departing for Molekane's eyot, you will find the girl, and you will bring her to me, dead or alive. Alive, preferably. Do you understand?"

"I do, lord!" Bill cried. "Thank you, lord!"

Bill crawled forward on his knees and began grabbing at the hem of Burkhalter's robe. It was a disgusting sight that would have made Burkhalter's stomach turn if he still possessed one.

"Now get out of my sight," Burkhalter said.

Bill stood and backed away, bowing frantically until he had reached the edge of the observation deck. Then he scrambled down the stairs and hurried off to obey his master's orders.

Burkhalter motioned for his lieutenants to join him. They did, shuffling across the deck with the dull clink of oiled joints and the solid thuds of metal footfalls.

"My Lord," said one of the lieutenants, "are you certain of your wish to attack the Talian's camp? We *are* under contract with her, and if word gets out, we will find it difficult to conduct further business with others of her nation. Even the Ahadi Syndicate will question the wisdom of trading with us if we fail to uphold our agreements."

It was Kruger who had spoken, the oldest and most senior of the lieutenants. He had fought alongside Burkhalter during the schism in St. Corbin, and they had been exiled together as heretics. Of the three, he was the only one who could so blatantly question his master's decisions without fear of punishment. It was a privilege that he understood and never made the mistake of abusing.

Burkhalter placed a heavy hand on Kruger's shoulder and laughed. Kruger was always concerning himself with negative possibilities. It blinded him to opportunities.

"I have no interest in the petty concerns of a few gangsters," Burkhalter said. "Even *if* they hear of this, who is to say that it truly happened? Molekane will not survive to tell the tale, nor do the terms of the contract bind us to her protection. She could have been killed by anyone, and the Ahadi will have the good sense to see things that way when money is on the table."

And, Burkhalter knew, once the punch card had been returned to him, such politics would no longer matter. The Ahadi would do as he instructed or they would be annihilated. And when the eyots of the Commonwealth burned with holy fire, all the world would see that those were the only two choices available.

"As you say, Lord," Kruger answered, and wisely left it at that.

Burkhalter looked out across the sky at his vast fleet of airships and smiled beneath his mask. What he was about to do was radical in nature, a complete diversion from the instincts of a regular pirate lord. With such a fleet, he could expand his territory, conquer free ports and eyots outside of his borders, or go to war with one of the great dynasties of the Badlands: perhaps Ney, the scheming Melmothian whose ancestors had battled the Commonwealth and lost; or Blücher, descended from fellow Corbinites who had fled into the wilderness rather than accept the faith of Sankt Korbinian. He could even assault one of the nations bordering the Badlands—the Commonwealth, Tali, or even St. Corbin to take revenge for his exile. No pirate lord in history had ever won a sustained invasion, but the successful raids always returned with booty and glory. He could do any or all of these things with such a fleet, and another pirate lord certainly would have done so. But Burkhalter had greater plans in mind, plans that would redraw the political map through a force even he could not fully fathom.

"Herr Vanderberg," he said, turning to the second of his lieutenants, "the fleet will be left in your care during my absence. I expect you to keep it in readiness for when the assault on the East must begin. We will begin with the Commonwealth and then move southward into Tali and finally east to Tentetsu and Jianguo. With their cities already flame, they will beg to surrender. Mercia will be a harder nut to crack. The men must be ready to hunt their forces down through the wilderness once their cities are in ruins."

"They shall be ready, Lord," Vanderberg answered.

Burkhalter turned to the youngest of his lieutenants, the ambitious Hewes, who had earned his final augmentation only half a year before. Burkhalter knew that Hewes was eager to prove himself, and he was filled to brimming with the vigor and ruthlessness common among Badlanders. The young man's aggression and ambition made him useful in a way that Kruger and Vanderberg were not.

"Herr Hewes," Burkhalter said, "you will lead the assault on the Talian's eyot. Spare no one but the woman, Steele. I would like her brought to me alive. I have *plans* for her. But," Burkhalter flicked his fingers dismissively, "if she must die, then she must die, in which case bring me her head. Above all is the punch card. Whatever else happens, it must be returned to me. I will send Adler to assist you."

"Yes, Lord," Hewes said, bowing.

Hewes extended his arm and Adler flew to it. The mechanical bird's heavy talons gripped Hewes's forearm viciously. If the limb had been flesh rather than metal, it would surely have been snapped into pieces.

Burkhalter turned away from his lieutenants and looked back out across the expanse of his fleet.

"Now go," he said. "You have your tasks. See to it that they are carried out."

The three lieutenants bowed and covered their masked faces with their hands.

"Yes, Lord," they all intoned as one. The dull, mechanical chorus of their voices made Burkhalter smile a little.

* * * *

"We should focus our defense around the central hill," Ray said to Wolfe, as they made their rounds of the camp. "We can use the height advantage to fire over the heads of our comrades in the front, which should allow us multiple lines of defense."

Wolfe nodded. "Aye, that's a sensible idea. We'll put gun pits down around it to handle the support weapons."

"How many do we have?" Ray asked.

He and Wolfe looked over at the *Resolute*, which sat rather forlornly on the ground some distance away. Some of Molekane's workers were already busy helping the gun crews unbolt the airship's weaponry and haul it off the deck with the aid of a small crane.

"Let me see," Wolfe said. "We've got the big 105mm naval gun and the two 75's from the prow. Let's put those up near the top in a triangle to cover as much ground as we can."

Wolfe studied the map in Ray's hands and then tapped three points around the hill. "Here, here and here, I think."

Ray gave an appraising look and nodded his agreement. It was a sensible layout that would allow them to defend as wide an area as possible. Ray was not a trained engineer, but he had spied on enough enemy fortifications over the years to develop a working knowledge.

With his pencil, he made some marks on the map.

"Put the 105 on the north side," he said. "That's where the air attack is likely to come from."

"Aye," Wolfe said.

"Smaller weapons?" Ray asked.

Wolfe tapped his fingers together as he made a mental count.

"Two pom-poms and four gatlings."

"Divide them up on either side?" Ray asked.

If the pirates made it to the ground—which was just about a foregone conclusion—the most likely directions of attack would be roughly east and west.

Primarily east, he thought. It had the best landing ground inside the tree cover.

"That's good thinking," Wolfe said, studying the lay of the land near the edge of the forest through the telescopic sight he had removed from his rifle. "Put one pom-pom in the middle of the two big guns on either side. Let's have two gatlings on the eastern side, one on the west, and the last to the south. Can't be forgetting our backdoor even if Burkey's boys won't think to use it."

A reasonable plan. Ray made the appropriate notes on the map and began sketching out possible trench lines around them.

"We'll have to tear those tents down," Wolfe said, putting his hands on his hips and surveying the main camp. "With them gone, we'll get a nice open view to fire across. Nothin' like a killing field to even the odds."

Ray lowered the map and looked off across the camp, imagining the view from behind a machine gun. Wolfe was right about it being a "killing field."

"What about your snipers?" he asked. "Should we put them in the command post on the hill?"

Wolfe shook his head. "We'll leave that as a fall-back point, but I've got a better idea for them to start with." He began looking around the camp intently, mumbling to himself, "Now where is that girl . . . ? Ah!"

Wolfe shoved his fingers in his mouth and whistled to draw attention. Ray winced a little and rubbed his ear. Badlanders were notoriously loud people, and Wolfe seemed to have picked up all their bad habits during his time in exile.

A dark-haired young woman in a leather coat had been walking across the camp in the direction of the woods, with a rifle slung over one arm and a bundle of rope over the other. Hearing the whistle, she turned toward them with an irritated expression.

"Hey! Zitkalasa!" Wolfe shouted, waving his hand. "Get over here!"

Zitkalasa began walking in Wolfe's direction, holding her hands out in a gesture of impatience and wonder.

"*What*?" she demanded in a tone that Ray had never heard any of the other Badlanders dare use with Wolfe. "What is it? I'm twenty feet away from you, old man. Why can't ya run over and tap me on the shoulder?"

It was a perfectly valid question from Ray's perspective, but Wolfe seemed to disagree.

"I need to talk to ya!" he barked, the Badlander side of his accent overpowering the Commonwealth voice that he had used with Ray.

"So you whistle and start shouting at me across camp like we're in a big city and you can't be heard over the hustle and bustle?" Zitkalasa asked.

Wolfe ignored the question and responded with one of his own: "Have you found a better sniping spot?"

Zitkalasa gave Wolfe a narrow-eyed look. "'Course I have. I found it ten minutes ago while you were larkin' about with your new friend here!" She turned briefly to Ray and added, "No offense, mister."

"*Larkin'*"? Ray thought. He would have to remember that expression next time he entered the Badlands in disguise.

He waved the apology away. "None taken."

Zitkalasa turned back to Wolfe. "Now if you'll excuse me, I've gotta go make sure Thompson hasn't shot himself in my absence."

"Don't be uncharitable," Wolfe told her. "Thompson knows his way around a gun."

"Maybe," Zitkalasa said, "but he sure doesn't know his way around a *tree*."

Ray and Wolfe both did a double take at this.

"Say again?" Wolfe asked.

Zitkalasa waved the bundle of rope. "He fell outta the tree I had him in, *again*, and he can't get back up. So now I've got to go hoist him in like he's a sack of grain!"

Ray coughed a little and covered his mouth with his hand to keep from laughing. Just when he thought he had heard every humorous Badlander story. . . .

Wolfe looked at her stone-faced. "Well then what are you standing around talking for?" he asked.

"You watch it, old man," Zitkalasa said, pointing a finger in Wolfe's face. "Just for that, I'm not telling you where we're set up. See if you can find it on your own!"

With that, she turned and headed back toward the forest.

"I'll have no trouble finding ya, girl!" Wolfe shouted after her.

Zitkalasa spun about in place and continued walking backward as she shouted back, "'Course not! 'Cause Thompson'll just fall out of the tree again, like he's been doin' every fifteen minutes! You could set a watch by him!"

Ray felt a titter coming on and coughed to hide it. He would have to meet this Thompson . . . assuming they both survived the next few hours.

When Zitkalasa had passed out of earshot, Wolfe gave a deep sigh.

"I'm so goddamn proud of that girl," he said. "Best damn sniper I've ever had."

"Your daughter?" Ray asked, expecting the answer yes. From the way the two had interacted, the relationship was obvious.

Wolfe shook his head. "I should be so lucky."

There was a pause. Ray opened his mouth to inquire further, then thought better of it.

"Ok then," he said. "So the snipers are *somewhere* in the woods to the east."

"If that girl's done her job right, we'll be lucky to find them before they start shooting," Wolfe said, sounding prouder than ever.

"Well that's . . . great." Ray sighed and drew a sizeable circle around the entirety of the eastern forest's edge on his map. So much for knowing where all the defending positions would be.

Glancing across the camp again, Ray suddenly saw Steele burst out of the communications tent and race toward the hill.

"Steele's got something!" he said to Wolfe, and rushed to follow her.

Ray arrived at the main tent right on Steele's heels. She paused just before entering and looked at him. There was urgency in her expression and a great deal of excitement. The news was good.

Ray followed Steele under the cover of the tent, where Molekane and Wren had been conducting their own logistical preparations. The two women looked up from their work.

"Welcome back," Molekane said. "I hope you have good news."

"We have to hold out," Steele said, breathless from running. "Troops are being assembled at Singhkhand as we speak. Some of them are to be diverted as reinforcements. ETA ten hours."

Ray exhaled. The news was very good. And if forces were already being assembled, it meant they understood and believed the urgency of the situation. The SSB priority code Ray had included had done its job.

"*Ten hours?*" Wren exclaimed. "Can't they go any faster?"

"Not if they want to maintain combat readiness, no," Steele said. "And something tells me they'll be flying right into a firefight."

Assuming we last that long, Ray thought. Wren had a point. Ten hours was a long time to hold out against an overwhelming enemy.

"What are they sending?" he asked. "Will it be up to the task? I don't think a few air frigates are going to be of much help."

Steele grinned at him.

"They're sending *Hellfire*," she said.

Ray felt his heart leap. If the Air Force had sent the *Hellfire* they would have a chance, whatever Burkhalter could throw at them. Steele was right: they had to hold out until it arrived.

"What is *Hellfire?*" Molekane asked.

"Our salvation," Steele answered.

SEVENTEEN

The first attack came by lunchtime. Outflyers from Burkhalter's fleet swept in from the northwest, bringing with them a horde of violent, eager men armed to the teeth. There were three ships in all, little different than the one that had brought Bill and his men the first time. The pirates were too enthusiastic to bother with any sort of covert approach, and Steele heard the lookouts shouting their approach as they came around the edge of an eyot a mile away. An alarm went up instantly, and Wren's troops rushed to the defense.

The 105mm was still mounted on the *Resolute*, waiting to be hauled off by crane and placed in one of the gun pits still being dug. Steele saw Wren's quartermaster, Joseph Hernandez, rush to man it, his best gunnery crew following at his heels. The men scrambled aboard and made the weapon ready to fire with all the speed and precision of military gunners. Steele was impressed. They were as good as anyone she had seen aboard an Air Force vessel.

Steele grabbed a pair of binoculars for a better view, raising them to her eyes just in time to see the first shot strike the middle airship in the side, just below the rim of the deck. The small craft shook violently, and several men were flung overboard. The pirate gunners tried to return fire, but the explosion had destroyed the two main guns on that side. A second shell with a timed fuse went off just above the deck, showering the pirates in shrapnel. The airship tilted off course and vanished from sight, a trail of smoke rising up past the edge of the trees.

Haha! Take that! Steele thought as she joined the mercenaries in a loud cheer.

She saw the lead airship came in low over the camp and drop ropes. It was a classic pirate tactic for ground assault. Men began scaling down while more on the deck put up suppressing fire against the defenders. Once the pirates hit the ground, they would swarm the guns to take them out and allow the rest of the mob to land. Steele had seen the tactic used time and time again.

"Landing party!" she shouted, racing for the nearest gatling team.

Wren's machine gunners saw the threat as well and strafed the deck with heavy fire, gunning down the pirates in droves. Those that made it to the ground charged for the entrenchments in a bloodthirsty swarm.

Steele twisted around and changed course, racing to meet them. The men and women in the half-dug trenches readied their rifles and pistols and began to return fire as she arrived. The pirates would not take them so easily!

"Stand your ground!" Steele heard Wren shout. She looked over her shoulder and saw the woman rush down the hill, already firing her pistols into the mob.

Steele raised her revolver and began shooting. A pirate went down, then another. The mercenaries kept up their fire, supported by the machine guns. The pirates shot back, but in the midst of the charge their bullets went wild. Only a few came close to their mark.

A man next to Steele cried out and clutched his chest. He stumbled for a moment before collapsing into the trench. Steele crouched and felt his throat. The man was dead.

Poor bastard. Steele knew that the man was a hardened killer, most likely a criminal of the worst description, but seeing him die at her side made her forget all that. As she looked at him, she saw only a man, an ally, killed by a common enemy.

Steele bolted to her feet and resumed firing. The pirate mob was closing in despite their horrible losses. Shots rang out from the trees—Wolfe's snipers had come to support them! More pirates went down, this time deep inside the mob. That would sap their fanatical morale in a way that even the machine guns couldn't.

Above her, the third airship came in clumsily and attempted to strafe the ground with its anti-ship guns. Being designed to hunt aircraft, it was poorly constructed for ground support, and its gun crews were not especially proficient at their task. As the ship came in, more pirates bounded off and rushed into the fray. Steele saw Hernandez and his gunners shift their fire to the next ship along, blasting its envelope open and sending it to ground in a torrent of flames.

The remaining airship turned and made for the edge of the eyot, abandoning the men still fighting their way toward the trenches. Steele heard the 105mm fire once again and saw a shell blow apart the airship's rudder and port engine. The pilot promptly lost all control of the vessel. It twisted sideways and rammed prow-first into a sizable chunk of floating rock. The hull splintered on impact, and the airship was knocked away into the open abyss below.

Steele turned back toward the pirate mob in time to see it reach the front trench line. Her revolver was empty—there was no point to reloading. Hefting the weapon like a short club, she let out a roar that shook her body and leaped at the nearest pirate.

The next few minutes were a confused mess filled with flashes of blood and metal. Steele lashed out about her, all the while screaming in rage. She expected to be overcome at any moment, but the wall of mercenaries around her held firm.

Suddenly the pirate mob disintegrated before her eyes, as the men at the rear forced their way forward only to discover that their comrades had not broken through.

"Counterattack!" someone shouted. It was probably Wren.

The mercenaries gave a great cry of "hoorah!" that rippled along from one end of the line to the other. Steele heard herself shouting the strange Badlander word along with them. Not quite a civilized "huzzah!" but it did the trick.

The mercenaries charged out of the trenches and rushed the dozen or so remaining pirates. Steele ran with them, holding her pistol aloft and savoring the adrenaline. The pirates, no doubt realizing their situation, began to flee for the forest in a confused mass. None of them reached the trees.

Heart pounding and gasping for breath, Steele sank onto the ground as Wren's mercenaries rushed onward to scour the field for survivors—any they found would not survive long. Steele looked down at herself and saw blood on her hands and sleeves. It was some of the most brutal fighting she had ever experienced, and it would only get worse as they day went on.

Steele walked back to the command post in a daze, hands shaking with excitement. The adrenaline slowly began to ebb, leaving her tired and dizzy. She felt more than a little sick.

Ray and Molekane were waiting for her in the command post on the hill. As ever, Mwai waited silently at Molekane's side, carefully eyeing the damage that had been done.

Ray set down his rifle and hurried to Steele's side.

"Are you all right?" he asked.

Steele threw an arm around his shoulders, laughing and gasping in equal measure. She had no idea what to do with this strange feeling of exhaustion and elation that still clung to her. The melee was such a mess, so chaotic. It was all vigor and instinct, like they were animals. Even the worst dogfight demanded calculation and tactics.

"So that's what the infantry go through, eh?" she said. "I'll stick to aeroplanes, thank you."

Ray shook his head at her. "Next time," he said, "try staying up here with me and a good rifle. You get a very different experience on the ground when you aren't making a bayonet charge."

Steele looked back toward the trenches and saw Wren, Wolfe and Hernandez rushing up the hill to join them.

"I am glad to see you all alive after our first taste of the action," Molekane said. "How did we perform?"

"Well," Wren said. "They caught us unready and we survived. That's something."

Steele nodded—survival certainly *was* something—but added, "I only hope we'll fare as well when Burkhalter attacks with his real troops, and in force."

"So this was not indicative of what we will be facing?" Molekane asked, a hint of uncertainty in her voice.

"I don't think so," Steele said. "Those men who attacked us were run of the mill freebooters, probably sent as sacrifices to test our defenses. They showed very poor tactics."

It was a safe bet that none of the pirates had ever faced a harder target than a half-armed merchantman.

"You think Burkhalter's had someone watching what happened?" Ray asked, scanning the horizon.

"Probably," Steele said. "There must be a ship somewhere far out of sight keeping track of us through telescopes."

Wolfe whistled at her. Steele turned and saw him peering at the sky through his scope.

"I reckon I've found it, though it makes no proper sense to me." He lowered his rifle and pointed at the sky. "I see a bird up there circling the camp. Now tell me, shouldn't a bird have been frightened away by all the gunfire?"

A bird?

Steele picked up a pair of field glasses and looked where Wolfe pointed.

"Oh damn and blast!" she swore. "That's no bird. It's a machine."

It was the same bird from the Vihara train; there could be no doubt.

"A machine?" Ray asked. He accepted the field glasses from Steele and took a look for himself.

"I don't know how it's possible, but that thing is mechanical," Steele said. "I saw it on Singhkhand, right before that assassin attacked me on the train. Burkhalter must be using it to keep track of things."

But how? she wondered. Maybe it had a camera inside of it or an aethercast relay.

"It would seem that Burkhalter has been interested in you since before your arrival," Molekane said.

"You heard Bill," Steele replied. "There's a price on my head."

"Out of curiosity, what's the going rate for your life?" It was Wren who asked, a sarcastic smile playing across her lips.

Cheeky devil, Steele thought, but she grinned in reply.

"You know what? I forgot to ask."

Molekane clapped her hands for coffee. It wasn't tea, but Steele appreciated the gesture. Even in wartime and with imminent death starting them all in the face, certain standards of civilization could not be ignored.

"Tell me, Ms. Steele," Molekane said, "how long has Burkhalter been pursuing you?"

"About two days," Steele replied without hesitation. She knew that being evasive about the point would only offend her allies, and in any event they deserved to have their questions answered.

"Has he a particular reason for it?" Molekane asked.

Steele exchanged looks with Ray. Should she tell them? The more people that knew about the card, the greater the risk. Steele still had no idea why Burkhalter wanted it. What if one of them knew something she didn't?

Bugger it, we're all in this together.

She reached beneath the hem of her shirt and pulled out the punch card.

"He's after this," she said. "I don't know why, but he's been hunting me for this for two days, and I don't intend to let him get his hands on it."

"Nor should you," Molekane said, nodding. After a moment, she extended her hand. "May I?"

Steele hesitated, then handed the card to Molekane. She saw Ray fold his arms and tuck his hands beneath his coat where they could reach the concealed pistols slung against his ribs. Steele hoped he was overreacting.

Molekane studied the card with intense curiosity for a few moments before handing it back.

"That is quite a remarkable artifact you have there," she said. "When we are safe again, I would be interested in helping you negotiate its sale to a museum."

"Museum?" Steele asked. Why would a museum want a punch card?

"Yes," Molekane said. She pointed at the card. "That is one of the best-preserved pre-Upheaval objects I have ever seen. It has not even the slightest hint of bending, wear or rust."

Pre-Upheaval?

Steele looked down at the punch card and asked, "What makes you think it's pre-Upheaval?"

Molekane tapped the markings on the card. "It has Cyrillic letters on it. Cyrillic is a dead alphabet. It has not been used in over a century and never with this level of craftsmanship since the Upheaval."

"Who ever used it?" Ray asked. He sounded amazed to have finally found someone who recognized the symbols. Steele knew how he felt. "I've never seen it anywhere else."

Molekane laughed. "That is hardly a surprise. It was used by the people of Rhossiya in the ancient days. Most of them are long gone now, lost to the Great Upheaval. If their culture survives, it is somewhere beyond the bounds of the Known World. I have found artifacts bearing those symbols in eastern Mercia and across the Sleeping Lands, and there are people with Rhossiyan names in those regions, but those who can read and write Cyrillic must be few in number."

"The Sleeping Lands?" Steele asked.

"Indeed. If there are any people alive who can translate it properly, you will find them there, most likely at Erkusk in Sibir."

"I'll bear that in mind." Steele put the card away in a document pouch strapped around her waist and tucked her shirt in to conceal it. "But let's save talk of relics for a time when we aren't facing a band of marauders who want to use our guts for garters."

"Words to live by," Wren said.

＊ ＊ ＊ ＊

The workers finished digging by mid-afternoon, during which time they had faced a strafing run by pirate fighters and a second attack by an airship landing party. Both attacks had been repelled with little difficulty, and they demonstrated the effectiveness of the entrenchment layout. Steele knew without a doubt that Burkhalter's mechanical bird had observed both incidents and had reported in to its master.

While the digging was completed, Steele joined Hernandez and a small group of mercenaries in the unsavory task of searching the pirate bodies and stripping them of their arms and ammunition. It was a necessary job—Steele knew their own supplies would not last long enough for rescue—but handling corpses was a disgusting task, especially in the day's heat. The flies were as bad as the smell, and the Badlands breed seemed both larger and more aggressive than their cousins in the civilized world. The more Steele swatted them away, the more they seemed to home in on her. At least there were no mosquitoes.

And at least the dead pirates had the decency to stay dead.

Steele shoved a handful of rifle clips into her bag and went to join Hernandez who knelt a few yards away, organizing their collection of salvaged munitions. Steele did not like the look of their haul. There was too much variety in the arms and ammunition and practically no standardization. It would have driven any self-respecting Commonwealth quartermaster to madness.

"How is it going?" Steele asked, unloading her bag on the pile of uncounted equipment.

Hernandez rubbed his face with his hands, leaving smudges of dirt and gunpowder on his cheeks.

"Slowly," Hernandez said. "These pirates have no sense of standardization. I've got a dozen different ammunition calibers here. For the pistols alone we're looking at 6mm, 9mm, .32-cal, .38-cal, .45-cal, and God knows what other homemade junk the pirates cooked up for themselves! I've got a 4 bore elephant gun with no ammunition, 8 gauge shotgun shells with no shotgun that will fit them. . . ." He sighed. "This is what we have quartermasters for."

Poor chap. He gets to make sense of it all. Steele patted Hernandez on the shoulder. "You get to have all the fun don't you?"

"You've no idea, Miss Steele." Hernandez reached into his pocket and pulled out a toffee sweet wrapped in wax paper. "Want one?" he asked.

"No thanks." Steele waved the offer away. She was in no mood for sugar, certainly not with the day's heat.

"Suit yourself." Hernandez popped the sweet into his mouth and grinned. "Better than a shot of whiskey." He knelt down and resumed his sorting.

Steele looked off toward the far end of the camp where Mwai and Wolfe were busy giving Molekane's excavators a few lessons in shooting. It was not the world's most impressive performance, but at least the Talians were giving it their best. Most of the workers had probably never picked up a weapon before in their lives, but the two soldiers were giving it their all with a dedication that made Steele proud to see. They made a good pair as well, trading off the roles of instructor and drill sergeant, each in turn demonstrating how to load and fire while the other barked instructions.

Mwai was a fine man, that was abundantly clear, and Steele was beginning to see more likeable things in Wolfe than she wanted to find. The Badlanders were criminals through and through, but the shared struggle was beginning to wear on Steele. She found herself thinking more and more of them as comrades rather than allies of convenience.

She turned back to Hernandez and said, "I'm going to check on defense plans."

Hernandez nodded without looking up.

Steele walked toward the command post on the hill. The trench network was almost complete, and the gun emplacements had been finished, reinforced with wood and metal for added stability. The support guns had the priority of position, of course. They were the only things that could threaten Burkhalter's aircraft, and they would be extremely important to repelling ground attack as well. If all went according to plan, the infantry in the trenches would be nothing more than defensive support for the machine guns and artillery. Not that things *ever* went according to plan.

An argument was raging as Steele entered the command post. Molekane and Wren were speaking with raised voices, and Ray stood to one side looking exasperated.

"I will *not* allow my soldiers to stand in the line of fire!" Wren shouted. "Armed civilians can't shoot straight. That's a fact! If your people get in behind mine and start firing off weapons, you're going to have a lot of dead mercenaries on your hands, followed by dead civilians when the pirates break through and fall on them."

"You cannot possibly suggest that I place my workers in the front line," Molekane said. "They are not trained soldiers. They will be overwhelmed and slaughtered at the first instance, and I will not tolerate so callous a dismissal of their lives!"

Steele sighed and took up a spectator's position next to Ray. It wasn't enough that they had a pirate lord out for their blood, now they were fighting amongst themselves. And worse, it was over a valid concern.

"Do we have to arm the civilians?" Steele asked.

It was a redundant question—they needed every gun they could get—but at least it stopped the argument. Wren and Molekane looked up at Steele and then at each other. No one had yet questioned it.

"We have to," Ray said. "We need the added firepower."

"It's only added firepower if they can hit their target," Wren said.

Steele glanced down the hill and saw Mawi and Wolfe walking toward them. Mwai looked satisfied but impatient, and Wolfe had an exhausted expression on his face. The Talians on the practice field were still taking shots at their makeshift targets, but it seemed they no longer needed instruction. Either that or Mwai and Wolfe had given up.

"What don't we ask our two drill sergeants?" she asked, pointing toward the men.

"A sensible suggestion," Molekane said.

Wren nodded. "How's the shooting gallery, Jack?" Wren asked, as Mwai and Wolfe entered the tent.

"Well, let me tell you, they've got *spirit*," Wolfe said.

Steele's heart sank at those words. It was Army slang for 'they don't have anything *but* spirit.'

Molekane looked at him. "Is that good?"

"No," Steele said. "It's pretty bad, actually."

Mwai nodded. "Unfortunately, that is the truth, ma'am. The workers are trying their best, but none of them are soldiers."

"What are your recommendations?" Molekane asked.

Mwai exchanged looks with Wolfe.

"We have been discussing that, actually," Mwai said. "And we have come to an agreement."

Well, at least that was something. If Mwai and Wolfe hadn't given up on their trainees, there might be hope.

"What is your suggestion?" Molekane asked.

"Put them someplace they don't have to move from and let 'em shoot until they run out of bullets," Wolfe said.

That was the best they could come up with? Steele scoffed. "There's positive thinking for you."

"I call 'em like I see 'em," Wolfe said.

"What do you recommend?" Wren asked.

"Organize the civilians into firing teams," Mwai said. "That is the system we have been using to train them. Give each team a sergeant from among Captain Wren's crew to ensure that they have someone to direct fire and keep morale up."

Steele considered the suggestion. It was sensible, she had to admit. Under the circumstances it was probably the best they could manage.

"Can you take care of that?" Wren asked.

"Can do," Wolfe answered.

Mwai looked at Molekane. "With your permission, ma'am. . . ."

"Attend to it, Mwai," Molekane said. "Make them ready to fight."

Mwai nodded. "Yes, ma'am." He gave Wolfe a nudge and headed off down the hill. "Come along, Mr. Wolfe. Time to earn your pay."

Wolfe spread his arms. "What do you think I've been doing all day?" he demanded, following after Mwai.

Steele watched them go, smiling in spite of herself at the exchange of words that continued as the two men returned to the firing range.

"Well they're getting along," she said.

"Thick as thieves," Wren agreed.

As they turned back to their planning, Steele happened to glance at the sky and saw a curious dark blot plastered against the blue and white. She already knew what she was looking at when she snatched up her binoculars for a better view. She immediately recognized the profile of airships and aeroplanes moving *en masse* from the northwest. There were seven airships: five were of a light structure similar in size and armament to a Commonwealth corvette, one was mid-sized similar to an air frigate, and the last was a massive command ship of some sort built on the scale of a battleship. A dozen or so fighters provided a skirmisher screen around the airships.

The attack had finally begun in force.

"Incoming!" Steele shouted and pointed toward the attacking flotilla.

Everyone looked where she had pointed and began swearing and shouting orders. Ray raced toward Hernandez, yelling at him to get the gun crews in position. Molekane called for Mwai and Wolfe, and when they looked at her, she pointed toward the approaching pirates. The two men exchanged looks and began barking orders to the armed civilians. It was a jumbled mess, but in the confusion the excavators managed to find their weapons and their supply of ammunition, get into their trenches, and hunker down with their appointed mercenary sergeants.

Steele grabbed a pair of rifles from the weapons supply and tossed them to Ray and Wren before grabbing a second pair for Molekane and herself. She ducked down behind an upturned table reinforced with earth and watched the pirates approach. At the bottom of the hill, she saw Wolfe rush off to the trees to rejoin his snipers. That was good. They would need that supporting fire once the pirates hit the ground.

In the trenches, Hernandez's gun crews positioned their weapons and waited for the pirates to come into range. They waited for a tense few minutes as the pirates advanced steadily on them, seeming to sense little danger in spite of the earlier experiences of their comrades. Perhaps the poor quality of the first marauders and the disorganized state in which the camp had been found had instilled overconfidence in the flotilla's commander. Regardless, Steele was grateful for the pirates' poor tactics.

"Wait for it . . ." she heard Wren whisper beside her. The words were addressed for the gun crews. "Wait for it . . ."

But Hernandez knew his business. He waited until the airships were all within easy firing range and the fighters had began to break formation and dive, committing themselves to a strafing run. Then the guns opened up in a torrent of thunder and fire. One of the pirate corvettes was struck full on by the 105mm gun, blowing its prow apart. The 75mm guns battered the remaining airships. As Steele watched in awe, one lucky shot managed to hit the command ship in one of its engines, causing it to list ever so slightly to the side and throwing off its course.

The barrage was followed by another and then another, blowing holes in the sides of the airships and tearing apart the envelopes of two corvettes and the frigate. They vanished from sight behind the trees, and Steele heard them crash somewhere further along the eyot.

The fighters were caught by the pom-poms in mid-dive, when it was too late for them to escape. The anti-aircraft fire ripped three of the triplanes to pieces instantly, sending them spiraling down to the ground where they smashed in clumps of burning wood and canvas.

The remaining aeroplanes were hit and damaged, but they kept together well enough to complete their run. Machine gun fire struck the trench lines in disorganized bursts, and Steele dropped behind cover as one plane strafed the command post. She heard men and women cry out in pain as they were hit. Peering out from behind the table, she watched as the pom-poms managed to down two more fighters as they sped away back into the clouds.

Under the intensive anti-aircraft fire, the pirate flotilla split in two. The battleship steamed away from view toward the long northeastern section of the eyot, while the corvettes headed to the shorter end to the west. As the group split, it became clear to Steele why the airships had been flying in such close formation. They had shielded from view a pair of freighter airships with large cargo holds slung beneath their envelopes. As the flotilla divided, they split as well, one going in either direction. Steele knew what their purpose was, and it did not involve supplies.

"Troop transports!" she shouted.

"Hell, we're in for it," Wren said. Bolting to her feet, she began waving and shouting at Hernandez. "Focus fire on the transports! Focus fire on the transports!"

"What?" Hernandez called back, unable to hear her over the sound of the guns firing.

"Focus fire on the—" Wren cut herself off and simply pointed.

Hernandez looked where she was pointing and started at the sight of the transport ships that hid just behind their escorts. He began shouting orders at the gun crews, who turned their attention toward the cargo ships. But the pirates had made their precautions well. One of the remaining corvettes went down as it was struck by a shell intended for the freighter behind it. One of the 75mm guns managed to hit the second freighter, but the ship was covered in thick armor plating, which absorbed much of the blast. The airships quickly moved out of sight behind the trees, and in their wake came the fighters on another strafing run.

"Get to cover!" Steele shouted.

From the angles of approach, she could see that the aeroplanes were making for the gun crews. Most of the teams dove for cover behind their earthen barricades, sparing them the worst of it, but the pom-poms kept firing in spite of the onslaught and lost two gunners in the process. In return, their fire tore apart four of the pirate planes.

Well, at least that was something, Steele thought as she watched the fighters go down in flames. Not compensation for their losses, but repayment in kind. War produced such a curious economy of human life.

Steele heard the fighters come around for another pass. It was a sound she was very familiar with. She looked up and saw Wren still shouting at Hernandez and the gun crews.

"Wren!" Steele shouted. "Get dow—"

At that moment a burst of machine gun fire from one of the fighters raked the command post. Wren was struck in the arm, and she tumbled onto the ground.

Steele broke from cover and rushed to Wren's side. Molekane joined them in a flash, carrying one of the medical kits they had stockpiled. Steele helped her pull off Wren's coat and watched as the Talian tore open the sleeve around the wound.

"It has gone clean through," Molekane said, sighing with relief. "And it has missed the bone."

Thank goodness, Steele thought. She wasn't about to have Wren falling to some pirate's bullet.

"You're not getting away from the law that easily," she said.

Wren laughed. "Looks like Lizzy's luck is wearing off on me, eh?" She hissed in pain as Molekane began cleaning the wound with disinfectant. "Oh Hell, leave it!"

"Be quiet, Miss Wren," Molekane said. "I am your employer, and I intend to bandage this wound before it turns you into a bad investment."

Steele turned away from them and peered over the barricade. The guns had stopped firing, and as she watched, the crews took the moment to remove the two dead gunners from their chairs and replace them with living soldiers. The determination of the mercenaries was inspiring to see as they shrugged off the deaths of two close friends. But, Steele knew, the gunners still grieved, and they would take out the loss of their comrades on the first pirates to show their faces. At least, it's what she would do in their place.

What about the civilians? They had just received their first taste of real combat.

Steele looked down at the trenches and saw fear on the workers' faces. But she saw something else as well: determination. They might be terrified, Steele realized, but they would not break so easily. Molekane had chosen her people well.

Steele spotted Mwai and a few others helping the wounded up toward the command post. It was the only reasonable place to take them for treatment. Steele bounded over the barricade and raced to help them. She took the arm of a Talian man and supported him as he struggled up the steep hill. Together they fell in alongside Mwai, who was carrying an unconscious Badlander.

"It's finally started," Steele said.

Mwai nodded. "Your reinforcements had better arrive on time."

"They will." Steele had no doubts about it. The Commonwealth was practically a byword for punctuality.

"I am trusting you and Mr. Ray to keep Miss Molekane safe," Mwai said. "I will be commanding the soldiers from the trenches under her orders, but the terms of my employment are to protect her at all costs. If something happens to her. . . ."

"I'll protect her with my life," Steele assured him. Molekane had risked everything so that she and Ray could warn the Commonwealth about Burkhalter. Steele would be damned if she let Molekane die for making an honorable choice.

"Good," Mwai said, and fell silent.

Steele knew that he had every intention of holding her to that agreement.

EIGHTEEN

The pirates began their attack by land about an hour later. The fighters tried one more strafing run in the meantime, but they were repulsed again by the pom-poms. Throughout the air fighting, the gatling guns had remained silent, conserving their ammunition for the inevitable infantry assault.

The first attack came from the northeast, heralded by rifle fire in the trees as Wolfe's snipers skirmished with them in an effort to delay the onslaught. The snipers managed to buy another twenty minutes as the pirates tried in vain to root them out.

Thompson and the fourth sniper, Davies, were killed in the exchange of gunfire. With ammunition running low, Wolfe and Zitkalasa retreated from the forest amid a hail of gunfire. Midway across the campground, Zitkalasa was hit in the leg and collapsed. Ignoring the pirate gunmen, Wolfe heaved her over his shoulder and carried her back to friendly lines as both of them returned fire with their revolvers.

Up in the command post, Steele spotted them as they made their retreat. Shouldering her rifle, she gave them whatever covering fire she could manage. Ray and Molekane grabbed their own weapons and joined her. A handful of pirates tried to break from the trees to pursue the fleeing snipers, and Steele turned her sights on them.

She kept firing until Wolfe and Zitkalasa reached the safety of the command post.

"How are we looking out there?" she asked Wolfe, as he set Zitkalasa down on the ground.

"Could be better," Wolfe said.

Zitkalasa winced in pain and clutched her leg. "You've got a talent for understatement, old man!" She looked up at Steele. "It's a small army they've got. We stalled 'em in the woods for as long as we could. . . ."

"You did plenty," Steele said, grabbing one of the medical kits. "Let's get this wound dressed."

"Don't think I'm sitting this out just 'cause of a little bleeding," Zitkalasa said, as much to Wolfe as to Steele.

Wolfe opened his mouth.

"Never in any doubt," Steele said. "We need every gun we can get. Why don't the two of you set up on either side of the command post. You can cover both sides of the hill from the same position."

"Aye," Wolfe said, not really agreeing. He waited for Steele to finish bandaging Zitkalasa's wound before he spoke again, "C'mon girl, don't dawdle. If you insist on getting yourself killed, at least be quick about it."

So saying, Wolfe hefted his rifle and walked off to take up his own firing position.

Steele watched him go and then looked at Zitkalasa. "Are you *sure* he's not your father?" she asked. Ray had made some comment to that effect earlier. Steele still did not believe it.

Zitkalasa sighed. "Positive, though Gentleman Jack seems a bit confused about it."

They were suddenly interrupted by an eruption of gunfire. Steele looked over the parapet and saw a fresh mob of pirates, about a hundred strong, rushing for the hill by way of the eastern forest. The pirates charged across the field, heedless of the gunfire from the trenches, screaming bloody murder with cutlasses and axes raised high in the air. Some of them even fired their pistols toward nothing in particular.

More marauders. Burkhalter was sending cannon fodder at them.

Steele opened fire with her rifle, as did Ray at the opposite end of the position. Zitkalasa crawled next to her and joined in as well, picking off pirates with much greater accuracy than Steele could ever hope to manage.

Below, the machine guns and pom-poms were tearing the mob to pieces. Steele and the others were just auxiliaries to Hernandez and his heavy weapons.

The first wave of pirates went down, disintegrating into a mass of death and confusion. Steele raised her binoculars and scanned the edge of the woods, ignoring the jubilant cheers from the men and women in the trenches. The attack had been a distraction for something else.

She spotted machine guns and light artillery among the trees, confirming her suspicions. Burkhalter's men must have moved them into position while everyone was distracted by the marauders. The pirate gunners looked to be consummate professionals, probably mercenaries bought with Burkhalter's ill-gotten wealth. This was going to get nasty.

"Enemy machine guns!" she shouted.

Beside her, Zitkalasa took aim. "I've got 'em," the woman said.

More marauders appeared from the trees, charging for the hill and screaming blood and fire. Steele knew their kind well. Most of them were drunk or invigorated by drugs, and they came on heedless of their dying comrades.

Under the pressure of the attack, a fourth of their number managed to reach the front trench where they were met by rifle and shotgun fire from the frantic civilians. Steele kept firing into the pirates in a futile attempt to keep them at bay. All she could see were the civilians about to be overrun.

Soon the pirate guns were up and running, and they opened fire on the entrenchments, tearing apart the remnant of the mob. The civilians and their mercenary sergeants scrambled for cover, flattening themselves in the ditches as bullets tore through the air overhead. Steele watched as Hernandez and his gunners returned fire in a vicious machine gun duel that tore holes in the trees at the edge of the forest and ripped apart sections of the earthen barricade. At her side, Zitkalasa took a more precise approach, carefully selecting the pirate gunners and shooting them one by one.

As the fighting raged on the eastern side, Steele heard a roar from the west. She ran to the opposite side of the command post in time to see another horde of marauders, easily two hundred in number, appear at the edge of the trees and charge. They were being encircled!

Steele loaded a fresh clip into her rifle and began shooting. The gatling gun and the pom-pom on the western side of the hill opened fire as well, and Steele saw Wren race for one of the gunnery pits, shouting orders. The pit's 75mm gun turned toward the western forest and began firing, blowing apart trees, guns and men in more or less equal measure.

The pirates had made the mistake of swarming on the side with the excavation pits, and the men were forced to drop down into the holes before running up the opposite side. The machine guns, pom-poms, and gunfire from the defenders caught them full on as they came in. Still, they came, and in tremendous numbers. They reached the first trench line with their vigor still intact. Faced with the terrifying onslaught, the first rank of defenders fled backward, blocking the line of fire from the second trench.

Cursing, Steele raced to reinforce them, drawing her revolver and a combat knife. Ray was a few steps behind her, carrying a pistol and his machete. In the second trench, she heard Molekane shouting for the workers to hold their ground. The roaring mass of pirates was almost on top of them, but the Talians held firm, waiting to be struck by the human wave.

There was nothing to do now but meet the pirates head on.

"Ready to do something stupid, Ray?" Steele asked. She could already feel the adrenaline rising again, making her giddy. Was this how soldiers felt in the rush of a bayonet charge?

"Always," Ray said, flashing her a grin.

Steele let out a cry of "huzzah!" and plunged into the fray.

The fighting was a bloody blur, filled with movement, violence and a torrent of faces. Somehow Steele kept her wits about her and managed not to strike or shoot anyone friendly. It was easy enough to tell the pirates and Molekane's workers apart, but the two groups of Badlanders were another matter. More than once, Steele leveled her revolver at a dirty, violent-looking combatant only to realize that he or she was on her side.

Suddenly, one of the attacking pirates appeared at her elbow and stabbed the mercenary fighting beside her. Steele spun about and leveled her revolver at the pirate, but when she fired, the pistol was empty. She had lost count of her shots. The pirate turned on her and lunged, knocking her to the ground with a blow from the flat of his boarding axe.

Steele hit the ground, stunned for a moment. *Get up! Get up!* she commanded herself, but her body refused to respond.

The pirate loomed above her, a cutlass in one hand and the axe in the other, weapons raised and ready to strike. Steele forced herself to move and lashed out with her knife, but the pirate jerked back just out of range. Grinning with a mouthful of rotting teeth, the pirate lunged at her, and Steele knew it was the end.

Not how I expected this to end, she thought. She had always assumed she would go down in flames, like any good pilot.

Suddenly, as the pirate dove forward, the long, thin blade of a bayonet appeared seemingly from nowhere and impaled him through the chest. The man flailed wildly for a few moments and went limp.

Steele stared upward in disbelief and saw Mwai standing over her, holding his bayonet-armed revolver out at arm's length. He fired once to dislodge the pirate and then kicked the body away.

"Thanks," Steele said, accepting the hand that Mwai offered her.

Mwai shrugged as he pulled her to her feet.

"I keep people alive for a living," he said. "I saw no reason to make an exception in your case."

As he spoke, he half-turned and fired into the pirates, gunning two of them down.

"Thanks all the same," Steele said as she reloaded.

She looked around to regain her bearings. The force of the pirate assault seemed to have broken, and the guns on the western side were still firing on the pirates in and around the excavation pits. With their comrades dead or wounded, the pirates on the front line began to flee. But as they did, they found the pits much easier to enter than to climb back out of. The defenders had no cause to show mercy.

As the last of the surviving pirates fled into the trees, Steele plopped onto the dirt above the trench and gasped for breath. Mwai joined her, snapping open his revolver and loading fresh cartridges. Each one was about the size of his thumb.

"How did things fare over on your side?" Steele asked. Presumably they had won, or else Mwai would not have arrived in time to save her.

"The support fire halted the pirates in short order," Mwai said. "With the eastern trenches secure, I came to lend a hand over here while the artillery attended to the enemy machine guns."

"I'm bloody well glad you did." Steele flexed her fingers. Her hands were sore from gripping her pistol and knife so hard during the fighting. "We managed that pretty well."

"We did, though I believe the greatest share of credit belongs to the guns from Captain Wren's ship. I have no wish to contemplate what will happen if they run out of ammunition."

Steele grimaced at the thought. Without the machine guns, they could never keep up the volume of fire necessary to repel the pirates. It was not an end she cared to contemplate.

Ray appeared from nearby, his machete dangling from his fingers. His coat was slick with blood, and he had a nasty cut across his forehead. Steele felt a twinge of sympathy. The wound was superficial, but it probably hurt like mad.

"Hey there, Ray," she said. "You've got a little something just there. . . ." She motioned at her own temple.

Ray touched his forehead and peered at his bloody fingers. "That's no good," he said. "I hope it doesn't scar."

Steele almost laughed. It was not the reply she had expected, and Ray's deadpan tone made it sound like he was complaining about the weather canceling a cricket match.

Mwai gave Ray a smile. "Vanity is unbecoming in a man, my friend. You men of the Commonwealth must learn to wear your scars with pride."

"Get it looked at, Ray," Steele said. "One of the medical kits should have some ointment you can put on it."

Vanity was probably the last thing on Ray's mind. Scars and other distinguishing features were a terrible liability for people in his line of work. You might be forgotten, but they would be remembered.

Ray nodded, then asked, "How much longer until the reinforcements arrive?"

That was a good question. Steele had all but lost track of time.

She checked her watch. "Three hours, assuming they arrive on schedule."

"Three hours." Ray sighed. "I only hope we last that long.

Always the optimist.

"You know just what to say to cheer me up, Ray," Steele said. "Now go get that pretty face of yours looked at. I don't want you getting all scarred up. I'll never be able to take you out in society again."

Mwai laughed boisterously at this.

"At least the defenses are holding," Ray said.

"'Holding,'" Steele said with a snort. "They just overran the first trench line."

"Yes, but at least we took it back," Ray said. "And thankfully we had the trenches in the first place."

He was right about that, Steele knew. They'd suffered casualties in the fighting, but it was a walk in the park compared to what they would have faced on an open field. At least they had someplace to go for cover when the enemy started shooting back.

"That is true, they will protect us," Mwai said, "so long as the enemy does not bring any artillery to the fight."

"They won't," Steele said. "Not so long as we keep the punch card out of their hands. If they wanted to simply obliterate us, they'd have done it with the airships when they first arrived. Burkhalter doesn't want to risk damaging the card, I'm certain of it."

"Then let's hope nothing happens to it," Ray agreed. "Our survival depends on it."

* * * *

Steele enjoyed a brief respite of about twelve minutes before the next attack. When the lookouts signaled movement in the trees to the east, she took up a position at the barricade, expecting to fight off another horde of marauders. But this time there was no great massed charge. Instead, she spotted small clusters of men with rifles lurking among the foliage in a skirmish order.

Steele realized that the pirates meant to suppress them with sharpshooters. A glance told her that these men were professionals—probably mercenaries. She was about to test their skill by returning fire when a sharpshooter's bullet struck the earthen wall half an inch from her hand. Steele quickly dropped out of sight.

That answers that question, she thought, as she tried to catch her breath. Narrowly avoiding death had shocked the wind out of her.

She sat there feeling helpless for a while, knowing that everyone else was probably doing the same thing. Here and there she heard snatches of machine gun fire as Hernandez's gunners tried to shoot back, but most of those attempts were followed by cries of pain as the sharpshooters sniped the gunner.

Steele sat in silence for the next fifty-three minutes, exchanging wordless looks with Molekane, Wren, and Ray and obsessively checking her wristwatch. At least that gave some momentary relief whenever she did it. All the while, she heard nothing but rifle fire—the sharpshooters in the trees dueling with Wolfe and Zitkalasa, no doubt. At least someone on their side was able to fight back.

She knew that the pirates had to be up to something, and sure enough they were. The gatling gun on the west suddenly began to fire again, and Steele crawled up onto the barricade on that side to see what was happening. She spotted a group of pirates in the western woods trying to creep around to the southern flank. The gatling was already making short work of them.

Steele smiled a little. The pirates wouldn't take them that easily.

"Steele!" she heard Ray call to her. "Get down before you get shot!"

Steele looked over her shoulder at him. "I'm fine! They aren't even shooting at me—"

But who were the sharpshooters firing at? Steele in her curiosity had just made herself an easy target, much easier than any of the people hiding in the trenches or gun pits. But in spite of that, she was untouched. She slowly stood, half expecting to be shot, but no bullet came. The pirates were too busy keeping the gun crews suppressed to pay any attention to her.

At that moment, more pirates emerged from the brush on the northeast side and charged the entrenchments in small packs. These men were different from the marauders and the skirmishers. Two in each group had large sacks that hung from around their necks, and it only took Steele a moment to realize what they carried.

Grenades! The sharpshooters were keeping the gunners under cover to make them easier targets for the explosives!

"Grenadiers!" she shouted as loudly as she could. She flattened herself against the earthen barricade and began shooting.

Even at such a distance, she could tell that most of the grenades were of a primitive make, effectively metal balls or empty cans packed with explosives and topped with a fuse. The pirate grenadiers carried all manner of burning objects to light them, including pipes, cigars, and even slowly burning bits of cord tied into their beards. That would slow them down more than a modern grenade, and Steele was thankful for it.

She kept firing as the pirates raced toward the suppressed defenses on the northeast side, hurling their grenades overhand in an attempt to get them over the barricade. A few fell short and exploded against the mounds of dirt, some went off in mid-air, and one even detonated scarcely a moment after it had left its thrower's hand. The explosion knocked the group of pirates down in a shower of blood and shrapnel. But the others continued on, racing around the northern side of the entrenchments.

The gatling gun nest on the northeast corner was the first to be hit. Steele watched helplessly as a pair of grenades from two different grenadiers tumbled into the entrenchment and went off. The crew, already huddled together low to the ground to avoid the sniper fire, were killed instantly. Another grenade managed to find its way into the eastern pom-pom position, killing the loader and severely wounding the gunner.

The injured gunner crawled to her feet and began firing into the flanking pirates. She tore through several of them until a sniper's bullet finished her off.

Steele kept firing, doing whatever she could to keep the grenadiers away from the defenses. Her rifle was a lever-action, which forced her to turn sideways after each shot to chamber a new round. It was frustrating work, and she cursed the people of the Badlands for not having the sense to use bolt-actions like the civilized world.

Ray and Molekane joined her, adding their shots to the fusillade, and together their combined weight of fire began to show. One of the pirates fell, then another, then another. Someone—Steele was not certain who—managed to hit a grenadier as he was in mid-throw. The man dropped the grenade and then, realizing what had happened, tried to scramble away. The explosion killed him and his team.

As the dwindling grenadier teams struggled to knock out the gun positions before they could be refilled, another cry arose from the western forest.

Not again! Steele cried inwardly as she raced to the west side of the command post.

She saw another mob of pirates appear at the edge of the trees, accompanied by support guns. It seemed they were trying to repeat on the west what they had tried and failed to do to the east. It was a serious miscalculation. The guns on that side were still active, and they began firing at the mob, cutting the men down just as viciously as they had done an hour ago.

Nearby, Zitkalasa crawled from her sniping position and slid down the hill into the second trench line and began picking off the pirate gun teams while they were still setting up their weapons. Steele was about to join her when she saw Hernandez break from cover and rush for the big 105mm.

He was going to turn the gun on the pirate mob!

Without a moment's hesitation, Steele rushed to the barricade overlooking Hernandez's position and began shooting at anything that came close to him, cutting down a grenadier in mid throw. Hernandez looked up and threw Steele a salute, before turning the 105mm toward the western wood. The first shell landed dead on in the midst of the pirate gunners, sending pieces of metal and men flying.

Steele could scarcely stand to watch more of the slaughter, and she turned away. It was a good thing too, for as she looked eastward she saw a grenade flying in the direction of the command post.

"Get down!" she cried, and pushed Molekane behind cover.

Nearby, Ray threw himself down behind the barricade a moment before the grenade exploded in the air a few feet from the earthen wall. Steele had scarcely enough time to think *Oh Hell!* before she was struck by the force of the explosion.

She hit the ground with a thud and lay there, wondering why the sky looked so particularly blue at that precise moment. Everything was at once both clear and blurry. She tried to move and found that she couldn't tell if she was doing so or not.

Ray appeared above her, shouting something that she could not quite hear. She tried to respond, but her lips would not move. Ray began tearing open her shirt and vest, and she swatted at him feebly. What the devil did Ray think he was doing? Now was no time to be taking clothes off!

A moment later, Molekane appeared next to Ray, holding a probe and a pair of tweezers. In spite of Steele's resistance, she felt Ray remove her leather belt and with it the punch card. Suddenly a hint of pain appeared in her side. She realized that it was probably worse than she felt.

Molekane began digging around for something in her flesh, and there was more pain. Steele gritted her teeth to keep from screaming as her vision blurred. What were they doing to her?

Her eyes focused again in time to see Molekane pull a bloody piece of metal out of her. Shrapnel? So that was it. Panic began to fill her. How bad was it? Had anything vital been damaged? Was the punch card intact?

The first piece of shrapnel was followed by another and then another, until no less than six fragments from the grenade had been pulled from her body. She felt another burst of pain as Ray doused the wounds with antiseptic and began to bandage them.

"Oh Hell that hurts!" Steele cried, finally regaining her voice and her senses.

Ray smiled at her and gave her a tender pat on the cheek. "Glad you're your old self again, Steele. You were looking a little glassy-eyed there for a few moments."

Steele groaned. Everything was crystal clear again, including the all but deafening sounds of gunfire.

"How bad is it?" she asked.

"You took some shrapnel in the abdomen," Ray said, "but thankfully it didn't hit anything vital."

Oh thank goodness!

Steele tried to move. A warm pain blossomed in her flank. Better to lie still for a few moments more.

"So that's why you were tearing my clothes off," she said, managing to grin. "I thought you were after something entirely different."

Ray smiled back. She saw relief in his eyes.

"Nonsense," he said. "I'm a well-bred citizen of the Commonwealth. I'd have invited you to watch me play cricket first."

Steele almost giggled. What a truly Ray thing to say.

"Well that's different then."

She forced herself to sit up in spite of the pain. The document belt lay nearby. She grabbed it and checked the card. It was intact. Good.

She quickly buckled the belt back on. The tightness made her wince, but she had no intention of leaving the card unattended.

"Oh, and Ray . . ." she said.

Ray had leaned up to look back over the barricade. He ducked back down and turned toward her.

"Yes?" he asked.

Here goes. . . .

She grabbed Ray by the lapels of coat and pulled him to her. She kissed him firmly, savoring the experience. After a few moments she released him, pulled herself to her feet, grabbed her rifle, and returned to the barricade.

Ray sat, stunned, for a time, blinking in surprise.

"What just happened?" he asked to no one in particular.

Steele glanced over her shoulder. "Ray, if you want any hope of getting another one, you'd better get yourself over here and start shooting!"

NINETEEN

At the top of the hour, the pirates withdrew again, repulsed by the concentrated fire. Steele took immediate stock of the situation. It was not good.

Three of the gun teams had been lost to the pirate grenades, and while volunteers rushed to replace them, they would never reach the same level of effectiveness. The pirates continued skirmishing on both sides over the course of the next hour, battering the defenders with sniper fire, explosives, and mob attacks concentrated on the weakened northern flank. Wren had the good sense to rotate her gun teams during the lulls in combat, keeping experienced troops near the heavy fighting, but the overall effectiveness of the support guns was suffering because of their casualties.

Whenever a brief respite presented itself, the wounded were helped up into the command post for medical treatment. By midway through the second hour of the attack, all of the proper supplies had been exhausted, and the impromptu medics—Molekane and Wren's ship surgeon—were forced to make due with torn cloth for bandages. Steele did not want to be in their place, choosing who to help and who to leave untreated. The wounded would have to receive proper treatment once the Commonwealth forces arrived, or they would certainly fall victim to infection.

By the end of the second hour, Steele was all but holding her breath as she counted down to the impending arrival of reinforcements. She suspected everyone else was doing much the same. The timetable was a beacon of hope, a promise of survival if they could only hold out long enough. As the pirates continued to press their attacks, that hope was becoming more and more the one thing that kept everyone fighting.

More pirate aircraft appeared as the sun sank in the sky, and throughout the third hour, strafing runs were resumed by the strengthened fighter wings. As she studied the pirate attacks, Steele realized their purpose. The point of the attacks—the strafing runs and the mob onslaught—was not to kill them. Far from it: only a fool would assume that he could throw men at entrenchments without horrible casualties, and Steele suspected that Burkhalter was not a fool.

No, Burkhalter was throwing the "expendable" fighters at them to force the pom-poms to burn through their ammunition shooting the planes down. The human wave attacks on the ground soaked up the machine gun fire and forced Hernandez and his gunners to waste shells from the big guns to keep the marauders from reaching the trenches. Each time an attack was repulsed or a fighter crashed to earth in flames, the defenders cheered their good fortune, but, in fact, they were doing exactly what the pirate commander wanted them to do.

And worse, Steele realized, they would run out of ammunition long before Burkhalter ran out of men.

* * * *

By the end of the third hour of the attack, hope was wearing thin. Even Steele felt it. The pirates continued their attacks without any sign of stopping, and with each skirmish or assault, the defending position was being ground down. Up in the command post, Steele kept firing away at any pirates who showed themselves beyond the tree line. Ray was constantly at her side, supporting her gunfire with his own. She was grateful for the company.

Though they were conserving ammunition, their supply was running short. Twice Steele had been forced to go for more ammunition from the improvised depot nearby. All along the line, similar shortages were occurring. Steele had heard Wren instructing her soldiers to hold their fire unless the enemy got in close. It made sense, Steele supposed. The brunt of the fighting was carried out by the support guns. The rest of them were just protecting the gun nests from attack.

Steele looked at her watch and sighed. *Hellfire* was late.

"How much longer?" Ray asked, dropped down beside her and reloading his few remaining cartridges.

"They should have been here fifteen minutes ago," Steele said. "Where the bloody Hell are they?"

"I know how you feel," Ray said. "I can't abide tardiness either."

Steele gave him a look.

"Quiet, you," she said. But she appreciated the sardonic humor.

She looked up as Wren clambered over the top of the barricade amid a burst of gunfire.

"How are things out there?" she asked.

"Uh . . . bad." Wren passed her a handful of cartridges, then did the same for Ray. "This is the last of the rifle ammo. After this, we're out. Pistols are going to go next."

Ray inspected the bullets to be sure that they were the correct caliber and then refilled his magazine.

"We're that bad, eh?" He chuckled.

"Getting there." Wren's reply was without humor.

Steele glanced out over the barricade to check on the situation below them.

"How are the support guns doing?" she asked.

"The gatlings are down to about a drum each," Wren said, "and the pom-poms are almost empty. The big guns have plenty of shells left, but they're all anti-armor." She brushed a lock of hair back from her face and asked, "When are the reinforcements getting here?"

"Fifteen minutes ago," Steele replied. The answer sounded worse each time she said it.

Wren exhaled loudly. "Oh great."

"So either they're running behind or—"

Steele did not really want to contemplate an "or".

"Or someone got them on the way," Wren said. "This is the Badlands. It's the sort of thing one expects to happen."

Steele shook her head. "No, *Hellfire*'s coming for us. With anyone else, I might worry, but I know Group Captain Giyorgis by reputation. He'll be here."

"The question is when," Ray said.

And whether we're still alive, Steele thought.

* * * *

A mile to the northeast, the pirate Hewes was in a foul mood. He stood at his camp's aethercast with a grim expression, listening as his local commander on the western side reported yet another repulse. This was not how the operation was supposed to have gone. He enjoyed overwhelming numerical superiority and some of the best illicit weapons money could buy, and yet his forces were being thrown back at every turn.

Hewes was desperate to prove himself to Lord Burkhalter, and he had done everything that an aspiring warlord could be expected to do. He had encircled his enemy, distracted and overwhelmed them with assault after assault, used expendable men as cannon fodder to protect the strategic attacks of his elite killers, and in spite of it all, he had been held back. He had been ordered to obtain the master's punch card without risk of damaging it, and to that end he had been denied the high explosives and air burst shells that would have made killing the Talian woman's forces so much easier. Hewes suspected that this was all more of a test than anything else; surely a punch card, whatever information was on it, could not be worth such a challenge.

Above him, his massive and ungainly command ship floated back and forth in the early evening breeze. The sun was going down, and it would be dark within a couple of hours. The darkness might allow him to infiltrate some of his best butchers to deal with the defenders up close, but he was loath to wait any longer than was necessary. Lord Burkhalter had expressed his wish to see this sorted out immediately, and further delays would only reflect poorly on him.

"Herr William!" Hewes snapped, motioning for Bill to join him.

Bill approached slowly, running his fingers through his hair with palpable nervousness. He had been shaken ever since facing Burkhalter's ire hours before. Hewes had placed him in charge of the forces attacking from the north, assuming that the fear would make his efforts more dedicated. In fact, it had not.

"What can I do for ya, sir?" Bill asked.

"I am displeased by this lack of progress, William," Hewes said, "as will be Lord Burkhalter when he hears of it."

Bill gulped. "The men are tryin' their best, sir."

"They are *not*," Hewes said. "If they were, they would be in those trenches right now, slaughtering those who defy the will of our lord. But you and I are going to fix that, William. We will show Lord Burkhalter that where the rank and file fail, the officers of his fleet earn their share of the booty."

Bill looked even more nervous. It made Hewes feel a little better.

"How are we gonna do that, sir?" Bill asked.

How indeed! Hewes smiled to himself. The plan was a masterstroke, the sort of thing that Lord Burkhalter would have done.

"The Talian woman's people are demoralized and wounded," he said. "The only things stopping us from overrunning them are those machine guns. They're low on ammo, and they have many wounded. According to the scouts watching them, they've massed their soldiers and ammunition in an arc from the west to the northeast, covering our main avenues of approach, thus leaving their southern flank weakened."

"I understand, sir!" Bill said, straightening up and doing his best to look confident. "I'll lead an attack on the south side immediately!"

"No you will *not*," Hewes replied. How presumptuous of Bill to assume that his failure would be rewarded with the easy task. "We should still have a few dozen scallywags and scurvy dregs left alive. You will take what is left of them and assault the northern side, distracting the enemy while I take a force of proper soldiers and attack the south. Herr Smith will do likewise, attacking with his forces from the west. They will be overwhelmed."

"But sir!" Bill cried. "An attack against the north? It's suicide!"

Hewes was in no mood to argue with a coward. He reached out with one heavy metal arm and gripped Bill by the throat. Lifting Bill as if the big pirate were nothing but a child, Hewes pulled him in close and spoke very slowly and precisely, copying a technique he had seen Burkhalter use to great effect many times before.

"No, William, it's not suicide," he said, almost echoing his lord verbatim. "If you attack the north as I command you, then you have a chance of survival, however slim it may be. Suicide would be standing here questioning my orders. Do you understand?"

"Y-yes, s-sir," Bill answered, shuddering in fear.

"Good," Hewes said, and dropped him.

* * * *

Hewes commenced the attack twenty minutes later. First came the assault on the west, which drew the fire of the support guns and even the artillery in an effort to cut the pirates down in the excavation pits. Moments later, Bill appeared to the northeast, driving the last remaining band of marauders before him. Most of them were drunk and thought little of charging machine guns so long as the promise of booty was offered. They were cut down in bloody swathes, but not before they reached the trenches. Bill dove in, sword and revolver in hand, and he began fighting his way up the hill toward the command post. His only chance for survival was victory.

As Hewes had planned, the defenders immediately rallied and began focusing their fire against the two beleaguered fronts. Once they were committed, Hewes and a dozen chosen men burst from the thin strip of forest to the southeast and charged toward the trenches.

The fighters on the south side of the hill had scarcely a chance. The lone southern machine gun burned through its ammunition rapidly as its gunner tried to cut down the attackers before they could reach the lines, but the soldiers of Hewes's bodyguard were not the soft, weak men he had sent at them before. These were chosen men, all augmented by prosthetic limbs of Lord Burkhalter's design. Hewes had faith that they would neither flinch nor fall in the face of the enemy.

In spite of Hewes's great confidence in his men, four of them fell to the defending fire. It could not be helped. They were acceptable losses if only Hewes could return to his lord in triumph. The rest of the men were shot and kept moving. Hewes himself took numerous bullets to the chest without flinching, as they struck and rebounded off his metal body.

Hewes and his men smashed through the first trench line and then into the second. As his bodyguards fell upon the defenders, Hewes continued his charge up the hill toward the command post unopposed.

Victory was at hand.

* * * *

Steele heard the sounds of gunfire from the normally quiet south side of the hill and turned toward it. What could they possibly be shooting at?

A moment later, the southern guns were abruptly silenced. Steele exchanged looks with Ray, who rushed to the barricade. She saw him stop short at the edge and let out a garbled cry of surprise.

A figure in heavy gothic armor and robes of rough black cloth appeared at the top of the hill, flanked by two more pirates whose bodies were distorted by implants of metal and mechanical limbs. Steele's breath caught in her throat as the armored man—she assumed it was a man—turned his masked faced toward her and pointed in her direction.

"There is the woman!" he shouted, with a voice that sounded dull and hollow. "Kill the others! She is mine!"

"Yes, Herr Hewes!" came the pirates' reply.

Steele shouldered her rifle and began firing, hitting one of the pirates in his torso. The first shot rebounded off the man's armor, but the second bullet found an opening a few inches below the heart. She saw Ray shoot the second pirate point-blank, hitting him in the forehead just above his monocular implant. Ray turned to fire on Hewes as he chambered his next round, but Hewes lashed out with the back of his hand and caught Ray in the chest. The force of the blow knocked Ray off his feet and threw him against the barricade.

Bastard! Steele looked toward Ray. It was impossible to tell if he was alive or not, but he wasn't moving. Steele felt a spike of anger blossom somewhere in the back of her head. Her vision blurred, and all she could see was Hewes.

Taking a breath, she raised her rifle and fired. It was one of the most impressive shots she had ever made, striking Hewes dead center in the throat. For a moment her heart leapt in triumph. But the bullet found reinforced metal rather than yielding flesh, and it ricocheted away.

A cold sensation fell over Steele. She had made a shot in a million. Hewes should be dead, but he was alive. Steele reloaded and fired again, and yet again the shot was deflected.

No! No! No! she thought with each new shot.

Hewes did not seem troubled by the bullets rebounding off his armored body. He paused for a moment, standing amid the clusters of wounded as he stared at Steele. He seemed amused at her failed attempts to kill him. The placid expression on the faceplate mocked her desperation.

Without warning, Hewes lunged at her. Steele managed to fire off one more ineffective shot before the mass of animated metal and clockwork barreled into her. Steele struck Hewes in the face with the butt of her rifle, dislodging his faceplate. The face behind the mask was human, but it was distorted and withered. The sight of it turned Steele's stomach.

Hewes spat blood and grinned at Steele. His teeth were metal. Of course they were, Steele thought. Even his heart was probably a machine.

She struck Hewes again, this time above the eye. Hewes flinched from the blow and snarled, his triumphant amusement gone.

Not used to people fighting back, are you?

Hewes tore the rifle from her hands and flung it away. He picked her up like a rag doll and threw her onto the top of the barricade. The air was pressed from Steele's lungs by the impact and she gasped for breath. She saw Hewes reach for the document belt around her waist and she kicked out with her feet to force him away.

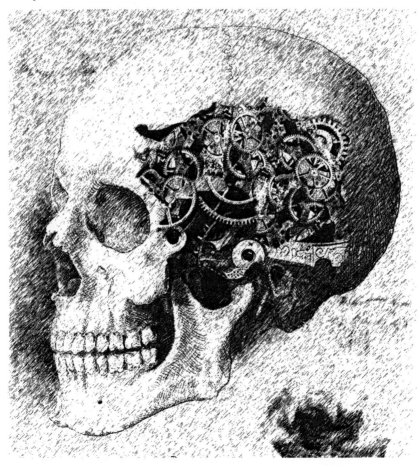

Gaining freedom, she rolled over the top of the barricade and down toward the second trench line. The rough ground battered and bruised her as she tumbled along it, but she needed to get away long enough to regain her senses.

She finally came to rest just above the trench and scrambled to her feet. Wiping some blood away from a scratch on her arm, she drew her pistol and looked around. The fighting on the north side was thick and violent, and it was impossible to tell how bad things were. The pirates had managed to break past the first trench, and Steele saw the Talians and Badlanders being driven back toward her.

She saw Mwai rush in from the west, catching the pirates head-on and knocking them aside with his tall shield. Spotting Steele, he began fighting his way through the mob to join her, stabbing and slashing with his revolver's bayonet as if it were a sword.

A shadow fell across Steele, and she looked up to see the pirate Hewes leaping through the air in her direction. She had barely enough time to roll aside and avoid being crushed as the mass of machinery hit the ground with a tremendous thud.

Steele's heart was beating furiously, almost painfully, but she fought back the instinct of fear and drew her pistol. She fired as she tried to stand. Her bullets bounced harmlessly off Hewes's armored chest.

The pirate closed the distance between them in a single stride and struck her in the stomach. The blow was like a hammer delivered by a piston. Steele gasped as she doubled over, and Hewes backhanded her. She stumbled sideways and collapsed in the dirt.

Laughing, Hewes grabbed her shoulder in a vice grip and reached for the document belt. Steele saw a long serrated blade extend from his wrist, poised to cut through the leather belt and her belly with equal ease. In spite of herself, Steele shuddered at the sight of it. Was this how it was to end? Gutted by a pirate who was only slightly more human than a locomotive?

"I'll be taking this, girl!" Hewes said, snarling.

Mwai appeared behind Hewes and struck him hard with his shield. In spite of his tremendous augmentation, Hewes was knocked aside by the force of the attack.

"Down, abomination!" Mwai shouted.

Steele saw Mwai aim his revolver at Hewes and prepare to fire. Then the big Talian jerked violently and his eyes widened in surprise. He stumbled half a pace sideways and Steele saw Bill standing behind him, holding a bloody sword. Bill fired two bullets into Mwai's armored chest and then tried to push past him to assist his commander.

Steele struggled to get to her feet again, her only thought of helping Mwai. He had just saved her life. She had to return the favor. But her head swam, and her limbs refused to respond. She watched as Mwai staggered and spat blood.

Get up! Get up! Get up! Steele shouted at herself. She caught Mwai's gaze and saw in his eyes a shared fury at a common enemy.

What passed between them in that glance Steele could not describe, but she felt it keenly. Anger boiled within her, and she let out a scream of hatred that Mwai echoed in booming tones.

As Steele scrambled to her feet, she saw Mwai grab Bill and pull the man back toward him. Bill punched Mwai twice with his augmented arm, but Mwai did not relent. He brought up his revolver and swung his bayonet at Bill, who barely managed to block it in time. Bill gripped Mwai's gun arm with his mechanical hand and pinned it.

"Gotcha, Tali!" Bill said, laughing.

In reply, Mwai smashed his forehead into Bill's nose and dove in for the kill.

Steele felt like cheering, but her voice had left her. In a violent daze, she picked herself up off the ground and fired at Hewes again. Most of the bullets pinged off Hewes's armor, but one cut across his exposed temple and drew blood. Hewes paused and touched his face, studying the crimson stain that came away on his fingers like a man who had never seen blood before.

It was all the respite Steele needed. She tore the punch card out of the document belt and raised it into the air. She saw Ray at the barricade above her, and her heart leapt. He was alive!

"Ray!" she shouted. "Catch!"

She threw the card toward Ray, spinning it sideways like a discus. She saw Hewes turn his head to watch as the punch card sailed through the air. He reached out as if to catch it, but it was beyond his grasp.

"Adler!" Hewes cried. "*Schnell!*"

There was a rush of air, the sound of taut metal, and a fluttering of wings. Burkhalter's mechanical bird swept in from above and snatched the card in its talons. Ray, inches away from catching the card, stumbled and stared as the machine began to fly upward again.

No! Steele thought. No, she would not let a glorified windup pigeon steal the card when she had fought so hard to protect it. But what could she do? How could she shoot down so small a target?

"Wolfe!" she shouted. "Shoot the bird!"

* * * *

Wolfe looked up from his sniping and saw where Steele was pointing.

"Aw, Hell . . ." he swore. Why were they always expecting him to work miracles?

Raising his rifle, he took aim at the bird and fired. It was a shot in a million—Wolfe was willing to admit as much—but the high caliber bullet hit the bird in the leg, smashing the mechanism at the foot joint and forcing it to drop the card.

"Ha! Take that, birdie!" Wolfe shouted.

The bird did not seem particularly troubled by the loss of its limb, but it did notice that the card was now falling toward the eyot beneath it. This was unacceptable, and the bird tilted downward and hurtled toward the ground like a bombshell. It caught the card in its beak about a dozen feet from the ground and narrowly avoided crashing as it leveled out and began its ascent again.

Wolfe let out a string of curses in as many languages as he could think of. Not only were they asking him to do the impossible, but the impossible was cheating!

He shouldered his rifle and began firing at the retreating bird, this time aiming for the much easier targets of its body and wings. Zitkalasa joined him, and together they tore apart the bird's extremities. As its wings gave out and it began to fall again, the bird lifted its tail feathers and a tremendous burst of fire erupted from a concealed rocket housed within its lower body. The bird hurtled skyward and then vanished into the clouds, traveling in the direction of Burkhalter's main fleet.

The damn thing had cheated *again!*

"That's not bloody fair!" Wolfe shouted as he reloaded. "I shot it down, dead to rights!"

"Get your eyes checked old man!" Zitkalasa called back, as she returned to firing upon the pirates. "While you were busy ticklin' its feathers, I took out the wings."

Wolfe glared at her. But she was right, of course. He'd been aiming for the body, as if it were a living animal and not a damned cheating machine.

"Fine, girl," he said. "Rematch. Winner takes all. Total kills in the next five minutes."

That'd show her.

Zitkalasa grinned at him. "You're on!"

Or maybe not. Wolfe dropped back into his firing position and began shooting pirates as fast as he could. The damn girl was going to give him a run for his money, like she always did. Why had he trained her so well?

* * * *

Nearby, Ray did not share their gleeful attitude. Instead, he watched as Hewes loomed over Steele, arms raised, ready to tear her apart. Unable to get a clear shot without risk of hitting Steele, Ray did a tremendously foolish thing. He threw his rifle aside and charged the augmented pirate like a man possessed.

* * * *

Burkhalter was on the top deck of his command ship when Adler returned. The bird was a wreck, its body and wings dented tremendously and falling apart in places. Scorch marks from the emergency rocket covered its legs and tail, and it had barely enough flight control to reach its master. It tried three times to come in and land before it finally managed to settle on Burkhalter's outstretched arm. It was only able to stand using one of its feet; the other was clutched close to its body, its talons hanging limply. In its beak it carried the punch card, which it dropped obediently into its master's hand.

"*Sehr gut*," Burkhalter said, stroking Adler's head with one massive mechanical finger. The bird closed its eyes and opened is mouth in a parody of the joyful expression of a living creature. The faint whirring of gears could be heard from inside its body.

"Herr Kruger," Burkhalter continued, "take Adler to the machine shop and supervise his repairs."

Whoever had dared to damage the poor creature would suffer dearly if they survived Hewes's attack. Burkhalter could not abide cruelty to his machines.

"*Jawohl*," Kruger said, bowing low and then extending his arm for the bird.

Burkhalter turned to his remaining lieutenant. "Herr Vanderberg, the time has come for me to put the card to its rightful use. Kruger will accompany me on the command ship. Once the men have finished loading the supplies, we will depart. I will leave the fleet in your care."

Vanderberg bowed. "It will be ready upon your return, Lord."

And it would be, Burkhalter knew. Vanderberg was unlike most Badlanders. He had a sense of duty, of order, of structure. He could be relied upon to manage things in Burkhalter's absence.

"What word have we received from the neighboring lords regarding my request for passage?" Burkhalter asked.

There was an awkward hesitation that conveyed clearly the ill news. Burkhalter was immediately displeased. Now was not the time for failure or disappointment, not when he was so close to his goal.

"Your request has been met unkindly, master," Vanderberg said. "Lord Ney and Lord Tecumseh both demand a substantial payment of tribute in money, ammunition, and canned food and an additional oath of submission to them. Lord Pryce asks much the same and also requires the secrets of your technology."

Was that all? At least they had not declared war. He would not have put it past them to do that at such an inconvenient time. And demanding the secrets of Sankt Korbinian's prosthetics? He had forgotten how presumptuous his neighbors were. Presumptuous and stupid.

"And Lord Blücher?" Burkhalter asked.

"Sir, Lord Blücher refused even to see our emissaries."

Burkhalter almost laughed. Of course he had, the paranoid fool. Like his fathers before him, the current Lord Blücher feared the machinery of Sankt Korbinian as surely as the faith. What a *dummkopf* he was.

"Very well then," Burkhalter said. "If no path through the Badlands is possible, we shall avoid it. Instruct the navigator to plan a course north of the Commonwealth, even unto the border of the Sleeping Lands. At least along that route our way shall be cleared. Do this before you depart the ship."

"As you will, Lord," Vanderberg replied, bowing low and backing away.

Burkhalter turned toward the edge of the deck and watched his fleet in all of its chaotic glory. Soon he would be master of the greatest power known to man, and after that, he would be master of the world. Where other pirate lords saw their fleets as extensions of themselves, as demonstrations of their glory and might, Burkhalter saw his merely as a means to an end. And that, he reflected, was the reason why he would succeed.

TWENTY

Steele was still trying to get a hold of her senses when Hewes grabbed her by the throat and hoisted her into the air with one arm. She made a choking noise as the pirate's grip tightened just enough to cause pain without fully suffocating her or causing her to black out. Hewes clearly knew what he was doing in that regard.

As if in a daze, Steele caught glimpses of the fighting around her as she struggled to breathe. All around the pirates were being beaten back by the determined defenders, but more cutthroats massed at the edge of the forest all around them. The machine guns were silent—they had probably exhausted the last of their ammunition—and Steele saw Hernandez lead his surviving gunners to join their comrades in the desperate fight.

Some distance beyond Hewes, Steele could see Mwai struggling with Bill in a battle of human flesh and bone against mechanical augmentation. Wren flashed into view near the edge of the western approach, firing her volcanic pistols into the pirates as she led the defense on that side. She kept her wounded arm in close to her body, aiming and firing from the hip with tremendous precision.

Steele's head swam, and she clawed at Hewes's hand in a futile effort to break free. The scarcity of air was keeping her from thinking properly.

Must stay calm. . . . Must not panic. . . . Think! Think!

"You've lost, girl!" Hewes shouted. "We have the card now, and I grow tired of this fight and its inevitable end."

He grew tired? Through the pain of suffocation, Steele was suddenly indignant. She had been fighting for hours! He'd only just arrived!

Hewes drew an ornamented flare gun from his belt and fired it into the air.

"With that signal," he said, "my men will overwhelm your companions and kill them all."

"What about me?" Steele snarled. She had to play for time until she could figure out how to get her hands on a weapon.

"You and I will return to Lord Burkhalter," Hewes said. "He has developed a great interest in you over the past few days."

I'll bet he has!

Steele caught movement from the corner of her eye and looked in that direction. She saw Ray charging down the hill with a long combat knife in his raised hand. What did he think he was doing? Coming to save her? He'd get himself killed trying!

Hewes followed her gaze and looked in Ray's direction. The pirate laughed and took a lazy swipe in his direction. Ray ducked under Hewes's arm and brought the knife down toward his throat. For a moment Steele felt a burst of hope. Ray had gotten in close. He might actually kill Hewes!

But the knife missed by barely an inch and stuck between two of the plates in Hewes's shoulder. Steele felt like screaming in frustration. On a living man it would have been painful and debilitating, just the thing she needed to break free, but Hewes scarcely seemed to notice. He simply punched Ray, knocking him to the ground in a heap.

The sun was going down over the horizon, casting a terrible crimson light over the eyot. As Hewes's flare descended through the sky, the air was filled with the sound of engines. As Steele looked upward, she saw two dozen pirate fighters and four mid-sized airships sweep in from the far end of the eyot where they had been hiding, shielded from the anti-aircraft guns.

She saw Hernandez and his remaining gunners fight their way toward the artillery to intercept the ships, but if the pirates were given leave to bombard the camp, there would be little that the mercenaries' guns could do before they were obliterated.

But as Hewes held Steele aloft and leered at her in triumph, another noise joined the cacophony in the sky. It was the unmistakable sound of the Kumar-Kent engines used by Commonwealth fighters. Against the pain of half-strangulation, Steele bared her teeth at Hewes.

She had gambled against time, and she had won.

"Checkmate," she said.

The sky split apart with a bright burst of blue-white light. Bolts of lightning arced sideways across the sky and struck the envelopes of two of the pirate airships. They exploded violently with a tremendous roar, spilling flaming wreckage in all directions. The two airships tumbled from the sky and vanished, the columns of smoke rising from their burning hulls the only thing to mark their passing.

Commonwealth fighters appeared in the sky. First came a squadron of Kestrels that darted in and out among the pirate aircraft, tearing them to pieces with precise bursts of machine gun fire. Behind them followed six larger twin-engine fighters that thundered along with less agility but no less speed. Steele stared at them in astonishment. She had never before seen such machines.

She watched with staring eyes as the twin-engine fighters wove their way around the remaining airships, dodging past anti-aircraft fire as they strafed the enemy. What were they? Clearly Commonwealth. They flew using pack tactics and dove at their targets like raptors moving in for the kill. As they zeroed in on the next pirate airship, bolts of lightning erupted from their noses and blew their target to pieces with cracks of thunder.

Behind the fighters Steele saw wings of military airships: mid-sized air frigates, packs of small corvettes and gunboats, and even a single flying battleship packed down with heavy guns. Reinforcements had arrived, and in force.

Finally, illuminated by the crimson light of the dying sun, the tremendous bulk of the sky tender *Hellfire* broke through the clouds. The *Hellfire* was something akin to a massive flying airfield kept aloft by tremendous gyro propellers and armored capsules of buoyant gas concealed beneath the flat landing pads that extended out from its central command structure.

Steele tried to cheer at the sight of the air group chasing the dying light onto the battlefield. As she watched, the airships turned their guns on the remaining pirate aircraft and opened fire, obliterating them in a shower of fire and burning debris.

She looked back at Hewes and saw him staring into the sky in shock. The bastard had probably never before experienced such a sudden and complete reversal of his situation.

"No!" he cried. "No! It's not possible!"

Now was the time to act! Steele saw her opening and took it. She grabbed the knife that sat lodged in Hewes's shoulder and yanked it free. Hewes turned his eyes back toward her and closed his hand to choke off her windpipe. Steele gagged but she forced herself to keep moving.

Die, you monster! Die!

Against the pain and the blurring of her vision, Steele thrust the knife into the flesh beneath Hewes's chin. The pirate dropped her and grabbed at his neck, gurgling hideously as he fell to his knees. A part of Steele wanted to relish the sight of the man-machine dying, but it was all she could do to think about breathing. Instead of savoring victory, she lay on the ground, holding her throat and gasping for air.

But she was alive. They were all alive. They had won.

She watched as a group of men and women leaped from the deck of the sky tender and dropped toward the eyot. They were dressed in Commonwealth uniforms, combining Air Force gold and blue with Army red. Only one regiment would have dared blur the line between the services so audaciously.

Flying Rifles!

The soldiers had oxygen masks and goggles covering their faces to protect them from the wind and high altitude, and heavy metal jetpacks were strapped to their backs. They activated these midway into their descent, releasing pulses of fire and steam from the exhaust pipes that brought them in to land safely around the camp. The jetpack soldiers were armed with short pump-action carbines, and they began firing while in midair, cutting down the remaining pirates and clearing the field.

The commander of the soldiers landed a short distance away from Steele and crossed to her.

Get up, Steele thought. *You can't greet a fellow officer if you're lying on the ground.*

She pulled herself to her feet, swaying slightly. The commander removed his breathing mask, revealing a sturdy Beylikite face with a narrow moustache.

"Major Shahin, Flying Rifles," he said.

"Wing Commander Steele, Commonwealth Air Force," Steele replied, her voice croaking a little. Well, she'd just narrowly escaped strangulation. It couldn't be helped. She exchanged salutes with Shahin and added, "Took you long enough to get here."

Shahin's mouth tugged up in a grim half-smile. "We hit a flotilla about fifteen miles out, and it slowed us up."

Well, at least they had a halfway decent reason for their tardiness.

Shahin paused to bark a few orders at his subordinates and then turned back to Steele. "What's your situation?"

"We've got *a lot* of wounded here," Steele said. "They need immediate medical attention."

"We have landing craft right behind us," Shahin said. "We'll get the wounded up to *Hellfire* immediately."

"Thank you," Steele said.

She heard Ray groan loudly as he regained consciousness. She staggered over to him and knelt to see how he was. A large bruise was forming on the side of his face where Hewes had punched him. A little worse for wear, but not bad under the circumstances.

"How you doing there, Ray?" she asked.

"Peachy." Ray blinked a few times and shook his head. "Oh," he added, "you've got a little something . . . everywhere."

Steele touched her head and looked at the blood that stained her hand. She could not tell if it was hers or someone else's.

"Thanks, I wouldn't have noticed," she said. Truth be told, she probably wouldn't have.

"Let me take care of that for you," Ray said, pulling a handkerchief out of his pocket.

Steele smiled. "Such a gentleman."

She leaned forward and allowed Ray to dab at her face to clean it. She had no idea if it was having any effect, but at least it seemed to make Ray happy.

Ray glanced at Shahin and the other Commonwealth troops.

"Ah, the Flying Rifles," he said. "Took them long enough to get here."

"I told him already," Steele said.

If Shahin heard them, he gave no indication. He was already busy shouting orders to his officers.

"Macallester!" he called to one of his lieutenants, a willowy young woman standing watch over two other soldiers as they disarmed and manacled a group of pirate prisoners.

"Sir?"

Macallester pulled off her mask as she responded and hitched her goggles up onto her forehead, revealing a rosy face dotted with freckles. She looked to Steele like the sort of girl commonly depicted as a cherub on postcards. What was she doing on a battlefield? Then again, Steele reflected, some people probably thought the same about her being a fighter pilot, so she decided to leave it at that.

"Get four teams together and check the woods to the northeast for any surviving pirates," Shahin said to Macallester. "And pay special attention to that landing site we saw coming down. I don't want any hidden guns opening up on the transports when they come down."

Macallester gave a smart salute. "Yes sir!"

"And tell Pinault to take another two teams and do the same over to the west. He's got less ground to cover so he can make due with a single squad."

"Sir," Macallester replied before shouting her own orders to the troops under her command.

Steele helped Ray to his feet, then walked toward Shahin and waved to get his attention.

"Major," she said, "you should know we've got a bunch of Badlanders working with us."

The last thing she needed was one of Wren's people being mistaken for a pirate.

"We were told," Shahin said. "A good thing you mentioned it in your distress call or we might have shot them on arrival."

"Might?" Steele wondered. "Would have" was more like it. She realized she should probably give Shahin the unpleasant truth about their new friends personally. It was the sort of thing that made a nasty shock.

"They're mercenaries under the command of 'Captain' Wren," she said.

Shahin's moustache twitched for a moment. Steele knew how he felt.

"Sarah Wren?" he asked.

"Yes." Steele leaned in close. "Under the circumstances, though, I'm inclined to treat them with clemency. They did keep us alive for you lot to rescue."

What was the world coming to, Steele wondered, when she was defending the likes of Sarah Wren from her own fellow officers? Still, Shahin seemed to understand the sentiment.

"Tell the Group Captain when he debriefs you," he said. "It's his call what we do with them."

"I'll do that," Steele said. "But in the meantime, I'd suggest keeping them under watch but not disarming them just yet. After the day we've all had, if you try to take their firearms, they're liable to start shooting."

"Understood."

Steele heard a groan and saw Ray stumbling toward them. She reached out quickly and pulled his arm over her shoulders to support him. Ray seemed grateful to lean against her. She was probably the only thing keeping him on his feet.

"We should get these wounded sorted out," Ray said.

Steele nodded. "We should indeed. Major," she said to Shahin, "let me take you to Ms. Molekane. She's the head of the camp, and she's risked a lot to protect us. She's with the surgeon, and they'll both have a better idea of who should be taken up to sickbay first, who can wait, and who needs to be treated here on the ground."

She did not mention the people who were already beyond help. It was not something she wanted to think about.

* * * *

Steele found Group Captain Giyorgis waiting for her on the bridge of the *Hellfire*. She liked him immediately. He reminded her of home and of why she joined the Air Force in the first place.

Giyorgis was a tall, striking man of Saba with ebony skin, a high forehead, aquiline nose, and a neatly trimmed beard of tightly curled hair. He was not a handsome man—his expression was too harsh and his eyes too severe for that—but he had a perfect figure for uniform and the countenance for command. In an instant, Steele could see why his air group was famous for high morale and confidence in battle. He looked like the sort of man people felt privileged to follow into Hell.

"Ah, Wing Commander Steele, I presume," Giyorgis said, turning away from the great glass window that looked out over the *Hellfire*'s forward landing platform.

"Yes, sir," Steele said, snapping a smart salute.

Giyorgis returned the salute and then looked at Ray, who stood at Steele's side.

"And this must by Amartya Ray," he said. "Namaste."

"Namaste, Group Captain," Ray replied, exchanging bows with Giyorgis.

Giyorgis motioned them to follow him over to the navigation table, where charts and maps of the surrounding region were already laid out next to barometric gauges, altimeters, flickering aetherscopes, a large compass, and a set of clocks with one set to the air group's local time and the others marking the time in the capital of each Commonwealth state. After the chaos on the ground, it was comforting for Steele to see the ordinary accoutrements of Air Force life.

The navigator on duty was busy plotting out the Air Group's return trip. He nodded to Steele and stepped to the side to give her room.

Giyorgis removed his peaked cap and set it on the corner of the table.

"Now then," he said, "you'll be making a full report to Belgaet once we return to Commonwealth airspace, but until then I'd like a summary of your operation and the particulars on Burkhalter's forces."

Steele gave a brief rundown on the events of their trip into the Badlands, placing the emphasis on their encounters with Burkhalter's forces. She also took care to note Molekane's decision to protect them from the pirates and Wren and the Badlanders' role in their defense. She realized that now was the ideal time to take Wren and Wolfe into custody, but after fighting for survival alongside them, the thought of it made her sick. Better and more honorable to take them in battle rather than by an insidious arrest in the dead of night.

As Steele told her story, Giyorgis's expression became more and more grave.

"A massive buildup, you say?" he asked when she had finished.

"Tremendous," Steele said. "On the scale of the Monroe Incident."

Giyorgis frowned deeply for a moment.

"Do you have photographs?" he asked.

"I do," Ray said.

"Show me."

Ray placed his surveying kit on the table. Opening it, he removed the photographs developed at Molekane's camp, which had been wrapped in a sheet of thick brown paper to protect them from light and wear. He unwrapped the bundle and spread the photographs out so Giyorgis could see them better. Steele leaned in with interest. It was the first time she had seen them. They would have been terrifying to look at had she not already seen the real thing up close.

Giyorgis picked up several of the photographs and studied them. His jaw muscles twitched as he saw the size of the fleet portrayed in even that limited view.

"By thunder . . ." he whispered. More loudly, he said, "Exactly like the Monroe Incident. Belgaet will definitely want to see these." He pushed the photographs aside to find their location on the map.

Holding up a pencil, he asked, "Can you fix the fleet's position for me?"

"As of when we saw it, yes," Ray said. He leafed through his notes for the exact coordinates.

"Are they likely to remain there?"

That was a good question.

"Possibly," Steele said, "though a fleet that size can't remain inert forever. Burkhalter's going to have to do *something* with it before it disintegrates. But even if he does leave it in harbor, the place is fortified and inhabited. It's at least a major supply center for him, if not his headquarters."

"It's a starting point." Giyorgis stroked his beard. "How heavily defended is it?"

Steele considered the question.

"They were pretty well dug in," she said. "Fortresses, big guns, anti-aircraft, everything. Burkhalter has money, and he knows how to spend it. We only got past because we were a single machine, and even then the patrols spotted us eventually."

That was the important part: any thug with money could amass a private army in the Badlands, but it was a rare type who could translate that into a real fighting force. And from what Steele had seen, Burkhalter had the ability to do just that.

Ray took the pencil from Giyorgis and began marking the location of the pirate fleet on the map.

"I know for certain they had weapons on these eyots here and here," he said as he drew in eyots and fortifications. "And I believe I spotted an airbase of some sort over in this area, but I was unable to confirm it. On the other hand, I *did* confirm a coaling station at this point. . . ."

There he goes, Steele thought. But, she had to admit, it was fascinating to see him at work. How could someone remember so many details so clearly?

At length Ray stopped and set the pencil down.

"I'm afraid that's the extent of my observations," he said.

"Mr. Ray, have you ever considered joining the service?" Giyorgis asked, after a lengthy pause. "My own navigation staff is bang-on, but I know a number of commanders who could use a man of your talents."

Ray coughed a little with proper Commonwealth modesty. It never did to be overly comfortable with praise when one was just doing one's job.

"Thank you, Group Captain," he said, "but I think the Air Force might be a little tedious for me after a career in the civil service, no offense intended."

Steele flashed him a look. *"Tedious?"*

"None taken, of course." Giyorgis leaned over to Steele and murmured to her, "Wing Commander, did he just imply that *bureaucracy* was more exciting than the Air Force?"

Yes, he did.

"Don't ask, sir," Steele said quietly. "He's a cartographer. They're all a little peculiar, if you ask me."

"By 'peculiar,' of course, you mean 'stark raving mad.'"

"Exactly, sir."

Giyorgis nodded. "Thank you both for this intelligence. I expect you'll need some rest after your ordeal. I'll have berths prepared for you, along with housing for our other guests. Wing Commander, as soon as the air group arrives at Rahul, you and I have been ordered to New London to present this information to Commodore Larken personally. You can prepare your official report during transit."

"I'd prefer to prepare it now while it's fresh in my mind, if it's all the same to you sir," Steele said. In spite of her fatigue and wounds, she was determined to finish her mission.

The corner of Giyorgis's mouth tugged up in a smile, but he merely said, "Very well. However, I do expect you to stop by the sick bay before you do anything else. You've both taken quite a beating today."

Sick bay? What sort of nonsense was that? A few cuts and bruises were no reason to go cluttering up the medical facilities.

Steele opened her mouth to speak but Ray interrupted her.

"Of course," he said.

Steele flashed Ray a look, but she could see that he was going to be stubborn about it. No point in arguing about that. A trip to the sick bay wouldn't kill her.

"Group Captain, if I may . . ." Steele said. Now was as good a time as any to bring up the issue of their allies.

"Speak."

"Among the defending forces that fought alongside us was a group of mercenaries working for Sarah Wren and Jack Wolfe," Steele said. Having spoken, she wondered how best to ask for their fair treatment.

Fortunately, Giyorgis seemed to anticipate what she was getting at.

"I assume from your tone that you are preparing to beg for clemency on their behalf," he said without batting an eye.

"Yes, sir."

Giyorgis took a deep breath. "Their assistance must have made quite an impression for you to make such a request. I know you've been hunting Wren for several years now."

Steele nodded. "Without her, we would have been killed. It's that simple. Wren even vouched for us when it was against her best interest to do so, and I believe that was one of the things that solidified Molekane's decision to protect us. It would seem . . . well, *uncivilized* to arrest her after such a decision."

Giyorgis took a deep breath and said, "Considering the state of their airship, leaving the Badlanders on the eyot would be an act of murder rather than mercy. I will take them back to Singhkhand with us in limited custody. The Air Force authorities will decide what is to be done with them, but you have every right to mention their service toward the good of the Commonwealth in your report."

"Understood, sir," Steele said.

"Very good, Wing Commander. You are dismissed."

TWENTY-ONE

Steele watched while the wounded from the eyot were brought up to *Hellfire*. Soon medical staff were transferred over from the battleship and the frigates to deal with the volume of injuries. Steele did not want to imagine what it was like for those doctors dealing with the barrage of battlefield patients.

Not everyone could be saved, and some people were already long beyond helping. Steele wanted to look away when the first corpses were brought up from the eyot, but she made herself watch. These people had sacrificed themselves to protect their comrades. To look away would be shameful.

The Talian dead—few, but still too many for comfort—were put on ice to help preserve them. They would be transferred to lead coffins at Singhkhand for the long trip back to Tali. The reverence for the departed was something Steele could understand, and she felt tears in her eyes as she watched Molekane lead her workers in a prayer for the departed.

Following the Talian display of grief, Steele was surprised, almost disgusted, by how abruptly the Badlanders treated their dead. The contrast could not be greater, she thought, as she watched Wren and Hernandez strip the corpses of their equipment and possessions, even down to their coats and boots. Only the most sentimental of trinkets were left with the bodies. Steele realized she shouldn't be so surprised. The Badlanders were used to death, struggle and scarcity. They were such a practical people, it only made sense that the living would take what they needed from the dead.

At least the brief funeral service was moving, filled with talk of damnation, redemption, and the short time that men had to live. Afterward, Steele watched as the bodies were thrown overboard in a dramatic burial at sky.

How strange it must be for them, she thought, casting aside their dead friends. There were no graveyards, no ossuaries, no urns of ash to remind the living of the departed. Just an empty piece of sky and the memory of a life ended.

* * * *

After the funeral, Ray went in search of Molekane. He found her in one of the mess halls where the uninjured and the ambulatory wounded were enjoying a much-needed meal.

He saw Molekane sitting at a private table with Mwai, who seemed to have lost none of his vigor in spite of his injuries. The man's torso was wrapped in heavy bandages to keep pressure on his wounds, but Ray marveled that he was standing at all.

The plate in front of Mwai was filled with food slowly going cold. He seemed to have lost his appetite. Well, Ray thought, two bullets to the chest and a stab wound could do that to a person.

As Ray approached, Molekane put down her fork and pushed the plate in front of Mwai.

"I am no longer hungry," she said. "Kindly finish this for me."

Mwai gave a slight frown and said, "I am your bodyguard, ma'am, not a *lap dog*. I have no interest in your table scraps, certainly not when I have my own meal in front of me."

"Yes, but you do not eat your meal, do you?" Molekane said.

Ray heard frustration and concern in her voice. Mwai was certainly a stubborn chap, even when his health was at risk. Dealing with him was probably a lot like dealing with Steele.

"I have no appetite," Mwai said.

"You have been *stabbed!*" Molekane exclaimed. "You should be in hospital, but if you insist on following me about, you must at least eat something!"

"I will eat when I am hungry, ma'am." Without warning, Mwai turned toward Ray and nodded in greeting. "Mr. Ray, hello."

Molekane sighed and looked up. "Indeed, hello Mr. Ray. Come, join us."

"Thank you," Ray said, sitting. "How are you recovering?"

"Well enough under the circumstances," Molekane said. "It is kind of you to ask. And yourself?"

Under the circumstances. What an appropriate way of putting it. Ray couldn't imagine any of them were doing particularly well by normal standards.

"Bruised but managing." Ray tapped the discolored mark on the side of his head.

He knew that Molekane was curious about his business but would not breech civility by asking about it directly. Best not leave her waiting. Ray knew better than to beat around the bush with awkward small talk.

"There was something I did wish to speak to you about, Ms. Molekane, if you have a moment."

"Yes?" Molekane smiled a little.

"When we make port in the Commonwealth, you'll be given official thanks by the government and the military: letters of gratitude, dinner with the Admiral and the Governor of Singh-khand, etc. I'm certain it's all familiar to you, but if you would like someone to give you a refresher on it, I can put you in touch with one of my agents experienced in the protocol."

"Thank you," Molekane said, "that would be most useful. It has been some time since my last visit to your country."

"Naturally, the Commonwealth will want to compensate you for the financial losses you've incurred in helping us. And, of course, your wounded will be given top medical care in Singh-khand until they're ready to resume their duties."

"That is most gracious of the Commonwealth," Molekane said with a measured smile. "I would expect nothing less."

Ray cleared his throat. Now time for the delicate bit.

"There is one other point that I feel ought to be addressed," he said, "and that is the unfortunate situation of those members of your workforce who were killed during the attack."

Molekane's smile faded.

"An unfortunate situation indeed," she said. "How do you propose to 'address' it?"

No point in dancing around the issue. Either Molekane would agree, or she would not.

"I will be filing a strong suggestion that their families be given funds to help compensate them for the cost of funerals and the loss of income," Ray said.

Money in exchange for the dead. Ray knew exactly how it sounded.

Molekane considered this in silence for a short time. "You know, Mr. Ray," she said, "a Badlander, a Mercian, or a Tentetsu might take your offer as an attempt to buy off a guilty conscience."

That was true, Ray knew, but it was not his intention. The question was, did Molekane think that was the case?

Molekane studied his eyes for a time. At length she said, "I suspect, however, that you are sincere in your intentions. In Tali we understand the great significance of financial concerns, especially where loss and bereavement are concerned. In time, the pain will eventually subside, though it will never leave. But through it all, the grieving family must be fed and clothed."

"My thoughts exactly," Ray said. It was all well and good to feel anguish over the dead, but what of the people who were most affected? They should not be made to suffer twice for their loss.

Molekane studied his eyes a little longer and then said, "What is more, something tells me that your conscience feels no guilt in this matter. Your generosity comes from sympathy at our sacrifice, not regret over your hand in it."

She was right about that, though Ray was surprised that she had realized it. Molekane was extremely perceptive. But, having been found out, he might as well be completely honest and save any lingering doubts.

"Ms. Molekane," he said, "given what is at stake, I'd have felt neither guilt nor remorse if you and every member of your camp had died so long as the information I carried got back to the Commonwealth in time to stop Burkhalter. And I would have suffered no regret or doubt if Steele and I had died for that same purpose."

Molekane smiled, apparently satisfied by these words.

"It pleases me that you confess the truth in this matter," she said.

"You knew all along," Ray said. There really was no reason for him to hide it.

"Of course," Molekane said, "but it still speaks well of you that you can admit it." Pausing only for a moment, she changed topics. "But can you be certain of all this generosity? It is my understanding that such things are a matter of decision, not standard procedure. Will the Commonwealth have the time to thank one small expedition of archaeologists in the grand scheme of things?"

"I intend to make certain of it," Ray said.

"I was not aware that cartographers had such influence."

"We don't, of course," Ray said, "but I am in close personal contact with certain people who do, and I believe they'll agree with me on this point."

After his superiors in the SSB saw the intelligence he had gathered, the Director-General himself would make sure of it personally.

"That is very kind of you," Molekane said.

"Well, I may feel no guilt," Ray said, "but I do have a great appreciation for your sacrifice, sympathy for the difficult position you were placed in, and gratitude for your aid. It would be wrong of me not to try to make amends however I can."

"It is appreciated."

"What will you do now?" Ray asked. That was always the difficult bit: deciding where to go after such an experience.

Molekane sighed. "My dig site has been abandoned. Even if the funds I invested are somehow returned to me, I will be unable to continue my work until Burkhalter's fleet is finished for good, and then only assuming that no other pirate group moves in to take his place."

A valid point, Ray thought, but if the problem of Burkhalter's fleet hadn't been resolved within the next few weeks, he dreaded to think what would become of the civilized world.

"If the field was to be cleared, what would you do?" he asked.

"Return and complete my work, I suppose," Molekane said. "Then I would publish my findings and attempt to sell the artifacts to a museum or other institution. Assuming, of course, that I possessed sufficient funds to carry it out."

"I may be able to help on that note," Ray said. "I have some associates at the University of Vihara, and I know they would be delighted to support such a dig. I can give you their information, if it pleases you. I'll arrange letters of introduction and let you take things from there."

Molekane's smile was tinged with the sorrow of the day. "Thank you, Mr. Ray. That would be most agreeable."

Ray nodded and stood. "Then if you will excuse me, I will begin preparations."

"Of course."

TWENTY-TWO

Steele was in the conning tower at the top of the *Hellfire* when Singhkhand came into view. It was well into the night and she could see the lights of the Sky-Yards and the airbase from miles away. They were like lamps in a window welcoming her as she returned from the wilderness.

She heard the observation officer in the tower speaking quietly into a voicepipe, reporting visual findings to augment the navigation information provided by the aetherscopes on the bridge. The shipboard routine was practically humdrum, and that made it strangely comforting.

"Home sweet home," said a soft voice at her elbow.

She turned and saw Ray. He had arrived unobtrusively, as he always did. She gave him a small smile.

"Quiet as a cat," she said.

Ray smiled back at her. "As only a public servant can be."

They fell silent and watched as the lights of Singhkhand drew closer and closer. At length, Ray spoke again.

"What happens now?" he asked.

Oh, what a question.

"Now?" Steele sighed. "Now we go to war."

She pointed at a cluster of lights that floated in the skies near Singhkhand like the distorted constellations of fallen stars.

"Do you see those lights there?" she asked.

"Yes," Ray said.

"That's the battle fleet being assembled. It's only preliminary, of course. It's still small."

The word of an Air Force officer went far, but it did not provoke general mobilization. Ray's photographs would do that.

Steele continued, "Once Belgaet sees the scale of Burkhalter's forces, that fleet will get very big very fast. They'll pull in wings and squadrons from all across the Commonwealth, weld us into a tactical force, give us some ambitious air commodore looking to make admiral and send us off to kill and be killed. It's Monroe all over again, but with luck we'll get away with only half the casualties. And *that* will be a great victory, if you can believe it."

Ray shook his head. "It's a chilling thought, the idea that the death of thousands is getting off easy. What a world we live in."

He was right about that. What a world indeed. But there were principles at stake, principles that neither Steele nor the Commonwealth could back down on.

"Better the sacrifice of the few than the massacre of the many," she said, arms folded and face set firmly against the thought of death. "It's what we all signed on for."

She looked up into Ray's eyes. He was upset. Steele felt like kicking herself. Of course he was upset. They'd just barely survived a day of heavy combat and here she was talking about rushing off to get killed. Best to change the subject.

"And what about you, Ray?" she asked. "What will you do now? Go back to Kilkala?"

"No, not yet," Ray said. Steele could tell he was relieved to be talking about something else. "I'll drop by the office to make sure that everything is in hand, but I'm not ready to leave the field yet. Too many things in need of addressing."

"Such as?"

"Well, that punch card to start with," Ray said. "I want to know why Burkhalter was so eager to get it. Molekane said the symbols could be found in the Sleeping Lands, so I think I'll go to Sibir and start looking into it. I have a contact out that way who knows where to look for that sort of thing."

"Sibir, eh?" Steele said. She had never been there. A part of her wanted to go, though. From the stories she had heard, she imagined it to be some vast frigid wilderness filled with giant redwoods, endless steppes, totem poles, and yurts. In reality, it was probably nothing like that.

"I hear it's rainy," she added.

"As you cannot even imagine," Ray said. "When it's not snowing, of course. I'll have to take you sometime when you have extended leave. It's quite a different sort of frontier. It will make a nice change from the Badlands."

Steele smiled at the invitation. If she survived the impending "Burkhalter Incident", she would gladly take him up on it. Not that she was likely to come back alive.

"You know something else that's interesting?" Ray asked.

"What?"

"I received a message from my man Smith when I checked in with the aethercast on Kilkala about an hour ago," Ray said. "Apparently the police have identified your mysterious old man."

"Really?" Steele raised an eyebrow. Now that was interesting. And surprisingly fast.

"Apparently it's Maxwell Boyde," Ray said.

Boyde? Why did that name sound familiar?

"Wait a minute . . ." Steele said. "The fellow you were going on about in the tunnels?"

Ray nodded. "The very same."

Steele blinked. Talk about improbable.

"Well that's a coincidence," she said.

"Isn't it just?"

"You said he was an aether scientist?" Steele asked.

"More than that," Ray said. "The top lecturer on aether physics at Melmoth University. Cream of the crop. That is until one of his more questionable experiments killed two of his lab assistants and drove three more insane."

"Charming." Steele made a face. Aether was such a nasty business. "I don't know why anyone would want to push the boundaries of this particle science nonsense," she said. "We've already got the aethercaster and the aetherscope: wireless communication and navigation. Why do we need anything else?"

"Because we can build them bigger and better." Ray laughed. "Why do we do *anything* in the Commonwealth?"

He was right about that. "Because we can" was so often the favored mantra of Commonwealth scientists.

Ray continued, "Apparently, Boyde was trying to create a device that could directly manipulate aether particles on a scale that would make aethercasting look like semaphore. Unfortunately, the side effects weren't pleasant. And his assistants weren't the only victims. When the government stepped in and forbade any continuation of his work, he carried on in secret. He was finally found out when his *entire neighborhood* began showing signs of mental instability."

Insanity by wireless. Steele shuddered at the though.

Ray noticed her shivering and wrapped his coat around her shoulders. "Cold?" he asked, gently placing his hands on her arms.

"No, I'm—" She stopped herself.

"Hmm?"

"Nothing," Steele said, smiling. "Continue. What did this Boyde fellow invent that was so terrible? A ghost machine?"

Ray chuckled at this. "No, although I think he claimed to have invented a 'ghost repelling' device at one point. No one took it seriously."

What a quack, Steele thought.

"I'm surprised they gave him tenure," she said.

"Oh, don't misjudge," Ray said. "Boyde was a genius, even if he had some rather esoteric theories. But there are limits, even for geniuses."

"What happened to him?" Steele asked.

"After he was dismissed from his post, he fled to Tali for asylum and then vanished off the map."

"Then what was he doing in the Badlands on the run from Burkhalter's men?"

"That," Ray said, "is a *very* good question."

* * * *

Several hundred miles away, Burkhalter stood on the observation deck of his flying fortress, watching as the last of the supplies were transferred to the cargo airships in his flotilla. He would be leading them to the very ends of the sky, to the place where all winds converged, and there was no guarantee that they would encounter communities or traders of sufficient size to support them on their journey. Burkhalter knew he would have to take precautions with the use of the supplies. Most of the pirates who served him had never before ventured into a place where they could not support themselves through theft or plunder. Without the aid of skilled quartermasters and rationing, they would quickly feast themselves into starvation.

Burkhalter held the prized punch card in one hand and stroked the top of Adler's head with the other. Repairs on the mechanical bird had been finished a short while ago, and now it showed no signs of knowing what an ordeal it had been through. Had the poor creature suffered permanent damage, Burkhalter would have been most displeased. He cared little for the suffering of people, but the unkind treatment of machines and his clockwork pets made him furious.

"My lord," Kruger said as he knelt at Burkhalter's feet, "the attack has failed. The scouts report that despite all efforts, the woman Steele remains alive, and the forces of the Commonwealth rescued the Talian's camp."

A disappointment, but ultimately of little consequence. Hewes would have to be punished, of course, assuming he lived.

"What of Herr Hewes?" Burkhalter asked.

"Hewes died among his men," Kruger said.

Well, that settled that. Hewes had already been repaid for his failure. All was in order.

"It is no matter, my loyal Kruger," Burkhalter said, stroking Adler's head with the same automatic tenderness as before. "Herr Hewes was too weak to accomplish his task. It is better that he has been stripped away, leaving us stronger."

"As you say, my lord."

Burkhalter beckoned to his lieutenant. "Rise, Kruger. Join me."

"Yes, lord," Kruger said, and did as he was bade.

"The punch card has been returned to me," Burkhalter said. "That was the only matter of consequence for Hewes to accomplish. The death of the woman was a secondary consideration."

"As you say, lord."

Burkhalter looked down at the punch card in his hand. "Herr Boyde's betrayal was a mere inconvenience. It has now been corrected."

"It is a pity that he turned against you," Kruger said. "His technical contributions showed great promise."

"A pity it is," Burkhalter agreed, "but his work has been enough for my purposes. On our journey, neither ghosts nor storms nor any other manifestation of the aether will trouble us."

Like Hewes, Boyde had already served his purpose. There was no longer any need for him. His death was irrelevant.

"Do you know why he fled with your property, lord?" Kruger asked.

Why indeed?

"Because he was a coward," Burkhalter said. "Because his fear of victory became greater than his fear of me. But in death, he was taught why he should fear nothing more than me. *No one* should ever fear *anything* more than me, for my wrath is more terrible than thunder or lightning and my reach greater than the winds." Burkhalter looked back out over the flotilla surrounding his flagship. "Are the men ready to depart?"

"Shortly, lord," Kruger said, motioning toward the last few cargo ships as they moved into position. "Very shortly." He paused. "Sire, do you truly believe that this undertaking will be worth the scale of your preparations? We stand ready to invade the East with a fleet of tremendous size and power. Yet, now we divide our forces and prepare to cross to the far side of the world in pursuit of a fantasy that may or may not exist."

Burkhalter paused. "Herr Kruger, are you questioning me?"

"No lord," Kruger quickly replied. "But my role is as your devil's advocate. If the artifact even exists, are you confident that it will do what the legend says it will do? Can it truly sunder cities and burn the skies?"

Burkhalter gave a hollow, mechanical chuckle. Such a question. Such doubts. Kruger should have more faith.

"Herr Boyde certainly thought so," he said, "or else he would not have risked my anger by stealing the card. And Herr Boyde was a genius. A fool, but a genius. His wish was to stop me, because he knew what I could do with such a machine at my command." Burkhalter paused and corrected himself. "What I *will do* with such a machine at my command."

Kruger bowed his head, no doubt recognizing the tone in Burkhalter's voice. There would be no arguing with him about this matter, just as there had been no arguing with him when they had made that fateful decision to rebel against the orthodoxy of the Church years ago.

"As you say, lord."

Burkhalter looked out across the midnight sky before him, smiling at the thought of the all-consuming triumph that awaited him only a few days hence.

"Go, Kruger," he said, dismissing his lieutenant with a flick of his hand. "See to it that all preparations are finished. We leave at dawn upon our great journey, our holy quest to obtain the power of God Himself and to harness it to my will. I have already remade flesh and bone with the perfection of the machine. When this task is done, I shall remake the world. And let all who have wronged me and all who stand in my way tremble with fear, for I shall bring my vengeance upon them and all that displeases me shall be burned with the unending fire until not even ash remains."

TO BE CONTINUED IN
BOOK TWO OF
THE HELLFIRE CHRONICLES

ASH

ON THE WIND

GLOSSARY

-A-

Aether

An elementary particle believed to have been released into the atmosphere during the **Great Upheaval**. Aether particles are known to clump together forming the substance commonly referred to as "aether", which in sufficient concentration can be tangible, visible and even solid. Aether exhibits particle-wave duality, appears to be affected by electromagnetic forces and is capable of transmitting energy (see **Aethercaster** and **Aetherscope**).

Aethercasting

Aethercasting is the process by which aether particles are used to transmit information wirelessly over long distances in a manner similar to pre-Upheaval radio. The word "aethercasting" has become the generic term for all wireless communications. Aethercasting is accomplished by a device known as an "aethercaster" or an "aethercast machine".

Aetherscope

An aetherscope uses aetheric waves to map out a surrounding region of airspace. It is similar in concept to the system of radar (still unnamed and in its infancy prior to the **Great Upheaval**), but is capable of greater accuracy and detail. In addition to navigation, aetherscopes are used to track the location of both friendly and hostile aircraft during combat.

Agar Gun

A single-barreled **machine gun** fired by turning a crank, which cocks and releases the firing pin when a new round is in position. Bullets are loaded from above, either dropping from a magazine or being carried on an ammunition belt. Spent casings are ejected by means of a rotating wheel that catches each bullet as it is being loaded. Because agar guns are single-barrel they are generally lighter than multi-barrel **gatling guns**, although they are also more prone to overheating. Most "light machine guns" carried as squad support weapons by elite infantry units are of the agar pattern. The generic term "agar gun" is taken from the name of Wilson Agar, inventor of the first Agar gun during the pre-Upheaval period, and is used to reference all single-barrel machine guns.

Autocannon

A rapid-fire gun comparable in function to a **machine gun**, but firing shells rather than bullets. Most autocannons are of the **agar gun** pattern.

Automaton (plural Automata)

A self-operating machine. A robot.

-B-

Badlands, the

A vast expanse of lawless and sparsely populated airspace located to the west of the Known World. Much of the Badlands represent the remains of the pre-Upheaval Americas. The region is characterized by extreme violence and criminal activity.

Belgaet (pronounced Bell-Gate)

Belgaet is a heavily fortified shipyard and airbase that serves as official home of the **Commonwealth** Air Force. It is located in the **Melmothian** region of the Commonwealth, and its name is used as shorthand for the Air Force administration.

Beyliks, the

The Beyliks are a cluster of **eyots** located in the northern section of the Commonwealth, which together comprise one of its member states. Prior to the **Great Upheaval**, the Beyliks were a part of the Ottoman Empire. The people of the Beyliks are Turkish in origin and are referred to as Beylikites.

Biplane

An aeroplane with two main wings.

Boxwallah

An itinerant merchant. Boxwallahs are named for the boxes they carry their goods in, which often double as portable display shelves. The term is derived from the **Londinian** word "box" and the **Mahari** word "wallah" (or "wala"), which references a person involved in a given activity.

-C-

Cacik

A **Beylikite** dish of yoghurt seasoned with salt, garlic, dill, mint and cucumber. A range of variants exist using modified ingredients, including olive oil, other vegetables like carrots, other seasonings like curry or black pepper, and lemon or lime juice.

Civil Servant

A **public servant** working directly for the government administration. In the **Commonwealth**, civil servants are always drawn from the academic class and they are capable of amassing tremendous power over the course of their careers.

Commonwealth, the

The Commonwealth is a large nation that comprises the northwestern corner of the Known World. It is a union of five different states (**Londinium**, **Saba**, **Melmoth**, the **Beyliks** and **Singhkhand**) that share a common central government and unified culture. The Commonwealth is home to a system of "enlightened scientific government" that places all political power in the hands of academics and intellectuals, who are selected as members of the Parliament based on test scores. Outside of its borders, the Commonwealth is sometimes unofficially referred to as the London Commonwealth after its capital, **New London**. Similarly, the people of the Commonwealth are colloquially called Londoners, although "citizen of the Commonwealth" is the official designation. The term Commoner, used especially in Mercia and the Badlands, is considered derogatory.

Corvette

A light attack airship designed as an escort for larger craft. Corvettes are intended to engage other aircraft rather than ground targets. Airships of a similar size class used for ground support and bombardment are referred to as **Gunboats**.

-E-

Effendi

A **Beylikite** word used to reference an educated gentleman or lady. It is applied as a term of respect for members of the **Commonwealth**'s academic class.

Envelope

The section of an airship that contains its buoyant gas. In non-rigid airships, the envelope is filled completely with gas to maintain its shape. In rigid airships, a framework maintains this shape and only part of the space is needed to hold the gas (which is contained in sealed cells). Consequently, in rigid airships the envelope can also contain crew areas, walkways, storage and even weaponry. All other sections of an airship are placed on or hang from the envelope.

Erkusk

The capital of **Sibir**. Formerly the pre-Upheaval city of Irkutsk.

Eyot

A floating piece of rock or land large enough to potentially sustain life (although not all eyots are inhabited). Following the **Great Upheaval**, the earth was fragmented into pieces, which ranged in size from small debris to chunks of land many miles across. Those of sufficient size to be of use to people are termed "eyots". The word itself is **Londinian** in origin, and references small pre-Upheaval islands, especially those found in the Thames River (now the Timaeus River on the eyot of **Londinium**).

-F-

Flechette

A small metal dart used to penetrate armor. Flechettes can be dropped from aeroplanes and airships or released from special artillery shells. They can also be fired from firearms by the use of **sabot** rounds. Flechettes are very good anti-personnel weapons, although their armor-piercing capabilities make them effective against aeroplanes and light vehicles as well.

-G-

Gardner Gun

A **machine gun** that uses a rotating mechanism to drive its firing pin forward to fire and back to advance the next round. Most gardner-pattern machine guns have multiple barrels, which allows half of the barrels to fire while the others reload. The generic name "gardner gun" is taken from the weapon's pre-Upheaval inventor, William Gardner.

Gatling Gun

A multi-barreled **machine gun** fired by turning the barrels in rapid succession. Bullets are loaded at the top of the mechanism and are then fired when the barrel passes the firing pin at the bottom. The generic name "gatling gun" is taken from the name of the weapon's pre-Upheaval inventor, Dr. Richard Gatling, and is used as the general term for all rotating multi-barrel machine guns.

Gondola

An enclosed compartment extending from the **envelope** of an airship, used for housing crew, passengers or control systems for the craft. Not to be confused with a **hull**, which is significantly larger than a gondola and hangs from the envelope with enough space for an exposed superstructure.

Great Upheaval, the

In the summer of 1908, a cataclysmic event shook the earth, causing unprecedented seismic activity and ultimately shattering the planet into countless fragments. Much of the world's population died in the incident and many who survived soon succumbed to starvation or the chaos that gripped the post-Upheaval world. After much struggle, some of the survivor communities managed to stabilize and rebuild, eventually returning to the same level of technology enjoyed by their pre-Upheaval ancestors, albeit modified for their changed circumstances. For dating purposes, 1908 is regarded as "Year Zero" and the year 1909 corresponds to Year One Post-Upheaval.

Gunboat

A light airship designed for heavy bombardment, primarily against ground targets but also against heavier aircraft. They are similar in size to **corvettes** but carry much heavier armaments and conversely are more vulnerable to light aircraft.

-H-

Hull

A large enclosed section of an airship that hangs from beneath the **envelope**. It consists of a single structure (unlike a **gondola**, of which an airship may have several) with a top deck and/or superstructure distinct from the envelope. A hull may have multiple decks. The hull system is used either in low technology regions where modern rigid-frame airships may be too difficult to produce, or to provide a modern combat airship with a stable firing platform to mount heavy guns and turrets. The term "hull" is used in reference to a naval ship's hull, which such structures often resemble. Many of the first post-Upheaval airships were constructed by attaching envelopes to old ship hulls, giving rise to the name.

-J-

Jianguo

Jianguo (the "Strong Country") is a vast and powerful nation that comprises the southeastern corner of the **Known World**. The founders of Jianguo were a survivor group of Han Chinese who quickly rebuilt their society and industrial base. Over the course of the first century Post Upheaval, the technologically advanced Jianguo expanded rapidly, absorbing many of its neighbors and acquiring survivor communities from other parts of Qing China, sections of Southeast Asia, Korea, Manchuria and Japan. After recent internal strife following the breakaway of the Korean and Japanese communities and the formation of the **Tentetsu Empire**, the Jianguo has entered a period of isolationism, allowing in only a small number of regulated merchants to keep up the flow of commerce as it struggles to protect itself from revolution and to regain its former glory.

-K-

Kestrel

The primary fighter aircraft of the **Commonwealth**. The Kestrel is a **monoplane** with an all-metal structure and an enclosed cockpit, both new innovations in aviation that let the aircraft operate at higher than average speeds with remarkable fuel efficiency. The Kestrel's long range allows fighter squadrons to serve as the mainstay of Air Force patrols, especially in areas like the Badlands where airships are either too expensive to operate or too vulnerable to ambush.

Kitali

Kitali is the universal language of the **Talian** people. It is derived from Swahili and it first began as a pidgin language to allow Swahili-speaking Talians to communicate with their Greek and Zulu-speaking neighbors. It has since become the primary language of Tali, and consequently the general trade language of the **Known World**. When two people of different nationalities are speaking to one another, chances are they will be speaking in Kitali.

Known World, the

The Known World is the principle area of civilization in modern times. It forms a rough circle centered on the nation of **Tali** and ringed by massive frontier areas such as the **Badlands** and the **Sleeping Lands**. While composed of many nations, several of which do not get along, the Known World is tenuously united by trade and by the shared belief that together they represent civilization surrounded on all sides by barbarism.

-L-

Londinium

Londinium is one of the five **Commonwealth** member states and one of its founding nations (along with **Saba** and **Melmoth**). During the Great Upheaval, the eyot that is now Londinium was formed from several different sections of the British Isles that were forced together around the city of London (now called Old London).

-M-

Machine Gun

An automated firearm capable of self-loading and able to fire continuously at a rate of hundreds or thousands of rounds per minute. All modern machine guns utilize some form of internal mechanism either to reset a spring-loaded firing pin or to push a fresh bullet onto a stationary firing pin. This can be accomplished manually, by turning a crank on the side of the machine gun, or automatically, by connecting the crank mechanism to a power source such as a steam engine. The gas-operated system developed by Hiram Maxim's prior to the **Great Upheaval** has since been abandoned in favor of the mechanical systems currently in use. Most machine guns are be classified as using either the single-barrel **agar** system or the multi-barrel **gatling** system. Volley guns such as the **mitrailleuse** are technically not machine guns (as new bullets must be manually loaded after firing each barrel), but they are colloquially referred to as such regardless.

Mahari

The Mahari are the people of the **Commonwealth** state of **Singhkhand**. Their name is derived from the term Maharashtra, meaning "Great Nation".

Melmoth

The Melmoth region is home to the eyot-cities of **New London** and **Belgaet**, which collectively form one state in the **Commonwealth**. Melmothians are descended from survivors from parts of French-occupied North Africa. During the pre-Commonwealth period, Melmoth became a significant rival to the **Londinium-Saba** alliance, ultimately resulting in warfare, annexation and the instillation of a friendly, predominantly Berber government, which co-founded the Commonwealth. Over the following century and a half, the Berber, Arab and French populations in Melmoth were integrated together into single ethnic group. Melmothians are regarded as natural aviators and have a disproportionately large presence in the Air Force.

Mercia, Kingdom of

A former **Commonwealth** colony, the Kingdom of Mercia is a major military power in the northeast of the **Known World**. The original colonists were **Londinians**, but their region of airspace also contained pockets of survivors from Eastern Europe and Scandinavia. Vehemently anti-**Commonwealth**, the Mercians are obsessed with the concept of purity, strength and a glorious Anglo-Saxon ancestry that was betrayed by Londinium in the forming of the Commonwealth. The Mercian language is extremely close to its English roots, albeit with many of the non-Germanic vocabulary words removed or more heavily anglicized.

Mitrailleuse

A multi-barrel volley gun used for support fire. Mitrailleuses are technically not **machine guns** as they can only fire one bullet per barrel before the ammunition block must be manually reloaded, although the term "machine gun" is still often applied to them. The mechanism is simple and uses minimal moving parts, making it extremely reliable on the battlefield even after long periods of continuous use. Downsides include the short firing time between reloading and the greater scattering of shots.

Monoplane

An aeroplane with one main wing.

-N-

Namaste

The general greeting of the **Commonwealth**, derived from an earlier **Mahari** greeting. It is often accompanied by a slight bow with folded hands. It is used in almost all situations where two or more people meet while speaking. It is not used in very informal situations, such as greetings between close friends (where handshakes are used instead), nor in wordless greetings such as on the street, which are often conducted by touching the hand to the brim of the hat or merely by exchanging nods.

New London

New London is the capital of the **Commonwealth** and one of the most modern cities in the **Known World**. Before the **Great Upheaval**, New London was French-controlled Algiers; after the Upheaval, it became the Port of Melmoth, capital of the Melmothian Empire. After being defeated by **Londinium** and **Saba**, the Port of Melmoth was remade into New London, the so-called "Capital of the Modern World". The name "New London" is derived from the writings of the pre-Commonwealth philosopher Lady Anne Timaeus, who used the metaphor of an enlightened "new London" contrasting the corrupt and chaotic "old London" of her time to outline her vision of an ideal society governed by science and reason. Today, Lady Anne is widely regarded as the architect of the Commonwealth's system of meritocracy and enlightened scientific government.

-P-

Pirate Lord

Pirate lords are warlords and military dictators who lay claim to vast amounts of airspace in the **Badlands**. They enforce their rule through ruthlessness and violence, often going to war with one another or attempting to invade the civilizations to their east. When not at war, pirate lords give their forces free reign to commit acts of piracy against anyone passing through their territory.

Pom-Pom

A quick-firing **autocannon** that uses 1 to 2 pound shells. Pom-poms are used primarily against fighters and light airships, but also noted to be effective against infantry.

Public Servant

An government employee working for an agency, department or public service not involved in government administration (see **Civil Servant**). In the **Commonwealth** all public servants are drawn from the professional middle class.

Raki

An anise-flavored spirit enjoyed in the **Commonwealth**. Also pronounced "rakou", especially in the **Beyliks** where it originated.

Saba

Saba is one of the five **Commonwealth** member states and one of its founding nations (along with **Londinium** and **Melmoth**). The people of Saba, the Sabai, are descended from the pre-Upheaval Ethiopians.

Sabot

A breakaway casing placed around a projectile, such as a **flechette**, that is smaller than the barrel it is being fired from.

Saint Corbin, the Holy Kingdom of

Located in the southwest of the **Known World**, the Holy Kingdom of Saint Corbin is an intensely religious society populated by survivors from the pre-Upheaval German Empire. Convinced that their survival was due to the intercession of God, and hardened by a series of plagues that nearly destroyed them in the early post-Upheaval days, the Corbinites are insular, fastidious and paranoid both of outsiders and of disease. They are known for idealizing the perfection of the machine over human weakness, which manifests in the practice of replacing body parts with mechanical prosthetics. The name "Saint Corbin" is the **Commonwealth** rendering of Sankt Korbinian, the nation's patron saint, who is credited with creating the first mechanical prosthetics.

Schnell

A Corbinite word meaning "quickly."

Sehr Gut

A Corbinite phrase meaning "very good."

Sibir

A loose confederacy of towns and trading posts in the **Sleeping Lands**.

Singhkhand

Singhkhand is the youngest **Commonwealth** state, having been a member for only just over a century. The eyot of Singhkhand represents the remains of north and central pre-Upheaval India. Its administrative region sits on the most volatile section of the **Badlands** border and serves as the first line of defense against pirate raids upon the Commonwealth.

Sky Yard

A place where aircraft are constructed and repaired. Sometimes hyphenated as sky-yard.

Sleeping Lands, the

A vast frontier located far to the northeast of the **Known World**. The Sleeping Lands comprise much of the remains of pre-Upheaval North Asia as well as parts of Russia and northwestern North America. While not as chaotic or lawless as the **Badlands**, the Sleeping Lands are still a harsh environment that breeds strong, self-reliant people.

Special Survey Bureau (SSB), the

The Special Survey Bureau is a government agency tasked with assembling maps and survey data for the Commonwealth. Officially, the SSB is merely the provider of a civic service, like the post office. In this capacity, it buys and sells cartographic information to prospectors, navigators and other interested parties. Unknown to the general public, the SSB also serves as one of the Commonwealth's three major intelligence services (alongside Army and Air Force Intelligence) and it is the only agency in the Commonwealth that manages non-military espionage. While not every SSB agent is a spy, most senior employees are, or at least have the necessary clearance to know about the Bureau's clandestine activities. The SSB's information is always filtered through military intelligence agencies or is classified as the result of the unofficial activities of isolated field agents, allowing the organization to remain innocuous.

-T-

Tali Consortium, the

The Tali Consortium is a wealthy and influential nation positioned at the crossroads of the **Known World**. The original Talians were a Swahili people from eastern pre-Upheaval Africa who soon came into contact with and absorbed a much smaller community of Greeks and another of Zulus. Although the Consortium is technically a company rather than a government, it legally owns all of Talian airspace and fills the same role as a nation-state in the lives of its people. The name Tali is an acronym for the four companies that merged to create the Consortium (the Tajiri Bank, Akukweti Agriculture, Leonidas Arms and Steel, and Impala Shipping).

Talian Bank Chips

The Bank of Tali is the single most powerful financial institution in the **Known World**, so much so that its credit receipts are accepted as a form of universal currency by most people involved in trade and business. The "chips" are actually small metal punch cards that register a certain monetary value and can be exchanged for any currency held in the bank's vaults.

Tentetsu Empire

The Tentetsu Empire is a young, dynamic nation located at the eastern edge of the **Known World**. Its people are descended primarily from the pre-Upheaval Japanese and Koreans. Until recently, it was under the domination of its larger neighbor to the south, the **Jianguo**.

Triplane

An aeroplane with three main wings.

-V-

Voicepipe

A metal tube used to transmit sound from one area to another, primarily for the purpose of communication. Commonly found in airships.

Volcanic Pistol

A configuration of pistol with a lever-action. The name "volcanic pistol" is a genericization of the original pre-Upheaval makers of the weapon, the Volcanic Repeating Arms Company.

ABOUT THE AUTHOR

G. D. Falksen (author, blogger, man about town) is rumored to neither sleep nor eat. Between blogging for Tor.com, writing numerous popular serials for publications such as *Steampunk Tales*, and working as the lead writer for Hatboy Studios and the AIR: Steampunk video game, one wonders where he finds the time even for a cup of tea. In spite of his busy schedule, he moonlights as an MC at events in New York City, Philadelphia, and along the East Coast, and makes numerous public appearances all around the country where he lectures on topics such as the history of the steam age. Having appeared in *The New York Times*, on MTV, and in countless other media, he appreciates the finer things in life, like Earl Grey and kittens. For those seeking more information on this particular eccentric, he can be easily located at his website, www.gdfalksen.com.